Closer Than the Bones

An Ernestine Carpenter Mystery

Dean James

SILVER DAGGER

M Y S T E R

An Imprint of The Overmo'
JOHNSON CITY, TEN

Hardcover ISBN 1-57072-182-3
Trade Paper ISBN 1-57072-183-1
Copyright © 2001 by Dean James
Printed in the United States of America
All Rights Reserved

1 2 3 4 5 6 7 89 0

*In loving memory of
some very special women:*

*my maternal grandmother,
Myrtle Williams Breedlove;*

*my paternal grandmother,
Leola Rosamond James;*

*her beloved sister, my great aunt,
Bennie Rosamond Searcy;*

*and my paternal great aunts,
Dottie James Carrithers,
Belle James Caffey, and
Anna Mae James Williams.*

*Thanks to all of you for helping
make Ernie who she is.*

ACKNOWLEDGMENTS

As usual, a number of people assisted with the writing of this novel, offering valuable input, taking time out of very busy schedules to read and critique. I wish to thank them publicly for never failing to be there when I need them.

Megan Bladen-Blinkoff, Julie Wray Herman, and Patricia R. Orr read the manuscript in various stages and offered advice. A writer couldn't ask for a more supportive critique group.

Kaye Davis, crime-scene expert, once again generously offered me the benefit of her experience to answer questions about fingerprints and other forms of trace evidence.

Deputy Wayne Wells (aka Cousin Wayne) of the Madison County (Mississippi) Sheriff's Department repeatedly answered questions about how a sheriff's department in Mississippi goes about investigating a murder.

Henry Lackey (aka Uncle Henry)—lawyer, judge, and Southern gentleman—once again answered questions of procedure, helping me head in the right direction.

Nancy Yost, my agent, answered questions about some fine points relating to rights.

Any errors or inaccuracies of fact and procedure are the author's responsibility, where he either forgot to ask a question or else bent the facts for his own literary purposes.

Finally, thanks yet again to the fine team at The Overmountain Press who have worked to make Silver Dagger a success, particularly Sherry Lewis (aka Eagle Eye), who is the most meticulous editor I've ever had the pleasure of working with. It's great to be part of such a family!

Chapter One

YOU DON'T NEED A LICENSE to be nosy. Besides, when you're sixty, unmarried, and retired, everybody thinks you have nothing better to do, anyway, than poke your proboscis into other people's business.

I just happen to get paid for it. Even though I don't do it for the money.

I'm not a licensed private detective. I've never even bothered to find out what you have to do, in the great state of Mississippi, to become one. The kinds of problems I like to tackle are usually best solved with a little discreet probing, here and there, asking questions of the right people at the right time. With a network of friends, relatives, and former students like mine, which reaches all over the state and beyond, in positions high and low, I can usually find out what I need to with a phone call or two.

I haven't gotten around to renting any kind of office, though I've had my eye on one of the old buildings on Main Street in Tullahoma. I think it has the right kind of ambience for what I do.

I think of myself as a problem solver, first and foremost, and word of mouth is my best advertisement. For the time being, if someone wants to talk to me about taking on a problem, I simply invite the potential employer to my house. It's a bit of a drive from Tullahoma, about fifteen miles, but I'd much rather have the first interview on my own turf. In exceptional circumstances, I'll go to someone else's home or office to talk things over, but today I was glad that I had insisted she come to me.

I'm not in the habit of slapping potential employers. Especially when the person wanting to hire me comes from a very old and established family and is reputed to have enough money to buy the entire state of Mississippi and have change left over. But nothing puts my back up faster than someone who considers most of the human race beneath her.

Mary Tucker McElroy had a good fifteen or so years on me, which put her around seventy-five. The years had etched her face without mercy, and her mass of hair—burnished a deep copper, streaked here and there with gray, and gathered in a loose large chignon—did little to soften what age had wrought. Cold blues eyes, on a level with mine, examined me as the silence stretched out.

I stood, meeting her gaze without flinching, refusing to let her intimidate me. I spent nearly forty years teaching senior English in the public school system in Tullahoma, and there are few people on this earth I can't stare down.

"Thank you, Miss Carpenter," Mary Tucker McElroy said, "for agreeing to see me on such short notice. Though I really would have preferred to talk to you at my home." Her right hand, covered in a dazzling array of rings, fluttered in irritation as she eased her six-foot frame into a chair, then arranged her shawl around her shoulders to her satisfaction.

"I regret the inconvenience of having you come here, Miss McElroy," I responded, my voice firm, "but here, at least, we have absolute privacy. When we talked earlier, you kept harping on the fact that the matter you want to discuss is very sensitive."

"I suppose it's of no consequence," she said, "though I'm not very fond of driving myself these days."

That I could well understand. I had been watching out the kitchen window as an ancient, but well-preserved, Buick had inched its way up the hill toward my house, off the two-lane highway. Several cars, unable to pass because of the incline leading up to where my driveway connects with the highway, had accelerated roughly the moment the Buick and its driver were safely out of the way. I just knew that Miss McElroy and her creaky old car had never gotten above thirty on the drive out from Tullahoma.

"Despite the inconvenience, I'm pleased that you could see me on such short notice," Miss McElroy said, though judging by her tone she couldn't imagine my doing otherwise. The McElroys of Idlewild don't wait for anyone to leap at their slightest command.

"I have no pressing matters at the moment," I said in my most gracious tone. No sense in letting her get the upper hand, just because she might employ me.

"Your references are excellent," she said. Her eyes roamed around the room, and her hands relaxed in her lap. Though my house is not of antebellum vintage like hers, it is substantial and impressive in its own way—and one of the reasons that I had insisted she come to me. She now had a better sense of whom she was dealing with, and that should reassure her.

Ever since she had called me yesterday, I wondered who on earth might have given my name to so venerable a personage. Mary Tucker McElroy was not known to mix much with the locals, even though she had been born and reared here. I couldn't imagine what kind of problem she might want me to solve for her.

"Who recommended me?" I said. "If you wouldn't mind my asking."

"I have known your cousin, Henrietta McLendon Butler, for many years, and she speaks highly of your abilities in handling difficult situations."

I never knew my cousin moved in such rarified circles. "I *must* remember to thank dear Retty the next time we chat." Retty, whose veins ran with vinegar, had probably found a soul mate in this aristocrat.

Miss McElroy sniffed; my flippancy did not amuse her. "She also happened to mention that, despite your lack of manners on occasion, you are eminently suited to handle the type of problem I find myself confronting."

I could have shown her the door then and saved myself a lot of grief, but I itched to know what kind of problem Miss McElroy needed someone like me to solve. I did my best to keep my temper in check.

She sniffed again. I resisted the urge to offer her my handkerchief.

She allowed a small smile to crease her mouth, only for a moment, and I figured I had probably passed some test.

"What is the problem you're confronting?" I asked.

Miss McElroy regarded her hands for a moment before she spoke. "You are aware of my patronage of Southern belles lettres." She paused.

Any literate Mississippian (and there are a lot more of those than folk outside the Magnolia State realize) could tell you about the McElroy Young Writers Prize, given annually to the most promising high school senior in the state. Then there was the McElroy Visiting Professorship at Ole Miss, which funded a writer-in-residence program at one of our best-known universities. Not to mention the occasional photograph in newspapers around the South, through which we could follow Miss McElroy's hobnobbing with literary celebrities like Eudora Welty, our own national treasure; Lee Smith; Pat Conroy; Anne Rivers Siddons; and the late Willie Morris, to name just a few.

I inclined my head. If she sniffed again, I was going to recommend that she consult an allergist.

"You are also no doubt aware," she continued, "that several times a year I invite various of my protégés to Idlewild. I offer them the opportunity to meet persons who might be helpful to them in their careers as writers. I also provide an environment in which they are free to explore their art without fear of mundane frustrations. At Idlewild they may seek the fulfillment of their potential while living in an atmosphere of intellectual stimulation and encouragement."

Despite the fact that she sounded like she was reciting a promotional brochure, I had to acknowledge the truth of what she had said. Though few outside the world of belles lettres were ever invited inside the portals of Idlewild, the house itself was a well-known landmark.

"You're certainly to be commended for your services in the cause of Southern literature over the years." I managed a bland smile.

Though her eyes narrowed, Miss McElroy otherwise ignored my little barb. "Next week I shall again play hostess to such a group, and I require some expert assistance during the two weeks that they will be staying at Idlewild."

I waited, resisting the impulse to tell her that I didn't do windows.

"With one exception, this same group was here with me six months ago, during the Christmas season. Something happened then which caused me great distress." She paused.

A memory stirred. I had spent Christmas in Houston, with my cousin Gerard McLendon, his daughter Maggie, and her fiancé, but when I came home just after New Year's, I heard something about a young woman who had died while staying at Idlewild. There had been a brief article in the paper, then nothing more.

"One of your guests drowned, I believe?" I frowned, trying to remember. "The paper said very little about it."

Miss McElroy nodded. "The editor of the local paper is one of my former protégés."

Maybe I should also mention that the current sheriff of our county is a distant cousin of Miss McElroy's. No wonder few details about the accidental drowning were made public.

"What does all this have to do with what you need me to do, Miss McElroy?"

For a moment, the mask of majestic indifference slipped, and I could see the fear of an elderly woman beneath it. She was afraid of something, and that made me warm to her, just a bit. It was the first time she had looked completely human since she had walked in my door fifteen minutes earlier. "I want you to be there with me while these people are at Idlewild because I want you to figure out which one of them is a murderer."

Chapter Two

THREE DAYS LATER I drove through Tullahoma on my way to Idlewild. I had spent those three days mulling over what Mary Tucker McElroy had asked me to do. She hadn't blinked at the outrageous fee I had quoted her. I guess she still had the deep pockets that local rumor had always attributed to her and her family.

After retiring from teaching I hadn't intended to specialize in murders when I had let it be known among family and friends that I would be available to help sort out problems. Though I'd had some luck in ferreting out killers, I wasn't all that keen on getting caught up in another murder investigation.

I couldn't help admitting to myself, however, that Mary Tucker McElroy's particular problem intrigued me. She had promised further details when I arrived at Idlewild to join her little "artists colony," as she called it. She had no concrete proof that murder had been done, but something she had discovered in the time since the "accidental" death made her suspicious. Before she told me the full story, she insisted, she wanted me to meet the various persons involved. Having my impressions of them unclouded by her own knowledge of them made sense.

I'd have preferred more information up front before I got involved in such an undertaking; but when someone was paying as much for my services as Miss McElroy, I was willing to bend my rules.

I inherited enough money from my parents so that I don't have to scrape by on my retirement, savings, and Social Security, thank goodness. I keep busy. I travel, I read a lot, I take care of my house and yard, and I do my bit for various charities.

All of that is pretty predictable, though, and I like challenges. Plus I'm good at figuring out things. And, as I've said before, I'm nosy. Finding a good outlet for one of my besetting sins means I don't have to squirm in my church pew on Sundays when the preacher talks about being overly concerned with one's neighbors' lives.

Or if I do squirm, I don't squirm that much.

The long, magnolia-lined drive to Idlewild stretched before me. I headed my red Jeep toward the house, and after half a mile, I drove over a slight rise. There below me stood one of the most breathtaking examples of antebellum Greek Revival architecture I've ever seen. Reminiscent of its sisters much farther south in Natchez, Idlewild had been built on a grander scale than all of them.

Over nearly a hundred and fifty years, successive generations of McElroys had lavished care and attention on the upkeep of the house, but they had rarely allowed the general public inside its walls, or even on its grounds. Miss McElroy, like her forebears, tended to keep to herself. As if I needed anything more to whet my curiosity over Mary Tucker McElroy's problem, I was looking forward to the opportunity to explore the place.

I drove past the house, marveling at the sparkling white columns and broad verandah, around the back to a converted stable, where I parked my car. After hefting my two bags from the back of the Jeep, I made my way along a path toward the back of the house. To my right lay a small vegetable garden enclosed by a waist-high brick wall. To my left stretched a broad expanse of well-tended lawn, a brilliant green in the morning sun. Over under the trees, beyond the lawn, stood what looked like a summerhouse, not a gazebo or folly, but a small house.

Wooden steps led up onto the back porch, where I set down my bags near the door. I knocked, and a few moments later, the door opened. Framed in the doorway, a rail-thin man, late seventies at a guess, dressed in what I'd swear was a white linen suit, glared at me. Perhaps he had misplaced his Panama hat and mint julep glass before he got to the door. Despite his picturesque appearance, he looked about as welcoming as the Pope inviting the barbarian hordes into Rome.

"Good morning, I'm Ernestine Carpenter. I'm here as a guest of Miss McElroy's."

One thin eyebrow arched and disappeared into a shock of abundant white hair as he frowned. "Yes, I do believe Mary Tucker said you were coming this morning. Please, do come in." He stood aside and bade me enter with an offhand gesture, as if he didn't care whether I came inside or not. "No, no, just leave your bags right there. I'll take care of them for you." His tone betokened his impatience.

"Thank you," I said, though I wasn't at all certain he was strong enough to hoist them. But I figured I couldn't insult the man by appearing to doubt him. Men have such tender egos, after all.

He stood with arms held stiffly at his sides. "Allow me to introduce myself, Miss Carpenter. I'm Morwell Phillips. During your stay here at Idlewild, please let me know if there's anything you need. We do hope your visit with us will be a pleasant one." I would have been more convinced that he meant what he said if he hadn't uttered the last two sentences in a monotone.

Maybe his feet were hurting, or maybe he was just rude. Whatever the reason for his less-than-gracious behavior, he was certainly high-class for an old family retainer. His voice was pure Mississippi gentry, and he had more the look of a retired lawyer or gentleman planter than that of a butler. I'm sure there was an interesting story here, and if I had the chance while I went about my job, I'd do my best to find out what his was.

"If you'll follow me, please," he said, as he shut the door behind us. My eyes had adjusted to the dimmer light inside the house, and I could see that we stood in a small room. On one side a half-closed door led into the kitchen. The murmur of voices and the aroma of something appetizing came from behind it.

To the left of us, through another doorway, were the back stairs, and ahead of us was a thickly paneled door. Morwell Phillips conducted me through it toward the front of the house.

The hallway, as was typical in houses of this kind, ran straight through from front to back, with the rooms off either side. The floorboards, covered in richly colored rugs, creaked slightly as we walked across them.

As we neared the foot of the broad wooden staircase, he waved a hand toward a room at the front of the house. "Mary Tucker is in there waiting for you. I'll show you your room first, and you just take your time settling in, then come on back down and talk with her when you're ready."

"Thank you," I murmured. Despite the admonition to take my time, I doubted that Miss McElroy would care to have me linger over the amenities, whatever they might be, in the room she had assigned.

We paused at the head of the stairs, and I beheld a wide and spacious hallway, like the one on the floor beneath us. Behind us, the stairs continued to the third floor. Along the walls were doorways, and in between the doorways were various oil portraits and occasional bits of statuary. In several places stood small groups of chairs and a couple of sofas. I remembered from tours of other antebellum homes that often the upper hallways were used almost as we would use living rooms or dens these days, and it appeared that Idlewild was no different.

Phillips conducted me down the length of the hallway. "There are six bedrooms on this floor," he explained, continuing to sound utterly bored with his task. "Most of them have their own bathrooms." He paused in front of the last doorway on the left. "The room there is Mary Tucker's"—he then pointed to the right—"and she's put you in this room, directly across."

Not the servants' quarters after all, I reflected wryly. I opened the door he had indicated and walked inside. My breath caught in my throat as I looked around the spacious chamber. The furnishings were enough to make any antique dealer swoon. At home I had a canopied bed much like the one here, but I didn't have the rest of the items that complemented it. Not the dresser, not the wardrobe, not a set of Duncan Phyfe chairs (if I wasn't mistaken). I sighed in sheer pleasure.

"I'll have to thank Miss McElroy," I said, and I meant it. I hadn't expected such comfort. "This is a lovely, lovely room."

Phillips remained aloof. "This was Mary Tucker's mother's room, and she rarely has anyone stay in it. I'm sure you'll find it eminently suitable." He gestured toward a door to our right. "Through there is your bathroom. On the bedside table you'll find a phone which connects with the kitchen, and if you need anything, anything at all, you just pick up that phone and let someone downstairs know."

"Thank you," I told him. "I'm sure everything will be just fine."

He inclined his head. "Then I'll leave you. Your bags will be here shortly, and please join Mary Tucker downstairs when you're ready. Perhaps later I can give you a tour of the house?" He added that last bit as an obvious afterthought; I'm sure it was part of his instructions from Miss McElroy, but he had no enthusiasm for the task.

"I'd like that very much," I said. "The house is spectacular, and I'd love to see it."

"Then it would be my great pleasure to show it to you." With a small, courtly bow, he was gone.

I wondered idly whether he treated everyone this way, or whether it was just me. Although my family wasn't as wealthy as the McElroys, we had been in Mississippi just as long. But that really didn't matter in the grand scheme of things.

Dismissing these thoughts as unproductive, I set my handbag down on the bedside table and hoisted my rump up onto the bed to test it. I'm six feet tall, but this bed was built high off the floor. Near the foot stood a two-step device for the use of those whose legs were too short to get them there on their own power. The mattress was firm and comfortable, and I resisted the urge to lie back and wallow.

Duty first. I inspected my face in the mirror, assuring myself that I looked presentable. No need to touch up the minimal makeup that I wear. The bathroom could wait until after I had seen Miss McElroy and found out what she wanted me to do today.

Down the hallway I went, taking a moment here and there to examine a portrait or a piece of statuary, but not lingering too long. The space was cool and quiet, as if the great house around me slumbered in the midday sun. Walking down the stairs, I listened to the small sounds the wood made. I'm a sucker for old houses. I had already fallen in love with this one, and I hadn't even been inside it for half an hour yet.

Shaking my head at myself, I approached the door of the room where Miss McElroy awaited me. The door stood a tad ajar, and I could hear voices from inside the room as I drew closer.

I was about to knock to announce my presence when I decided that it wouldn't hurt to stop and listen for a moment. Something about the tone of the voices behind the door alerted me.

". . . respond to threats," Miss McElroy was saying, her voice frosty.

"But, my dear Mary Tucker," the other person said, oozing honey, "I wouldn't exactly call it a threat. Think of it more as a promise." A throaty chuckle. "And you know, dear heart, I *never* go back on a promise."

"Come in, Miss Carpenter," Mary Tucker McElroy called out, startling me so that I almost stumbled into the door. I'm afraid my face was a bit red as I came into the room.

Miss McElroy frowned as she said, "My hearing is quite acute. You'll do well to remember that."

As humiliated as I felt at the moment, I doubted I'd ever forget it. "Duly noted," I said, with what composure I could muster.

As discreetly as I could, I examined the other woman standing near Miss McElroy. Short, plump, and homely were the first three adjectives that came to mind. She wore a Laura

Ashley dress that did its best to lend her appearance some kind of charm but failed miserably. Her faux-blonde hair framed her face in a mass of curls better suited to a woman forty years younger.

Miss McElroy sniffed. "Miss Ernestine Carpenter, I'd like you to meet one of my other guests. This is Lurleen Landry. I've no doubt that you've read her work. Lurleen, this is Ernestine Carpenter, who is joining us this week."

Lurleen Landry! I examined her more closely while I tried to keep my mouth from hanging open. The woman in front of me looked very little like the pictures I had seen on the dust jackets of her more recent books, and I wondered how on earth a photographer had managed to turn this little dumpling of a woman into the sleek authoress in the photos. I would never have recognized her.

Miss McElroy covered the looming awkwardness by continuing, "Miss Carpenter's assisting me with my memoirs." That was the fiction she had insisted upon to explain my presence among her select little collection of literary lions. I believe she *was* working on a memoir, but whether I'd be privy to any of it was anybody's guess.

"How do you do, Miss Carpenter," Lurleen Landry said, inclining her head in acknowledgment.

"I'm delighted to meet you, Miss Landry. I've enjoyed your work, ever since your first book, *Down on the River Road*." My composure had begun creeping back.

"Thank you, my dear. So many these days seem to have forgotten about my dear little first novel." She preened in happiness at my words.

I wasn't quite so bold as to tell her that, as far as I was concerned, her first book was without a doubt the best thing she'd ever done. The thirty or so books she'd penned in the forty years since had become progressively bloated and stale, peopled by brittle stereotypes whom it was difficult to like. Not, of course, that these problems kept the books from riding high on the best-seller list.

"*Down on the River Road* is a classic," I said, "and before I retired from teaching, I had it on my required reading list for my senior honors course. Few writers have ever been able to capture what it was like growing up Southern and female in the 1950s the way you did in that book. The friendship between the two girls and the racial tensions which eventually drove them apart are so beautifully done. I reread the book every two or three years, and it has never lost its impact."

"I can't tell you how gratifying it is to hear that," the beaming author replied.

Miss McElroy saved me from having to perjure myself on the topic of her later work by dismissing Lurleen. "I'm sure you'd like to go and rest a while before luncheon, my dear, and Miss Carpenter and I do have a number of things to discuss."

"Why, of course, my dear," Lurleen purred back at her. "We can always continue our little discussion later on." She gave me a demure wave as she walked out of the room, leaving the door open behind her.

I moved to close it, then came back and sat down across from Miss McElroy in a large armchair. She contemplated me in silence, and I wondered whether I had annoyed her by my clumsy attempt at eavesdropping. Would she fire me? I hoped not, because I was increasingly intrigued by the setup at Idlewild, and leaving now would disappoint my sizable bump of curiosity.

I'm a voracious and eclectic reader, and one of the reasons I had decided to take on Miss McElroy's job was the chance to meet several writers whose work I had enjoyed. Spending time in close proximity with the likes of Russell Bertram, Brett Doran, and Lurleen Landry was enough to get me to take the job, though unless you charge a healthy fee, people don't always take you seriously.

Lurleen had, in our initial meeting, surprised me. She seemed nothing like the glamorous author portrayed in the media, more like a dowdy Southern grandmother. Would the others be completely different from their public personas as well?

"I do understand your need to gather information," Miss

McElroy spoke at last, "but if you feel compelled to listen in on conversations, you might do well to remember that this is an old house with floorboards that creak. Not to mention the fact that, tall as you are, you do cast rather a long shadow."

And, with chagrin, I remembered that the mid-morning sun had shone through the front windows of the hallway toward me as I stood in front of that cursed door. I managed a smile. "Thanks for the reminders. I won't make those mistakes again."

"Very well." Miss McElroy allowed a small smile in return, and I relaxed a fraction. "My remaining guests will be arriving throughout the day, and I would like you to be on hand as they do. Russell Bertram will be accompanied by his wife, Alice." Her voice allowed the slightest inflection of distaste to surface as she pronounced the final three words of the sentence.

"One thing you should know in advance. Alice has for some years been reduced to walking with the aid of a walker, due to problems with her hips and lower back. She will ask you to fetch and carry for her, and you may decline as you see fit. You are not here as a personal servant, but as my guest—but that will not matter to her." She sniffed.

"I believe I know the type," I said, and indeed I did. I had once had a principal who was inclined to think that her teachers—in particular the unmarried female ones—existed solely to cater to her whims, like buying her groceries, picking up her dry cleaning, and so on. She had lasted at our school less than three months.

Russell Bertram, unlike Lurleen Landry, seemed to shun the spotlight. His last novel had been published nearly ten years ago, and since that time his name had seldom surfaced in the news. I had supposed he had retired from writing, but Miss McElroy informed me three days ago that he at last had a novel nearly ready for publication and that he would have a manuscript with him when he came to Idlewild.

According to Miss McElroy, the new book would carry on the story of his classic, *The Philosophy of Love*, an international best-seller of thirty years ago. The earlier book told the story of a man torn between his love for two women, one of them exotic and erotic, who brought out his sensual side, the other staid and prim, but his intellectual match and the one who encouraged his art. His solution was to bring the two women together under one roof, not unlike the way the late Georges Simenon had kept his mistress in the same house with his long-suffering wife. I had found the book provocative upon a first reading; but reading it again some years later, I found myself irritated by the main character's boorish self-indulgence and his whining about society's disapproval of his dubious sexual ethics.

Would I read the sequel to *The Philosophy of Love*? I had to admit that I would, in the hopes that the author and his creation would have learned something valuable over the last three decades.

Miss McElroy broke in on my reverie. "Brett Doran will no doubt be late, as usual, so I do not expect to see him before this evening. He might be bringing with him the final member of the group, a man named Hamilton Packer, a literary agent and advisor. Until a few years ago, Hamilton was dear Russ's agent. They did not part amicably, but they seem to have smoothed over their difficulties recently."

Brett Doran was something of an enfant terrible on the literary scene. His debut novel, *Music to Slaughter By*, had aroused a storm of controversy because of its graphic violence against women. Many critics had castigated the book for the perverse glee with which the author had described the torture and murder of several victims, at the hands of the novel's main character, a sociopathic professor of musicology. I had abhorred the gratuitous violence, but what most critics seem to have neglected was the book's stinging criticism of the way our society glorifies violence in all its forms, but particularly violence against women and children, for the titillation of the masses.

The author had something important to say, but the message seemed to have been lost because of the way in which he tried to say it. Since the book's publication six years earlier, he had not yet published another novel, only a handful of stories and a couple of screenplays.

"I'm very much looking forward to meeting Mr. Doran," I said. "I wonder if he can possibly be as provocative in person as his work."

One eyebrow arched as Miss McElroy regarded me. "I think you will find Brett most interesting, Miss Carpenter. As I think he will also find you most interesting." She again permitted herself a small smile, and I wondered, just for a moment, if I had gotten myself in over my head without realizing it.

"That brings us," she resumed, her tone brisk, "to the final member of this gathering." I gave her a blank look, because I couldn't remember her mentioning another guest. Miss McElroy frowned. "The final member is *not* someone who will be with us in the physical sense, Miss Carpenter. I refer, of course, to the reason you are here. Sukey Lytton."

Ah, yes, I thought. *The accident victim.*

"Though Sukey will not be with us in body, she will most certainly be with us in spirit," she said. A shadow—of pain? of regret?—passed across her face. "Every one of us here in this house will be thinking of her, and of the last time we were all together here. I will be regretting the waste of a young talent of great promise. But one of us will be gloating over the satisfaction of having her dead and out of the way. I want you to discover which one of my guests brought about her death. And why."

"If one of these people truly is a murderer," I said slowly, "then I'll do my best to help you figure out which one of them did it." I paused for a moment. "But we need to tread carefully. If someone killed once, he or she might not hesitate to do it again."

"What? Are you afraid someone will harm you?" Miss McElroy glared at me as if I had just announced my intention to quit.

"Or you," I pointed out equably. "Either one of us could be at risk."

"Do you want to quit, before you've barely started?" The

disgust in her voice stung me.

"No, that's not what I'm saying," I responded with as much patience as I could muster. "But we both have to be prepared to face the risks."

Miss McElroy sat and stared at me for what seemed a long time. Finally she spoke. "I have to know. No matter what happens."

Chapter Three

I CLEARED MY THROAT. "In that case, let's get on with it." There seemed no reason to belabor the point any further. Miss McElroy had chosen her course, and we'd both stick to it. "I found one of Sukey Lytton's short stories in an anthology I have," I said. "Very much influenced by Eudora Welty, I thought. She had a lot of promise."

"Yes," Miss McElroy said. "Sukey had so much left to write, so much to say. Her death was a great loss to the future of American letters."

"Most likely," I said. "Right now I need to know more about Sukey Lytton and the circumstances surrounding her death. I'll reserve judgment on the others until I've had a chance to meet them all. Now, the account I found in the local paper, and even the ones in the Jackson and Memphis papers, weren't much help."

Miss McElroy sat back in her chair, hands clasped together. "Sukey was a bundle of contradictions. Mercurial, insecure, overbearing, endearing. Exasperating. Yes, that's a good word for her. Exasperating. Just when you thought you'd want to wash your hands of her, because she was so obstinate and irritating, she'd do something unexpected, something tender and thoughtful, and you'd realize all over again what a dear child she was."

The unfortunate girl had aroused Miss McElroy's protective instincts, that was certain. *Frustrated maternal love?* I speculated. Perhaps.

"But she wasn't all that young, was she?" I asked. "I believe the newspaper stated her age as thirty-three."

"That's correct," Miss McElroy said. "Chronologically, at

least, she was thirty-three when she died. Intellectually, she was more sophisticated, but emotionally, well. . . ." She sighed. "Emotionally, she was still a bruised adolescent, hungry for approval and unconditional love. I tried to give her what I could, we all did, but that was sometimes difficult."

"Tell me more about what happened when she died," I said. "I need to know what wasn't in the newspaper."

She regarded some spot on the wall behind me. "It was Christmas. A time of joy and celebration. Yet it turned to ashes for me. Sukey had come to visit, for the first time in a year and a half. She seemed a bit more like her old self. But still a bit distant." Miss McElroy shook her head. "Something was clearly on Sukey's mind, but she couldn't bring herself to tell me." Her hands moved restlessly in her lap. "Something that the papers didn't know," she continued, her tone taking on an edge, "which in fact only a few people knew. Sukey had been working on a novel—had actually finished it, I believe—and she was on the verge of a contract with one of the major publishers. Hamilton Packer had been negotiating it for her, but of course that all evaporated when she died and we couldn't find a completed manuscript among her things."

My nose almost quivered at the scent of a possible motive for murder. "You mean the manuscript just disappeared? Didn't this agent of hers have a copy of what she had already written?"

"He had only the first three chapters, and that's what he was using to sell the book. Which is rather odd, of course, for someone like Sukey who was not known as a novelist. She had a good reputation, however, for her short fiction, and sometimes that's enough to sell an editor who likes the partial."

"It's odd, though, that the manuscript didn't turn up."

Miss McElroy shrugged. "Sukey was very secretive about her work, at least about any work-in-progress. I thought she had completed the book before she arrived here at Christmas, and I expected her to show it to me. But she didn't. So I don't know what could have happened to it."

Another lead to investigate, I thought, though it could prove to be nothing but a tantalizing red herring. "What about the circumstances surrounding her death?" I asked. "Was there anything about it that made you think it was murder?"

"If you'll remember," she said, "the weather was unseasonably warm at Christmas. We had the windows open, and everyone was wearing clothing more suitable for summer than for December. Sukey was restless that morning. It was Christmas Eve, and I saw her briefly at breakfast, when she said she was going out for a walk. To me she seemed much the same as usual, though afterwards the others claimed that she had acted despondent, depressed." Miss McElroy fell silent.

"What happened then?" I prompted.

"Sukey never came back from her walk." Miss McElroy laid her head back against the chair and closed her eyes. "When she didn't appear for lunch, I sent Morwell out to look for her. Sometimes she would fall asleep outside somewhere, or else sit and scribble under a tree, losing all track of time. I thought that was all that had happened, as it had happened many times in the past."

"But this time was different," I said, regarding her obvious distress with sympathy.

"Yes. Morwell soon came back, very shaken, to say that he had found her in the pond, in the woods beyond the back of the garden. Behind the house. She was floating facedown in the water." Miss McElroy paused for a deep, steadying breath. "Sukey often went there to sit and think—she said she found staring at the water very soothing. She seemed to have a fascination for it, which in retrospect made the place seem like an obvious choice if she really intended to kill herself."

I pictured the scene all too easily, and though I was impatient to know more, I did not prompt Miss McElroy when she fell silent this time.

"Morwell had waded into the pond to try to help her," she finally said, "but he realized, despite his deep distress, that she was beyond his help. He laid her body on the ground, then came back to the house. But before that, he found something." She paused, then went on as if forcing herself to speak. "On the ground near the edge of the pond, he found a piece of paper, containing one of her poems. A short poem about despair and a longing for release from it."

How appallingly sad, I thought. And how appallingly clichéd. Whether it was suicide or murder, it was an unoriginal way of accomplishing either. Simple and effective, but predictable.

"Why don't you think it was suicide or just a dumb accident?" I asked. "And if it wasn't suicide or an accident, why wasn't it investigated as murder?"

"At first I was too deeply distressed by it all to think clearly," Miss McElroy said, her voice tired. "It was entirely in character for Sukey to have done something so spiteful, so selfish, I'm afraid. One line in that poem was directed at me, and it upset me so badly that I simply couldn't cope with any of it. I retreated, mentally and physically."

I wanted to ask, but the pain was obvious on her too expressive face. I waited in silence, deciding to let her continue at her own pace.

She drew a ragged breath, then quoted from the poem. "'Mothered by Medea, I long for death. . . .'" Her eyes closed, she turned a blind face toward the wall. "She once called me Medea. It was one of the worst moments in our relationship. So, you see, I thought the note was left there specifically for me."

What a little monster was my first reaction. If Sukey Lytton had left the poem there deliberately in order to wound Miss McElroy, she had succeeded. What a vicious thing to do, even if one is in utter despair.

Yet, I couldn't resist thinking, how clever of a murderer to choose something which would have hurt Miss McElroy so badly, keeping her from thinking clearly about Sukey Lytton's death. But who might have known that the Medea reference would have been directed toward Miss McElroy?

As gently as I could, I probed further. "I can certainly understand why you'd be upset by something like that. And it would keep you from thinking too much about her death and whether it was really suicide or something else. But at some point you must have had second thoughts about it all. Why?"

Miss McElroy pulled a handkerchief from her sleeve and dabbed at her eyes before she answered. "The sheriff's department sent a man out to investigate, and he concluded rather quickly that Sukey had killed herself. In the circumstances, of course, there had to be a postmortem. I couldn't bring myself to ask much about the results, not at first, but I was assured by the sheriff's man that the findings were not inconsistent with suicide." She gave a grim little laugh. "It was only later that I thought about how he had phrased it. 'Not inconsistent.' To me that sounded just a little too ambiguous. Three weeks ago, I nerved myself up and made arrangements to get a copy of that autopsy report."

She shuddered, and I couldn't blame her. Having to pore through the grim details—and pictures, to boot—would be grisly, to say the least.

"What did you find?" I asked, my voice quiet and even. "Obviously, something made you change your mind about the suicide."

Miss McElroy nodded. "There were two things, actually. Two things I hadn't known before, which convinced me that Sukey was murdered. The first was that there was some bruising about the back of her head. That could have happened if she had slipped and fallen in the water, because there are some quite large rocks around the edge of the pond."

"Suggestive, certainly," I said.

"Yes," Miss McElroy said. "The report stated that the blows which caused the bruises might have been enough to render her unconscious. But the end result was that she drowned."

"Odd" was my only comment. I waited to hear the rest.

"The other thing which I hadn't known before, and which convinced me that Sukey did not kill herself, was the poem. Or rather the paper it was on."

"What do you mean?" I asked, puzzled.

"I had just assumed, as I suppose anyone would, when I was told the poem was found near her that it was in Sukey's own handwriting. Wouldn't you?"

I nodded. "Seems logical to me."

Miss McElroy suddenly seemed to relax. "Then you see my point. The poem wasn't handwritten. It was on a page torn from a book. Sukey would never have done that. She considered books precious objects, and she would never have damaged one in that way." She looked away for a moment. "She might damage a person, but not a book."

"Did anyone test the page for fingerprints?"

"Yes. That was in the report I got from the sheriff's office. There were no fingerprints at all on that piece of paper except for Morwell's, from where he picked it up off the ground."

"Because Sukey didn't tear it out of the book," I said, watching her face.

"Exactly. The murderer did that, hoping it would be passed off as a suicide."

"It worked. At least for a while."

"But no longer," Miss McElroy said with grim satisfaction. "Together, we'll see to that."

"Why didn't you tell the sheriff's investigator your suspicions?"

She waved a hand in the air, dismissing that idea summarily. "Can you imagine what would happen if a good ol' boy came galumphing around here, asking questions of these people? Absolutely nothing, that's what! This situation demands more finesse, and from what I've been told, you have the kind of skills I need."

I was both flattered and intrigued. There seemed to me room for doubt that Sukey Lytton had committed suicide, and I was willing to find out what I could. Miss McElroy no longer seemed as distant and supercilious as I had at first found her, which was a small blessing. "I'll do my best."

"Good enough," she said, her voice stronger as she regained her customary aplomb.

Behind us, the door crashed open and a voice assaulted our ears. "Nonsense! Of course she's ready to receive us.

Don't be ridiculous, Russell. And hurry up and help me to a chair. You know I can't stand for very long, not the way my hip is hurting."

Miss McElroy leaned forward, whispering. "And here, right on cue, are two prime suspects."

Miss McElroy stood to receive her visitors, and I followed suit, turning to face the newcomers. I had to admit to a bit of excitement at finally meeting Russell Bertram face to face. No matter how provocative and occasionally misogynist I found some of his work, he was still one of the preeminent men of American letters. I didn't often have the chance to meet literary celebrities of his magnitude.

It was his wife, however, whom one first noticed. Her face drawn in pain, Alice Bertram limped across the room, her heavy body supported by a walker. Jet black hair threaded thickly with white was coiled into a tight bun at the nape of her neck; and as she looked up at me with a glance of cold assessment, I almost took a step backwards. I couldn't recall a time when I had seen a face so full of spitefulness.

"Don't just stand there gawking like an idiot! Can't you see I need help?"

For a moment I was too stunned to move, then my face flushed in anger. No one speaks to me that way. At least, no one who has ever lived to boast about it afterwards.

I was just opening my mouth to retort when Russell Bertram stepped into the fray. "Now, Alice dear, here's your favorite chair, right beside you. Let me help you into it . . . there you go. Just ease yourself down, and you'll be quite comfortable in a moment." He had moved beside his wife, towering over her, as he guided her gently but firmly into a well-padded, straight-backed chair an appropriate height for her short stubby body.

"Not so fast, Russell! You know how my hips ache when I have to sit down." She grimaced, as if in excruciating pain, while she settled herself in the chair.

"No need to ask how you're doing, Alice" was Miss McElroy's greeting.

Alice Bertram glared across at her hostess. "As you can

see, Mary Tucker, I'm still in just as much pain as ever. I should have stayed home, because driving long distances in a car just makes everything so much worse. We left Nashville at the crack of dawn." Her voice had taken on an unpleasant whining quality. "But of course, the minute Russell knew you wanted us here, nothing would do him but coming here. Just like a little lap dog obeying his mistress's commands."

I heard a muffled intake of breath, and I wasn't sure whether it came from Miss McElroy or Russell Bertram.

"Now, Alice dear, you really shouldn't say such things to Mary Tucker. She wouldn't have asked us here if it weren't for something important."

"Exactly," Miss McElroy said. "I appreciate the sacrifice you've made to come here, Alice, and naturally we'll do our best to make you as comfortable as possible." She was making a remarkable effort, I thought, to keep her voice even.

I, on the other hand, would gladly have poured something cold and unpleasant over the woman's head. The days ahead suddenly seemed much, much longer.

"But I'm forgetting my manners," Miss McElroy continued. "Let me introduce my guest, Miss Ernestine Carpenter. Miss Carpenter, I'd like you to meet Alice and Russell Bertram."

"It's a great pleasure to meet you, Mr. Bertram," I said, holding out my hand to him while doing my best to ignore his harridan of a wife.

He clasped my hand in his and exerted a gentle pressure. Lightly tinted glasses masked his eyes, but his mouth quirked in what I assumed was a mute apology for his wife's behavior. He wore a dark suit with a white shirt and plain gray tie which contrasted sharply with the peacock nature of his wife's attire; the garishly colored pantsuit she wore seemed more suited to a fashion-impaired teenager than it did to a woman of fifty-odd.

Deep lines had etched the man's face, giving him the appearance of a man nearer the century mark than his true age of sixty-four. He nevertheless maintained the distinguished appearance which had graced the photographs on his book jackets for several decades.

"I'm delighted to meet you, Miss Carpenter," he said.

Miss McElroy motioned for us to be seated. "I'm sure, after your drive here, you'd like something to drink. What can I offer you?"

"We've already taken care of that," Alice said. "When Morwell greeted us at the front door, I told him what to bring us. You'd think he could have managed by now. I'm simply parched after that drive." She shook her head in disgust. "I don't know why you just don't go ahead and hire some young and capable person to take over."

Miss McElroy offered a tight-lipped smile. "When Morwell feels that he no longer wants to do such things, then I will of course do as you suggest, Alice. But until that day, I prefer to let him do as he pleases."

"Which is to take his own damn sweet time while I sit here dying of thirst," Alice complained.

I was going to have to work hard to keep a rein on my temper, I realized, or else this job would be over, with me in jail, before it ever got started.

Russell sighed as he stood up. "Don't fret, Alice dear. I'll just go and see what's keeping Morwell. Perhaps he needs help with the drinks tray."

The door opened then, and the butler walked in carrying a silver serving tray, arrayed with an assortment of bottles, glasses, a pitcher, and an ice bucket. He moved forward and set the tray down on the table beside Miss McElroy. With a flourish, he picked up a glass and presented it to Alice Bertram. "I'm sorry it took me so long, Alice, but I had forgotten to have the cook slice up any lemon before you arrived. Here's your iced tea with lemon."

"And?" She eyed the glass with deep suspicion.

"And laced with just a smidgen of bourbon, the way you like it," he responded.

I shuddered.

"Thank you, Morwell," she said. "At least someone around here makes some effort on my behalf. Though it certainly took you long enough to get it here."

Phillips caught the outraged expression on my face as he

turned back to the drinks tray. One eyebrow rose in a delicate arch, then his face disappeared from view. "Here you are, Russell," he said, turning back with another glass in his hand. "A bit of whisky and soda."

"Thank you, Morwell." As Russell took the glass with quick gratitude, I noticed for the first time the network of fine red lines in his nose. Perhaps a plentiful supply of whisky and soda was all that kept him from pushing his wife under the nearest eighteen-wheeler. I suppressed the urge to ask for one myself. It was way too early in the day.

"Miss Carpenter? What would you like?" Phillips had handed Miss McElroy a glass of iced tea. With a gesture, he indicated the tray.

Spotting a bottle of Diet Coke, I made my choice. With a deft hand he dropped several cubes of ice into a tall glass, added a twist of lemon, then poured in the liquid.

"Thank you," I said.

He ducked his head slightly in acknowledgment and said, "Now, can I get anyone anything else?" Assured that everyone was content, he turned to the Bertrams. "Well, then," he said, "I'll just go and take care of getting your bags out of the car and up to your room. If you'll excuse me."

"Well, this is cozy," Alice said as the door closed with a soft click. "Why are we here?"

Miss McElroy chuckled, deep in her throat. "Alice, dear, do I really need a reason to invite old friends here for a few days?"

Alice knocked back the contents of her tea glass, then thrust it in her husband's direction without even looking at him. Russell set his own glass down on a coaster on the table near him, before he got up to pour more tea and bourbon into his wife's glass.

"I know how much you adore Russell's and my company, Mary Tucker," Alice purred. "In fact, I'm sure you'd just love it if we lived here. That way, you and Russell could talk all you wanted to about what a brilliant writer he is and what a wonderful patroness of the arts you've been, all these years. He could even dedicate another book to you—if he ever finishes another one, that is."

Her face hardened, making her look even more unpleasant than before, if that were possible. "But that dog won't hunt. What's the real reason you wanted us here?" Alice took a long drink from her glass before setting it down with a thunk on the bare table beside her.

I was watching Miss McElroy with great attention, otherwise I would have missed the brief tightening of the muscles in her face.

She forced herself to laugh, a light sound of amusement. "I have to confess, Alice, that I did have an ulterior motive in asking you and my other guests here this week."

"Other guests?" Alice almost barked the words.

"It's going to be quite a reunion," Miss McElroy said. "Brett and Hamilton will be joining us sometime today, and Lurleen's already here." She beamed at husband and wife. "Won't that be delightful?"

"You're nuts," Alice said. She struggled to rise from her chair. "I'm not playing this little game. Russell, help me out of this chair. Now! I want to go home."

Russell sat frozen in his chair, looking helplessly back and forth between his wife and Miss McElroy.

"Now, Alice, don't be too hasty," Miss McElroy said. Her voice was so sweet you could have frosted a cake with it. "I'm sure you wouldn't want to miss a minute of the next few days. We're going to have such a grand time, reminiscing about old times, and I know how you hate not being at the center of things."

Alice ceased her crab-like struggles to get out of the chair. "And what, pray tell, are you talking about? Reminiscing? About what? The times Russell was nominated for the Pulitzer but never managed to win?" She cast a scornful glance at her husband.

"Always so tactful, Alice dear," Miss McElroy said. "How do you manage it? You might as well know, I've decided at last to write my memoirs, and of course I need my nearest and dearest friends around me to help me remember some of the most significant occasions."

Alice laughed, a harsh sound. "You've got gall, Mary Tucker. But then, women with money their daddies earned for them usually do. What if we don't want to stay here and play this little game with you? What if we go back home right now?"

"Now, Alice," Miss McElroy said, her voice mild. "I don't think you really want to do that, do you? After all, I just might not remember some things the way I should, and it would be a shame for the wrong information to make it into print. Don't you think so?"

"Like what?" Alice said, her eyes narrowing. Her husband and I sat there, watching the duel without saying a word.

"Like the time," Miss McElroy said, her voice even sweeter than before, "some of my checks disappeared. Then later on they reappeared, but someone else had signed my name to them. Remember that?"

Alice Bertram howled with rage. She picked up her glass of tea and threw it straight at Miss McElroy.

Chapter Four

MISS MCELROY MOVED FASTER than I would have thought possible. As the glass of tea arced through the air in her direction, she stood. The glass hit her just below her ample bosom, and tea spilled down the front of her lavender silk dress. The glass fell on the carpet at her feet, ice cubes splaying out in front of her. A faint scent of bourbon perfumed the air.

"'A hit, a palpable hit,'" Miss McElroy quoted, with understated irony. I couldn't help but admire her considerable sangfroid. She mopped at the stain on her dress with a handkerchief.

"Alice!" Russell Bertram choked out in a horrified whisper. "How could you?"

"Is this a private party, or can anyone join in?"

All heads swiveled toward the door, and there stood a stranger. At least he was a stranger to me, though I recognized him from the book-jacket photographs I'd seen. Brett Doran, in the flesh. Handsome flesh, too. If only I were about thirty years younger.

Stepping over the mess on the carpet, having forgotten her sodden dress, Miss McElroy moved forward with hands outstretched. "Dear, dear Brett! How lovely to see you. And handsome as ever, despite the fact that you seem unable to find your razor more than once a week." She chuckled.

He clasped her hand in his and raised it to his lips. Dressed all in black, with jet hair and a five-day stubble of dark beard on his face, he looked dangerous, like a man more at home on the mean streets than in the drawing room of a genteel Southern mansion. Which effect no doubt he intended to enhance his image as one of the "bad boys" of American letters. His face, however, lit with a big smile as he looked down at Miss McElroy; and danger receded, leaving only a bit of the playboy behind.

"What have I missed?" he asked, his voice low and husky.

Miss McElroy turned to face the Bertrams and me, tucking Brett Doran's hand into the crook of her left arm as she did so. "I've just been introducing my guest, Miss Ernestine Carpenter, to Alice and Russell. I'm afraid something I said caused Alice to have one of her little temper tantrums, but I'm sure that's all over and done with. Isn't it, Alice?"

The steel in Miss McElroy's voice made that last sentence more of a command than a query. Alice Bertram was seething, but all she said was, "Yes, sorry, Mary Tucker. I don't know what came over me."

"How do you do, Miss Carpenter?" Brett Doran held out a hand to me, and I clasped it in mine. He was trying hard not to laugh at Alice, and I grinned at him. He gave off a warm, masculine scent, a mixture of expensive cigars and an understated cologne.

"A pleasure to meet you, Mr. Doran. I've read your work, and I find it very provocative. And misunderstood, I'm afraid."

Whatever he was expecting, it wasn't that. Pleasure lit his face, making him younger and less jaded than he appeared to be. "Please, call me Brett," he said. "I think we're going to be good friends, Miss Carpenter."

"And call me Ernie," I told him. "That's what my friends call me."

"I'd very much appreciate it," Alice Bertram's voice cut through like the scritch of a diamond on glass, "if someone would refill my glass. I'm terribly thirsty, and it's time for another of my painkillers. My hip is excruciatingly painful."

"Let me do the honors," Brett said as he shepherded Miss McElroy back to her seat. As she reached for a bellpull near her chair, he stooped down, picked up Alice's glass, and began refilling it from the drinks tray. "In this world where few things are certain except death and taxes," he said, turning to Alice with a debonair flourish, offering her the newly filled glass of tea and bourbon, "I'm ever delighted at how certain things remain constant, my dear, dear Alice. One does so regret the pain you are forced to endure, but we do all so much appreciate the efforts you make in sharing it with us at *every* possible moment."

I braced myself for a repeat of the earlier glass-tossing scene, but Alice said nothing. Instead she knocked back half the contents of the glass. Since I had seen Brett pour a liberal dose of bourbon into it, I wondered whether she'd choke. But the woman was made of sterner stuff than I had estimated. She didn't even breathe hard as the tea-laced bourbon slid down her throat.

Brett held out a hand to Russell Bertram. "Russ, it's great to see you, as always. How are you?"

"Fine, Brett, just fine. Good to see you." Russell shook the proffered hand with greater enthusiasm than he had hitherto demonstrated. "We must talk later. I'm eager to hear about what you're working on now."

"It would be a pleasure," Brett said, as he sat on a sofa across from Miss McElroy. "Now, tell me what I've missed."

Miss McElroy smiled. "Just before you arrived, Brett, I had been explaining to Alice and Russell the reason for our little get-together. I've finally decided to work on my memoirs, and Miss Carpenter is assisting me with them. Naturally I wanted my nearest and dearest here to help me remember some of the important occasions in my life."

"I suppose," Brett said in a quiet tone, "that you know what you're doing, Mary Tucker." He looked at her, and some sort of unspoken message seemed to pass between them.

"What harm can a little reminiscing do us?" she responded, flirting shamelessly.

"Indeed," he said. The amusement he invested in that one word was palpable. He caught my eye and winked.

Miss McElroy had at least one ally among her guests, I supposed. That might make my job a bit easier. If Brett Doran was more willing to talk than I suspected either of the Bertrams would be, so much the better.

I kept staring at the puddle of tea and bourbon which had

soaked into the carpet. I seemed to be the only one worried about it, however, because Miss McElroy hadn't spared it a second glance after Brett's entrance into the room. I decided that, if she wasn't worried about her carpet being ruined, I wasn't either.

The door opened, and Morwell Phillips entered. Miss McElroy indicated the carpet with a flourish of her hand and said, "Morwell, I'm afraid there's been a bit of an accident. Alice spilled her tea. Could you send someone with a towel to mop it up, there's a dear."

"Certainly, Mary Tucker." He turned and left the room, closing the door behind him.

Our hostess stood. "I'm afraid, my dears, that I must retire for a little while. I really should change, so that someone can get the tea out of this dress before it's completely ruined. Please stay and chat, if you like. But you all know your rooms, of course, so just make yourselves at home, as always." Head held high, she proceeded out of the room. I resisted the urge to stand and curtsy. She did have such a regal way with her.

I caught Brett Doran's eye, and he winked again. Before I could say anything, Alice announced in a peevish tone that she wanted to go to her room. "Help me up, Russell. You know how difficult I find those stairs. You'd think Mary Tucker would make some effort to consider the comfort of her guests and have some kind of lift installed. But I suppose I'll just have to force myself upstairs, as usual."

Russell grimaced as he leaned over his wife, assisting her up and out of her chair. Neither Brett nor I offered any comment. Instead we watched in silence as the Bertrams proceeded at a sedate pace from the room, Alice giving ill-natured comments with every step. For someone in as much pain as she claimed to be, she had little trouble drawing breath to speak, that's for sure.

As the door closed behind the couple, Brett broke the silence. "So, Ernie, how did Mary Tucker rope you into this little shindig? Have you been 'discovered' like the rest of us?"

I laughed. "I have no claims to being a literary light, Brett. I did teach high-school English for nearly forty years, and I have several former students who are quite gifted writers. But I'm here merely as an assistant to Miss McElroy. Nothing more."

"Assisting her in doing what, I wonder?" Brett smiled as he stood up. He pulled a leather cigar case from his inside jacket pocket. "Would you care to join me on the verandah while I indulge my filthy habit? I'm afraid Mary Tucker doesn't allow anyone to smoke inside the house."

Out on the verandah, he guided me toward a shaded corner with several comfortable chairs. An old and venerable magnolia tree shaded us from the noonday sun. Thank goodness there was a bit of a breeze, otherwise the sultry day would have driven me back inside in a heartbeat. But I figured Brett had a reason for inviting me outside, and I might as well hear what it was.

I watched as he chose a short, fat cigar from his case, then clipped and lit it. He exhaled a cloud of fragrant smoke, being careful to direct it away from me, even though I didn't mind. "My one vice," he said, a boyish grin on his face.

"Somehow I doubt that," I said in a wry tone.

"I'd better not forget those years you spent teaching." He leaned back in his chair and stretched out his long legs. "No flies on you, I'm sure."

"Not many," I agreed, watching and waiting.

"You said something very interesting when we were introduced," Brett said after a brief silence, expelling more smoke.

"What was that?" I prompted when he failed to continue.

"That I was misunderstood. What did you mean by that?" He examined the glowing tip of his cigar with care, but his attention was focused on me, waiting for my reply.

"I read your book, and I read a lot of what the press had to say about it. I also saw a couple of the interviews you did, the one with Barbara Walters, for example, and that idiotic piece on 'Entertainment Tonight.' Seems to me most of them missed the point of what you were saying, completely."

"And what was the point, do you think?"

I watched him for a moment, through the haze of smoke circulating in a lazy pattern around his head. He reminded me of so many students I'd had over the years, bright, talented young people, aware of their gifts, yet insecure. Despite his success, he still wasn't quite certain of himself.

"I'll grant you that the level of violence in the book was almost too much," I said. "But I thought it was fairly clear you were making a point about how our culture these days seems to glamorize violence against women. The way violence against women demeans and diminishes us all. The satire was mordant and pointed; but most of the men, and even the women, who reviewed the book didn't get it all."

He exhaled a plume of smoke into the air with great satisfaction. "Thank you. Knowing that someone who read the book got what I was trying to say makes me feel better, believe me. I thought I was being pretty obvious, even a bit too heavy-handed, but I was surprised. I never thought the book would be that controversial." He grinned in self-mockery. "But that just goes to show you how much a writer really knows about his own work. The most important thing I learned in all this is that you have no control over how the public will perceive and construe what you've written. You might as well try to herd cats."

I laughed. "A good point. I do hope you didn't take too much of the silliness to heart and let it interfere with your writing."

Brett leaned over and tapped some ash off the end of his cigar into the flower bed beneath the verandah. "Wish I could say I had, but I have to admit it's taken me a while to get a sense of perspective on it. The last few months I've finally been able to write again without feeling like the whole world was staring over my shoulder, goggling at every word I typed onto the computer screen." He grinned.

"Good for you. You have to forget about them and write for yourself."

"Yeah," he said. "It's taken me a while to remember that." He drew on his cigar again and watched the smoke he emitted. "I think maybe I'm going to adopt you as my guardian angel. How's that?"

Absurdly pleased, I forced myself not to blush. "If you're

not careful, I'll have you in the principal's office for insubordination, young man."

Brett laughed. "I wonder if Mary Tucker realizes just what she has on her hands."

"I doubt it."

"I reckon Mary Tucker may have finally met her match, but she probably doesn't know it yet."

He laughed along with me, then told me a few amusing anecdotes about his first book tour, which I relished. He was a superb raconteur, and I relaxed and forgot about the job at hand while he talked.

"But enough of that." All at once serious, he leaned toward me. "So," he asked, his voice dropping to a stage whisper, "who do *you* think murdered Sukey Lytton?"

Chapter Five

I COUNTERED WITH ANOTHER QUESTION. "What makes you so certain she was murdered?"

"No fair," Brett sputtered, laughing. "I asked you first."

Smiling, I watched him. He attempted to stare me down, but he wasn't in my league. He smoked in silence for as long as he could stand it, which wasn't very long, then he broke.

"You win!" He threw up the hand holding his cigar. "I knew Sukey as well as anyone of this demented group Mary Tucker is gathering together. She sure wasn't the type to commit suicide." He shrugged. "I finally figured someone helped her along to the pearly gates."

"Why wasn't she the type to kill herself?"

"Sukey was a selfish little beast," he said, his voice flat and hard. "She didn't care how much she might hurt someone else, as long as she got what she wanted. She had a lot in common with Alice Bertram on that score."

"Sounds like you're speaking from personal experience. What did Sukey do to you?"

He expelled more smoke before answering. "Actually, she didn't do all that much to me, except make my life miserable for a while by following me around like a puppy." He looked away, staring blindly out at the lawn for a long moment, before turning back to face me. "I'll tell you now, before someone else, like Alice, does it for me. Sukey was infatuated with me at one point, although I was quite a lot younger than her usual targets. She liked them older and more influential generally. She wasn't very subtle about it. But I was never attracted to her, and I tried letting her down gently." He trailed off.

"She refused to be let down?" I guessed.

"Right. I finally had to get brutal with her." He frowned. "I'm not proud of how I handled it, even now. She was a gigantic pain in the ass about it, but in light of what happened, I feel guilty that I was such a bastard to her."

"Sometimes, when feelings like this are involved, people are wilfully blind, and there's no way you can let someone down without being brutal, as you put it."

Shrugging, he drew one last time on his cigar before pitching it into the flower bed below us. "That may be, but I wasn't too proud of myself afterwards. She wasn't my type and wasn't ever going to be. She was just so damn persistent!"

I watched him for a moment while I thought back over an article about him I had read not too long ago, when one of his screenplays had made a splash at the box office. The article had made a couple of coy mentions of a roommate, never named, but obviously male. Now I drew a rapid conclusion about what his type might be, and I spoke before I thought much about the consequences.

"Did you tell her you're gay?"

His eyes widened in surprise. "Speaking of brutal!" He laughed, a shaky sound which somehow put a barrier between us when before there had been none. Once again, he turned his face away, refusing to look at me.

I waited. He had to be willing to tell me the truth, or else he'd be of no use in my efforts to get at the facts behind Sukey Lytton's death.

He didn't try to bluster, as I had thought he might. When he turned back to face me, the naked pain there almost brought me to my feet. But I sat and gazed into his eyes, hoping he would find the reassurance that was there. Slowly, the pain receded, and the beginnings of trust replaced it.

"No, I didn't tell her I'm gay," he said, "which is the reason I continue to despise myself for what I did to her. I couldn't bring myself to tell her the truth, so instead I made her feel it was all her, the reason I wasn't attracted to her."

"Not a very nice thing to do," I observed in a quiet tone.

"It was a cheap, shitty thing to do," he said without heat.

Then he looked chagrined at his choice of words, which I ignored. "But at that point, I was having a hard time facing the truth myself, and I sure wasn't going to admit it to her, of all people. She could be horribly vindictive. I didn't think it through very clearly, I'll admit, but I figured it would be better to brush her off that way than with the truth."

"Better for whom?"

"How did you suddenly turn into my confessor?" he asked, a trace of his normal humor creeping back in.

"Comes with the job of guardian angel," I said, smiling. I figured it was time to offer a little of the milk of human kindness, now that we had passed the worst of it. "Brett, dear, you should know that one of the people I love best in this world is a young cousin who is gay. You can be yourself with me without having to worry about it."

He grinned at that. "Hey, has he got a boyfriend?"

I laughed. "Actually, he does, and they're very happy together. But they might have a friend who's looking for a handsome, talented, and successful writer to romance." I winked at him. "What about your 'roommate'?"

He looked puzzled for a moment, then his face cleared. "Oh, don't tell me you read that article in *People*." He snorted. "I guess everybody who read it figured that one out. So much for being in the closet. . . . Anyway, that's over and done with. I'm single. . . . Again." He laughed. "Seems to be my fate."

The sound of his laughter reassured me. "One of these days, the right one will come along," I said. "Now, back to business. Who do *you* think could have wanted Sukey dead badly enough to murder her?"

"Like I said before, Sukey could be really vindictive when someone crossed her. Figure out who pissed her off the most, because she probably pissed off that person even more. Then you'll have your murderer."

And that was all I could get out of him right then. I felt sure there was more he could tell me, but for now he was done. He stood and essayed a bow, shooting me an unrepentant grin once he was again upright. He strode toward the door without asking me to accompany him.

Rolling my eyes at his retreating back, I got to my feet and followed him inside. The cool dimness brought blessed relief from the humidity I had been ignoring while we talked on the verandah. Ahead of me, Brett disappeared through the door to the kitchen, probably seeking refreshment of some kind. I was tempted to follow him but decided that he could be allowed to get away from me for the moment.

As I made my way to the stairs and started to climb, I glanced at my watch. Luncheon would be served soon, and I might as well freshen up a bit before having to face the assembled guests at the dining table.

The house seemed oddly quiet as I moved up the stairs, except for the whisper of my shoes against the runner covering the steps. Then, as from a distance, I could hear faint sounds of conversation and the chink of crockery and cutlery. The staff must be preparing the dining room for the coming meal. Someone laughed, and the sound faded as I emerged from the stairs onto the second-floor landing.

The door to my right opened as I was passing by, and Lurleen Landry stepped out. She closed the door behind her before she spoke. "Shall I see you at lunch, Miss Carpenter?" Her face had stretched into a polite smile.

"Certainly, Miss Landry," I said, stopping before her. "Did you have a chance to rest a bit?"

"Why, yes, thank you," she said. "The heat of summer fatigues me so. But now I feel refreshed and ready to face the rest of the company." She made a small moue of distaste, quickly suppressed.

I had to grin. "Yes, I've met the Bertrams."

She permitted her face to crease in a quick smile. "Dear Alice," she said. "She does find life such a trial, doesn't she?"

"I can just imagine how it must feel, to be in constant pain like that."

"Yes, I don't know how poor Russell abides it." She giggled at her own cattiness. Then she clapped a hand over her mouth. "I can't believe I said that! Whatever must you think of me, Miss Carpenter?"

"Perfectly understandable," I said.

She glanced down the hallway before moving a step closer to me. "Tell me," she said, her voice dropping to little more than a whisper, "do you find it interesting to work for dear Mary Tucker? I know these memoirs of hers must be fascinating. She's known so many of the important writers of several generations, after all."

I wondered just what it was she was fishing for, but I decided to enlighten her on one thing. "I'm afraid I've not worked for Miss McElroy that long, so I haven't had a chance to read any of the memoir yet."

The calculating expression on her face made her look, for the moment at least, less like an overstuffed dumpling and more like the successful best-selling writer. "Well, I'm sure you'll find out all sorts of fascinating little tidbits about all the people Mary Tucker has known in her long life. Once you get to working on the memoir, that is."

"No doubt you're right," I said. "If you'll excuse me, I'd better just go freshen up before lunch."

"Certainly," Lurleen said. "I'll see you downstairs, Miss Carpenter."

I strode on down the hallway, speculating with every step. I recalled the fragment of conversation I had overheard earlier, between her and Miss McElroy. There was tension between them, that much was obvious. But what was the cause? What could Lurleen have to threaten Miss McElroy with? Or was it the other way round?

Opening the door to my room, I was still lost in thought and not completely aware of my surroundings for a moment. Then I stared in horror at what I glimpsed, stretched out across my bed, on top of a pillow.

Someone had taken my good red silk dress, spread it out over the pillow, and impaled it there with a large butcher knife.

Chapter Six

I DREW A DEEP BREATH and let it out. Someone had underestimated me—badly—if he or she thought I would be intimidated by such a tactic. The sight of my good red silk defiled in that way made me not only uneasy, but also angry. Someone was obviously concerned about my presence at Idlewild—someone who had a shrewd idea that I was here for something other than assisting Miss McElroy with her memoirs.

At the moment, the only person I could exonerate from this nasty little trick was Brett Doran. He had been downstairs in my sight the entire time since he had arrived at Idlewild today. Anyone else could have done it. Anyone who had either brought along a butcher knife as part of the luggage or who had sneaked into the kitchen here and taken one.

What should I do with it now? I wondered. For the moment, I turned my back on the bed as I thought it through. I could go downstairs and pitch a big fit, insisting that Miss McElroy do something about it. Just what she *could* do, I wasn't certain. No one would admit to having done it, and I doubt the party responsible would have been clumsy enough to let anyone see the knife being taken from the kitchen, if indeed it had been.

I could hide the knife somewhere, in case I needed it later for the sake of evidence, but again I doubted that the person who had done this would have been foolish enough to leave his or her fingerprints on it.

Going into the bathroom, I washed my hands, checked my face, and decided to touch up the bare minimum of makeup that I wear. The dress I was wearing was presentable enough, though I might have to change for dinner later on. My hair, which is short, thick, and with just enough body to curl a bit on the ends, looked as close to tamed as I can get it. Satisfied with my appearance, I went back into the bedroom.

I went over to the bed and pulled the knife out of the pillow, freeing my dress and scattering some of the feathers from the pillow. I grimaced at the desecrated red silk as I did so. I had paid more than I cared to admit for that dress, and now it was ruined. Miss McElroy might have something to say about the holes in her good pillow as well.

Slipping the knife into my handbag, I went to the door and opened it with care. I peered outside, but I could see no one in the hallway. More than likely, everyone else was downstairs waiting for me to show up so lunch could be served. I might look a bit odd, bringing my handbag with me, but it wouldn't hurt if Miss McElroy's guests thought me a bit eccentric.

My mood was not its sunniest as I marched down the hall and down the stairs. I stood at the foot of the steps for a moment, trying to figure out where the dining room was. A door to my right opened, and Morwell Phillips came out into the hall.

"Ah, there you are, Miss Carpenter. I was just about to come to call you for lunch." He motioned with his right hand. "Please join us."

"Thank you," I said as I approached him. "I was just wondering which might be the right door."

"Sometime after lunch, if you like," he said, "I'll give you that tour I offered earlier." He had thawed marginally; he no longer sounded grudging, at least.

"That would be lovely, thank you," I said, walking into the room before him.

The rest of the house party were already at the table. Miss McElroy was seated at the far end, at the head, with Brett Doran on her right hand and Russell Bertram on her left. Alice Bertram occupied the seat next to her husband, and Lurleen Landry sat next to her. The seat next to Brett was empty, so I decided that was where I would sit. Miss McElroy nodded as I took my place. I set my handbag down on the floor beside my chair.

"Please ask the girls to serve now, Morwell," Miss McElroy said.

He inclined his head, then went to the sideboard. He pressed a button in the wall before coming back to the table and sitting down beside Lurleen. Moments later, a door in the corner near Miss McElroy opened, and a smiling young woman in uniform came in bearing a tray with several dishes on it. She was followed by another young woman, similarly attired, who also bore a tray. Without speaking, they set their trays down on the sideboard and commenced setting bowls of various vegetables and one large platter of fried chicken on the table in front of us. Still smiling, they departed with their empty trays.

We bowed our heads as Miss McElroy said grace—a brief prayer to the Deity, invoking His good will and protection—then she urged us to help ourselves. "We are somewhat informal at mealtime, as you will see, Miss Carpenter," she explained to me as I began helping myself to the mashed potatoes sitting in front of me.

For a few minutes the only conversation consisted of inquiries as to whether someone needed the creamed corn or fried okra or corn bread or variations thereof. I soon had a heaping plate, vowing to myself that I'd take a walk later that evening, when the heat of the day had receded a bit. Too much of this cooking and I'd not fit into any of the clothes I had brought with me.

I waited until everyone had full plates, then I reached for my handbag. I pulled the butcher knife out and into my lap where no one could see it yet, covered as it was by the exquisite linen of the tablecloth, and placed my bag once again on the floor.

Waiting for a lull in the conversation, I scanned the table briefly. No one looked nervous or anxious. Alice Bertram was scowling at something, but that was hardly unusual, I decided. If the woman ever smiled, I'd think the Day of Judgment was upon us. After a couple of minutes, I had the opportunity I needed.

"I believe I've found something that one of you must have mislaid in my room," I said, my voice loud. With a flourish, I pulled the knife from underneath the table and dropped it with a clatter onto the table beside my plate.

"How extraordinary!" Miss McElroy said. I didn't see the expression on her face which accompanied this pronouncement because I was glancing around the table, trying to catch surprise on someone's face. But everyone more or less mirrored the puzzlement expressed by our hostess.

"What was this doing in your room?" Brett asked, reaching for the knife. He picked it up and turned it in his hands. "It looks wicked sharp."

"It is," I assured him, my voice grim.

"May I see that, please?" Phillips asked.

Brett handed the knife to me, and I passed it across the table.

"It looks like one which belongs in the kitchen here," Phillips said, after examining it.

"Just where in your room did you find it, Miss Carpenter?" Miss McElroy asked.

"It was on my bed," I told her. I would explain later, in private, just how I had found it on my bed. For now, I preferred not to broadcast the details.

"How extraordinary," she said again, looking straight at me. I raised my eyebrows at her, and she took that as a signal that I had more to tell her. "Something like that shouldn't be left lying around. Morwell, please speak to the girls and see what you can find out."

"Certainly, Mary Tucker," he said. "I can't imagine that one of them took it upstairs, so I'm curious to know how it got there." He glared at me as if he suspected I had taken it myself, but I gazed blandly back at him.

"I don't see what all the fuss is about," Alice Bertram said, her voice peevish. "So you found a knife in your room. Since no one stuck it in you, there's nothing to complain about. At least you can climb the stairs without feeling like you've got knives sticking in your back and legs every step of the way."

Her husband gazed down at his plate, his face ashen. How did the man live with this, day in and day out? No wonder he wasn't publishing much these days. How could anyone create if he lived with such a complaining harridan twenty-four hours a day?

"I did offer, as usual, Alice dear," Miss McElroy said, her voice deceptively mild, "to have a bed made up for you downstairs, but you insisted that you'd be more comfortable in one of the rooms upstairs."

"The rooms downstairs are just too drafty, even in the summertime. In the winter, it's too cold downstairs, and in the summer, it's too hot, and all sorts of bugs seem to get in. The last time I tried staying downstairs, I had bugs in my bed all the time."

"I should think that was better than sleeping alone," Lurleen said.

I nearly spit out the mouthful of tea I had just put in my mouth. When this woman turned catty, she did so in fine style.

"Speaking of sleeping alone, Lurleen dear," Alice said, "where is your *charming* young secretary? Did she decide not to come with you on this trip? How could you bear to be parted from that sweet girl, even for a few days?"

Beside me Brett snorted, and I watched in amazement as Lurleen's face suffused with red. What on earth was Alice trying to imply? I had never heard that Lurleen was a lesbian, though she had also never been married, as far as I knew.

Lurleen took a deep breath before she spoke. "I believe it was Oscar Wilde who said that although we're all in the gutter, some of us are looking at the stars. Have you ever, for even one moment in your life, my dear Alice, seen the stars?"

Bravo! I thought. I would probably just have poured my glass of tea over the woman's head, but Lurleen had class.

"As you can no doubt tell by now, Miss Carpenter," Miss McElroy said, "things are never dull here at Idlewild. We do tend to have such amusing conversations, don't you think?"

While I was trying to muster some sort of reply, the door

of the dining room flew open and almost banged against the wall from the force. "Hello, everyone! Sorry I'm late, but I missed my ride and had to come on my own. Blasted rental car broke down about two miles away, and I had to walk the rest of the way here."

The newcomer stood in the doorway, clutching a bulging briefcase in one hand. Almost as wide as he was tall, in his mid to late sixties, he wore a crumpled and sweat-stained dark suit. His florid face perspired heavily, and with a handkerchief, he mopped ineffectually at the moisture beading his forehead. Wisps of gray hair clung to his sunburned head. He had the face of a predator, with coldly assessing eyes and a lupine grin. I didn't like him, just looking at him.

"Hamilton!" Miss McElroy spoke his name in an exasperated tone. "If only you'd buy a cell phone, you could have called, and someone would have retrieved you. You must be the only literary agent in the world without one."

"Who needs 'em?" he said. "Just another way for idiot writers to bug you when you don't want to hear from 'em." He walked around the table, pulled out the empty chair next to me, and plopped himself down in it. "Damn, but I'm still hot."

Morwell Phillips retrieved a glass from the sideboard and filled it with water from a pitcher on the table. "Here, drink this. You're probably dehydrated by now." His nose wrinkled in distaste as he spoke.

Judging from the state of his clothes and the odor emanating from them, I'd say the new arrival was dehydrated, at the very least. I wouldn't want to take bets on the last time he'd bathed, that's for sure. I tried not to breathe too deeply and wished he had chosen somewhere else to sit.

Brett Doran whispered quietly in my ear, "Meet Hamilton Packer, world-class asshole."

"Wonder Boy here was supposed to bring me with him," Packer complained, as if he'd heard what Brett had said to me, "but he never showed up this morning. So I had to drive here in that banged-up piece of rental trash."

Brett muttered something under his breath. "I tried calling you this morning, Hamilton, before I left Memphis," he protested. "But you never answered your phone, and the staff at the hotel didn't know where you were. I just figured you'd decided to come on your own."

More likely, I thought, Brett didn't want the inside of his car smelling like a skunk's jamboree and had left the odiferous Packer to his own devices. I cut Brett a sideways glance, and he winked at me. I couldn't blame him. I was going to have to leave the table before much longer.

"Yeah," Packer said, "you wouldn't want to be doing me any favors these days, would you, Brett? Not after leaving me high and dry two weeks ago. Guess you forgot about that high six-figure advance I got you for your first book."

"Now, boys," Miss McElroy said, "can we leave such discussions for later? That's not why I invited you all here this week, after all."

"Why the hell *did* you invite us all here, Mary Tucker?" Packer asked. "This is one hell of a reunion, if you ask me. But of course there's one person missing, isn't there?" He turned in his chair to look at me. "But looks like we got some fresh blood, though. Who the hell are you?"

Before I could answer, Miss McElroy responded for me. "Hamilton, this is Miss Ernestine Carpenter. She's here to assist me with my memoirs. That's why I've invited you all here, too. I want you to help me, too."

"That's a crock of shit," Packer said, "if you don't mind my saying so, Mary Tucker. I know what y'all are after, but it's too late." He pulled his briefcase from under the table and set it in his lap. "I got it right here"—he patted the briefcase lovingly—"and nobody else can lay a hand on it."

I could feel the tension in the air after Hamilton Packer's announcement. I might not know what he had in his briefcase, but the rest of the group around the table sure did. Every eye in the room, except for mine, was fixed on the crude-talking, smelly man sitting beside me.

"And how did you manage to get hold of it?" Russell Bertram asked, his voice sounding rusty from either disuse or great stress.

"A very interesting question," Miss McElroy said, when

Packer failed to respond. "Do enlighten us, Hamilton. How *did* you get it?"

Get what? I wanted to scream.

"And how do we know it's really what you say it is?" Brett asked.

"Yes, Hamilton," Lurleen Landry said, her voice hard enough to cut a diamond. "How do we know that you didn't write it yourself? After all, it's taken long enough for you to *find* it!"

"Temper, temper, Lurleen, my love," Packer sneered. "A lady of your years shouldn't raise her blood pressure too much, you know." He laughed, a raucous sound that made me want to punch him. "But what I've got here is going to raise blood pressure all over the place. Not to mention my bank balance." He gloated at all of us, while the rest of the people in the room sat there, fuming in silence.

I had had enough, however. "All right, you odious little man, what are you blathering about? Either tell us what you've got there, or go take a bath. Preferably both!" I gave him my best glare, one that has served to quell several generations of unruly students, and he looked as if the tablecloth had reached out and slapped him in the face.

But only for a moment. He laughed again. "Damn, Mary Tucker, where'd you find this old bulldog here?" Then he had the temerity to leer at me. "You may be a bit long in the tooth, sweetie, but I like 'em scrappy."

He had nerve, I'll give him that. I almost had to admire the way he refused to be browbeaten. I've yet to meet the man, however, who gets the last word with me. "Well, *sweetie*, I like 'em clean and with something it doesn't take a microscope to find between their legs or their ears. You lose on both counts."

Beside me, Brett Doran convulsed helplessly with laughter. Lurleen Landry was giggling, Morwell Phillips looked totally scandalized, and even Alice Bertram had the ghost of a smile playing about her lips.

"Miss Carpenter, I do believe you have achieved what no other female of my acquaintance has ever been able to," Miss

McElroy said, the amusement evident in her voice. "You've left poor Hamilton speechless—at least for a moment—probably for the first time in his life."

"A dubious distinction," I said, angry with myself for having lost control long enough to say something like that, and in front of these people. What must they think? My sainted grandmother was no doubt spinning in her grave this very moment.

"The question remains," Miss McElroy said, "just how did you come into possession of Sukey's manuscript, Hamilton? At the time of her death, it couldn't be found anywhere."

Once again the level of tension ratcheted up noticeably, and the levity of what had taken place moments before was quickly forgotten. I could imagine that everyone here was curious about Sukey Lytton's last work-in-progress, but why should they be so uneasy about it? It almost felt like they were afraid of it.

Packer glanced at me, then his eyes shifted away. Maybe I had gotten my bluff in and he wouldn't try anything further with me. I sat back in my chair, leaning as far away from his noxious odor as possible while I waited to hear what he had to say.

"I guess I might as well tell y'all the story," Packer began, his voice smug. "It's almost like something out of one of those mystery novels you're always reading, Mary Tucker." He paused to drain his water glass, then held it out for more. Phillips grimaced in distaste, but he filled the glass from the pitcher on the table.

"Sukey didn't trust any of you not to interfere with the book she was working on," Packer said, "because she knew none of you would like it. So before she came here last Christmas, she bundled up the manuscript and sent it to a friend of hers. Problem with that was, this friend of hers was working with the Peace Corps somewhere in Africa at the time, and it took the package several months to arrive. By that time, of course, Sukey was dead, but the friend didn't know that. She stuck the manuscript away without even reading it, because Sukey asked her not to.

"Then this friend became deathly ill and had to be rushed out of whatever hellhole in Africa she was in, and she was in a hospital in Spain for six weeks. After that, she got sent home to the good ol' US of A. When she finally felt like unpacking her stuff, she came across Sukey's manuscript. That's when she discovered that Sukey was dead—when she tried to call her. She didn't know what the hell to do with the manuscript, but she remembered Sukey talking about her agent, namely me, and she decided to send it to me, not knowing what else to do with it. I got it in the mail three days ago."

"What an extraordinary story," Miss McElroy said.

The rest of us sat in somewhat stunned silence. *Extraordinary* was certainly the right word for the story. *Bizarre* also came to mind. Why on earth would Sukey Lytton send a manuscript off to a friend in Africa? The whole notion seemed preposterous, but of course I had no personal knowledge of Sukey Lytton or how her mind worked.

Writers had been known to do stranger things. I had a friend who stored the research notes for his dissertation in the freezer, of all places. Though I had thought it peculiarly appropriate to store notes on a book about Nathaniel Hawthorne in such a manner, it was still odd.

Had Sukey Lytton feared for her life to such an extent that she had taken extreme measures to safeguard her manuscript? What could she have been writing that was volatile enough to merit doing something like Hamilton Packer had just described to us?

"It's crazy, that's what it is," Brett said flatly. "But, then, that was Sukey all over."

"Yes, the poor girl had a persecution complex a mile wide," Lurleen agreed. "She thought we were all out to get her for some strange reason. I could never figure it out myself."

"That's a rich one!" Packer snorted in amusement. "None of you ever really liked the poor girl, and she knew it. She knew most of you despised her, and her poetry, but she's going to have the last laugh, and I'm going to see to it."

"And you'll be laughing all the way to the bank, I'm sure,"

Russell said, with more animation than I had yet seen him display. "You can cut out the self-righteous act, Hamilton. All you cared about was how much money Sukey could make from her work. You wouldn't have wasted any time on her if there wasn't something in it for you."

"And you should have been spending your time on someone who deserved your attention a lot more than that vicious little whore did," Alice added. "That last contract you negotiated for Russ, before he wised up and fired you, was nothing short of insulting."

"Alice! This is neither the time nor the place." Russell said; and, miracle of miracles, she shut up.

"Then I guess you think you have a surefire best-seller on your hands?" I said.

Packer cut his eyes sideways at me. "Yeah, I do. No doubt about that. Once the publishing world gets a hold of this juicy little masterpiece, there's gonna be a bidding war like you ain't never seen. Tom Wolfe and Norman Mailer will be crying their eyes out when they read this book."

"Just what is this book?" I asked. "Novel, autobiography, poetry? What?"

Packer didn't respond. From the head of the table, Miss McElroy sighed heavily. "I imagine it's a roman à clef, Miss Carpenter. I believe I told you earlier of Sukey's tendency to turn on those who had befriended her. I suspect that this book of Sukey's is a thinly veiled portrait of everyone in this room, with the exception of you, naturally. I've no doubt that, were we to read it, we would find characters who are barely disguised versions of us. And, it goes without saying, each of these characters is somehow vicious or unspeakably tainted, if not both. Sukey could be horribly vindictive."

Hamilton Packer laughed, again spewing forth that raucous, unpleasant sound. "That about sums it up."

"I don't suppose there's any way we could persuade you not to try to publish this thing," Russell said, his voice once again weary and defeated.

"Not a snowball's chance in hell," Packer assured him gleefully.

"If you're not careful, Hamilton," Lurleen said, "you may be meeting that snowball in hell before too long." The words sounded incongruous, coming from her dumpy, suddenly too-elderly face, but the glint in her eyes convinced me, at least, that she was angry enough to kill.

"You know," Packer said, pushing his chair back and standing up, "that bath sounds like a pretty good idea about now. Wanna come along and scrub my back?" He leered at me again.

I stared at him for a moment, then reached over and picked up the butcher knife from where Phillips had placed it. I held it up in front of me. "Sure. As long as you don't mind if I use this."

Packer's laugh wasn't very convincing. "See y'all later," he said, making a hasty exit from the room.

When I did see him again, he was no longer in any condition to threaten anyone.

Chapter Seven

THOUGH THE AIR SMELLED CONSIDERABLY FRESHER once Hamilton Packer left the room, no one seemed to have much appetite left.

"I don't suppose anyone would be interested in dessert, after that little announcement?" Miss McElroy asked in a voice laden with irony.

"The colossal nerve of that man!" Alice said. "Surely there must be some way to stop him from selling that, that *travesty* of a novel!"

"Good luck," Brett said, his voice harsh. "I don't know whether any of us has enough money to stop him. If the book is what we all think it is, it'll go for millions, and we'll all be the laughingstocks of the literary world." He grinned suddenly. "But maybe it'll get us on 'Oprah'!"

"I think I'm going to be ill," Lurleen said, pushing herself back from the table and standing up. "Brett is right, though I hate to admit it. Nothing short of murder is going to stop Hamilton from selling that book."

I decided it was time to do a little digging for information. "Now, I'll admit that I don't know for sure how these things work, but are you all certain that Mr. Packer has the right to represent this book? Did Miss Lytton leave a will, for example? Who was the executor of her estate, such as it was?"

Miss McElroy sighed heavily. "You bring up good points, Miss Carpenter, but unfortunately, Hamilton does have the right to represent Sukey's work. There is very little we can do. Short of murder, as Lurleen so succinctly put it."

"How certain are you that this manuscript is what you think it is?" I persisted in my questioning, because it seemed to me I had finally hit upon a convincing motive for believing that Sukey Lytton had been murdered. If, that is, this book was what the assembled company seemed to think it was.

Russell Bertram, sounding inexpressibly weary, responded. "If you knew Sukey Lytton the way we all did, Miss Carpenter, you'd have no doubts whatsoever. She was like one of those creatures that devours its own offspring. No matter how you tried to help her, to befriend her, sooner or later she turned on you."

"Even dying didn't stop her," Alice said, her face twisted in hate.

Lurleen, who had been standing all this time, announced, "I'm going to my room. I have a sick headache." She walked away from the table and out the dining room door.

"I'm not feeling particularly chipper myself," Miss McElroy said, and indeed her face had turned pale. "I think I'll have a bit of a lie-down in my room. Miss Carpenter, would you see me in the drawing room, about four, perhaps?"

"Of course," I said.

Brett Doran and the Bertrams followed Miss McElroy out of the room, while I lingered behind in hopes of talking further with Morwell Phillips. I caught his eye, and with a barely suppressed sigh, he waited to hear what I wanted.

"When would it be convenient for you give me that tour?" I asked. "I know you must be quite busy, but if you have time this afternoon, I'd love to see the rest of the house."

He consulted his watch. "Perhaps in half an hour?"

"That would be fine," I said. "Where shall I meet you?"

"At the foot of the front stairs, if you wouldn't mind." Without waiting for a response, he turned on his heel and headed for the kitchen.

Maybe at some point I would find out why he didn't seem to want me here. Not that it mattered all that much, since Miss McElroy wanted me here. He was just another employee, as far as I could see. I frowned. Maybe he was just jealous.

I shook my head as I grabbed my bag from beneath my chair. What could I do for the next half hour? I thought for a moment, then headed for the front door.

Just as I had thought. Brett was out on the verandah, smoking an after-lunch cigar.

"Mind if I join you?" I asked, walking over to him.

He stood, waving toward the chair I had occupied during our earlier conversation. "Please," he said, resuming his seat as I made myself comfortable in mine. He grinned as he held out his cigar case toward me. "Would you like one?"

"Some other time, perhaps," I said, surprising him. I had been known to enjoy a good stogie, upon occasion, but right now I didn't have the time to enjoy one properly. I had a little digging to do, and I figured Brett was more likely than some of the others to answer my questions.

"Your former agent is quite a piece of work," I said.

He snorted. "Yeah, ol' Hamilton is a bundle of joy." He frowned at the tip of his cigar. "But despite the act you just saw, he is pretty good at his job."

"Surely he doesn't behave like that with the publishing folk in New York."

Brett shook his head. "No, he reserves that kind of behavior for his nearest and dearest. I know it's hard to believe, after what you just saw, but he's completely different when he's dealing with an editor or a publisher. He's all charm." Grinning again, he said, "But he's all barracuda underneath."

"That's probably a good quality in an agent," I observed.

"Definitely," he said. "You want someone who will go to the mat for you and get you the best deal possible. Hamilton does that."

"But you've apparently parted company," I said. "Though of course it's none of my business."

Brett shot me a look which informed me he wasn't buying that one. "Yeah, I fired him about two weeks ago. If you must know, I found out he was doing a little extra dealing on the side, trying to get himself more of a percentage than he was entitled to. I told him I wasn't going to put up with it, and he laughed. So I fired him. End of story."

Somehow I wasn't surprised to hear that Hamilton Packer was ethically challenged. I decided to change tack. "When we were talking earlier, something you said made me curious."

He cocked an eyebrow at me as he exhaled a plume of smoke. "I think I may start calling you George instead of Ernie." He laughed.

"Fair enough." I grinned at him. "So I'm nosy. Anyway, you said something earlier about Sukey Lytton. About how she usually liked men older than you."

He nodded. "Yeah, she had this real daddy complex. Most of the time she went after guys in their fifties or older. Maybe it had something to do with the fact that she was an orphan, grew up in foster homes. I don't know." He shrugged. "But she was definitely into older men."

"Like Hamilton Packer?"

Brett twisted his face into an expression of disgust. "Even him, if you can believe it. But I think things had cooled off between them before she died. She had her eyes on someone else, I think, but I don't know whom."

"Maybe Russell Bertram?" I suggested.

"No, she'd already done that," Brett said before taking a long drag from his cigar. He exhaled smoke and watched it drift lazily into the humid afternoon air. "You could hear at lunch just how fond Alice was of Sukey. And that's why. Sukey and Russ had a little thing going two or three years ago."

"Quite an incestuous little group you have here," I said, watching his face.

He rolled his eyes but made no other comment.

Deciding that I had dug in the muck long enough for now, I changed the subject to the hit movie he had recently written. I knew how much most writers love talking about their work, and Brett was no exception. His face lit with pleasure, and he was off and running, telling me more juicy tidbits about some of his Hollywood acquaintances.

He was in the middle of an amusing, but highly scandalous, anecdote about a producer and his three girlfriends when the sound of a clearing throat interrupted us. I looked up to find Morwell Phillips standing near me. I had been so absorbed in Brett's story that I hadn't heard the butler approach.

"Are you ready for your tour now?" he asked, his voice more than a bit frosty.

"Yes, of course," I said, a little flustered as I stood up. "I'm sorry, I got so involved in talking with Brett I lost all track of time."

"You know me, Morwell," Brett said, standing beside me. "When I get going, I just keep babbling away."

Phillips allowed a small smile at that, but then he turned toward the front door and said pointedly, "If you're ready, Miss Carpenter?"

Smiling at Brett, I said, "Certainly, Mr. Phillips," though I had been tempted to say something entirely different.

We left Brett on the verandah to finish his cigar in peace.

Back inside the house, Phillips paused near the foot of the stairs. "I'm afraid we won't be able to see inside some of the bedrooms just now, but perhaps later on you'll be able to see some of them and their special features."

I nodded.

"Idlewild is, as you know, a house in the Greek Revival style," Phillips began, warming to his task the longer he talked. "This style became extremely popular in the eastern United States between 1820 and 1840, chiefly in our capital, and then the style began to spread northward and westward. Idlewild was begun in 1851 and completed in the summer of 1852 and is one of the finest examples of Greek Revival architecture in the South."

"It's a magnificent structure," I said, "and from what I've seen in Natchez and in other places, it's also one of the largest Greek Revival houses still standing."

"That's correct," Phillips said, looking very pleased. Apparently complimenting the house was one way to get in his good graces. "Idlewild was designed by an architect who had designed a number of public and private buildings throughout the South, and he was given a free hand by Mary Tucker's great-great-great grandfather, Belisarius McElroy. Old Bell had been to Greece as a young man, and he was very taken with the Greek style. He wanted his own little bit of it here, in north central Mississippi."

"It's a very imposing sight as you come up the driveway and see those twelve columns across the front of the house. And the doorways are wonderful, too, so large." I laughed. "At my height, I often have to stoop a bit in older houses, but not here."

Phillips smiled. "Doorways are important in the Greek Revival style, as are columns, since the form is based on that of a Greek temple. Much use of pillared porticoes and pediments, for example."

"A bit of Athens right here in Mississippi."

"Exactly." He beamed at me, and I felt like I had passed some sort of test. He took great pride in his employer's home, and I couldn't blame him. I've always been fascinated by houses, and I could quite happily spend several days or weeks getting to know every nook and cranny of this grand old girl.

"The rooms are laid out on each of the three floors basically as large squares," Phillips continued with his explanation. "The dining room is a bit larger than any of the other rooms on the ground floor. The kitchen is right next to it, with a small butler's pantry off to one side, and a rear staircase on the other. Across the hall are three rooms, each the same size as the other. The front room is, as you have seen, Mary Tucker's sitting room. It was once the main drawing room."

I followed him as he moved down the hall. "This second room here," he said, as he opened the door, "is a library. Feel free to borrow whatever you might like to read while you're here. There are some items"—he indicated a set of shelves enclosed by glass and secured by locks—"which are too precious to be left out in the open, but if you'd like, I'd be happy to show some of them to you."

Standing in that room, I stared lustfully at the shelves lining the walls around us. There must be fifteen or twenty thousand books in this room, I estimated, many of them dating from the mid to late nineteenth century, to judge by their appearance. The rich aroma of leather bindings tantalized my nostrils, and I wanted nothing more at this moment than to spend the rest of the day here, seeking out the many treasures housed in this room.

"A room like this is sheer heaven for a bibliophile," I commented.

Phillips gave a gentle laugh at the wistfulness of my tone. "I understand completely. This is my favorite room in the house."

With great reluctance, I followed him back out into the hall. The final room on the ground floor turned out to be another sitting room. "It has been a bit modernized, as you'll see," he explained. "If you care to watch television, you'll have to come here. This room has the only television set in the house. Except for the servants' quarters in the courtyard wing, that is."

The room, somewhat disappointingly, looked much like a room in my house, except for the high ceilings and large windows. "Mary Tucker has endeavored to keep as many of the furnishings intact as possible, throughout the house, but since this is a private home and not a museum, one has to take into account the fact that there will be wear and tear. Many of the pieces of furniture you see throughout are originals, but of course the fabrics in most cases are not. They simply couldn't stand the daily usage by several generations of McElroys and their guests."

I nodded my understanding. I could give a catalog of the many beautiful pieces of furniture I saw during that tour, but after a while, one could exclaim "How lovely!" only so many times without sounding ridiculous. Since all the bedrooms on the second floor were now occupied by guests, we went up to the third floor, where Phillips was able to show me most of the rooms. One room, however, we did not look into. Perhaps it was his own room, and I couldn't blame him for not showing it to me, though I'll admit I was more than a bit curious to see it.

After we completed our tour of the third floor, I followed Phillips back down the stairs. We walked into the kitchen where he introduced me briefly to the cook, Mrs. Greer, and the two young women who had served our lunch, Betsy and

Katie. I expressed my thanks for the delicious food (at least, what little of it I had gotten a chance to eat), and they beamed their thanks back at me.

A door on one side of the kitchen led us into the hallway of the courtyard wing of the house, as Phillips called it. Most of the ground floor of this wing consisted of the ballroom. We walked into the vast space, and I stood once more in awe. Hanging over the center of the room was a magnificent crystal chandelier. Thousands of pieces of crystal sparkled and danced before my eyes as the afternoon sun shone through the large windows on the west side of the room. When Phillips told me how much it had cost, when Belisarius McElroy had had it imported from Europe, I gasped.

The butler gave a wry grin. "We couldn't afford one like it these days," he said. "I'm still not quite certain how old Bell afforded it in the first place, but it is amazing, isn't it?"

We stood in the echoing space of the ballroom, about half the length of a football field, while Phillips gave me a verbal tour of the rest of the wing. The upper two floors of this wing consisted chiefly of the servants' quarters. Many of the rooms were no longer used, since the complement of staff had been sharply reduced over the years.

"I've talked to Mary Tucker about using this wing for a bed and breakfast, but she won't hear of it. We do use some of the rooms on occasion, for example when she hosts one of her writers retreats here, but that's not very often these days. I hate to see the rooms not being used. A house should be lived in, don't you think?"

I nodded. "Particularly a wonderful house like this. I know it's seen its share of tragedies and triumphs over the years."

Phillips sighed. "And there will be more to come, I suspect."

"Yes, this new situation promises to be full of drama," I said, trying to decide just what I could say to get him to talk to me. He had thawed considerably during our tour. Would a direct approach work? Or would he revert to his earlier coolness toward me?

Evidently the urge to gossip a bit won out. "Hamilton is an old hand at stirring things up," he said, "and I just hope this time he doesn't stir up more than is good for him. And for the rest of us."

"He's certainly being provocative," I said, "but it sounds to me like Sukey Lytton, may she rest in peace, is the one who was really trying to stir things up."

Phillips's face contracted in a brief spasm, whether in pain or annoyance I couldn't decide. "Sukey was a difficult girl, there's no doubt about that." He trailed off and stood staring at something I couldn't see, out one of the windows of the ballroom.

"But was she really as awful as everyone says she was?"

He sighed. "She was an outsider here. She struggled to fit in, but she came from the trailer park, literally, and she never felt truly comfortable in surroundings like these." He gestured broadly with his right arm.

"You seem to have a bit more sympathy for her than some of the others," I said.

Shrugging, he said, "Perhaps. Partly because I could understand how she felt. I didn't grow up in a place like this either. Far from it." His tone had turned bitter.

That didn't surprise me. He was Miss McElroy's butler, after all. But I was intrigued by his air of sympathy for the dead girl. Thus far, Miss McElroy was the only person in the house who seemed to have actually liked Sukey. "But you liked her," I said.

"Yes, I did," he said, sounding almost surprised by the admission. "She wasn't an easy person to know, but she could be very sweet, sometimes." He shrugged again. "The problem was, whenever she was here, she had a gigantic chip on her shoulder, and she did her best to dare everyone here to knock it off."

"And someone finally did it," I commented without thinking about what I was saying.

"What do you mean?" His tone was sharp, and he once again focused on the here and now. His eyes bored into mine.

"Her death," I said. "Do you really believe it was suicide, or even an accident?"

"So that's why Mary Tucker brought you here. I was wondering," he said, his tone grim. He walked away from me, his long stride rapidly lengthening the distance between us. I hurried to catch up to him.

"Well, what do you think?" I asked as I followed him back into the kitchen, nodding at Mrs. Greer and Katie, who were busy with after-lunch cleanup.

Before he could answer me, we were all startled by shrieks coming from somewhere in the house.

Chapter Eight

AT THE PIERCING SOUND of the first scream, Mrs. Greer dropped the bowl she was holding. It shattered all over the stone floor of the kitchen. She started babbling an apology, but Morwell Phillips brushed that aside as he ran toward the door leading out into the hall. I was right on his heels.

The screams continued for a moment longer, then they ceased abruptly, as the screamer seemed to be cut off in the middle of another ear-splitting wail. Once we were out in the hall, I could tell that the screams had been coming from the second floor. I pounded up the stairs behind the butler, passing him after the first few steps. Even though I'm sixty, I'm in pretty darn good shape, and I almost sprinted up the stairs. I could hear him huffing along behind me.

At the top of the stairs, Brett Doran held a sobbing Betsy in his arms. Even though her face was buried in his chest, she was talking, but her words were unintelligible. Down the hall, Miss McElroy had come out of her room and was moving toward us, while Lurleen Landry and the Bertrams were standing in the hallway.

"Betsy, my dear, what on earth is the matter?" Miss McElroy called out as she approached.

"In there, in the bathroom," Brett said in a terse voice. He jerked his head toward the room behind him.

While he continued to try calming the hysterical girl, I brushed past them and entered the bedroom. The door was ajar, and the moment I went inside, I could smell the identity of its occupant. This was Hamilton Packer's room, and his pungent stench lingered, no doubt emanating from the clothes strewn without care across the bed. To the right a doorway led into the bathroom, and I approached it with caution.

A grisly scene met my eyes. Hamilton Packer, his naked flesh obscene in its puffy whiteness, sat slumped forward in the bathtub, which stood to the left of the doorway, under a window. The water was stained red with blood. My gaze focused on the large knife protruding from Packer's back. I swallowed, trying not to vomit right then and there. I took one step closer, to gain a better view of the knife, then I retreated.

I hadn't noticed it, but the others had crowded into the room behind me. "Out! Now! Every one of you," I said, using my best bossy schoolteacher voice. Without even thinking about it, they did what I said. I followed them.

"Dear Lord," Miss McElroy said, collapsing on one of the chairs on the landing. "Who could have done such a thing?"

I stared at each of them in turn, but all I could read on their faces was shock and horror. As far as I knew, none of them had an alibi, at least until we knew more about when the man was killed. One of them had killed Hamilton Packer. Could it be the same person who had killed Sukey Lytton? Surely it must be.

"He was almost begging for it," Alice Bertram said in triumphant tones. "The bastard asked for it, and he got it."

"Alice!" Russell Bertram made the token protest, but he knew as well as we all did that his wife, for once, was absolutely right. She, however, was the only one to be completely open about her feelings.

"We need to call the sheriff's department right away," I said, taking charge, since no one else seemed inclined to do so.

"Right." Phillips snapped out of his reverie and made for the stairs. "I'll go call them right now."

"Brett, dear, please take Betsy downstairs, away from all this, and get her some brandy. I think that will help restore her a bit." Miss McElroy, after a few moments' distress, was once again taking over her role as lady of the manor. "Betsy, my dear, please go with Brett and try to remain calm."

Betsy's tearstained face appeared from the shelter of Brett's broad chest. "Yes, ma'am," she said. The poor girl didn't look to be a day over nineteen, and I doubt she'd ever seen anything like the ghastly scene in the bathroom, outside of those hideous slasher movies young people seem to adore these days. You'd think they'd be inured to violence, but when the real thing occurs, they are just as shaken as the rest of us.

"One quick question, Betsy, before you go downstairs," I said, casting a look at Miss McElroy. She inclined her head slightly, so I continued. "Why did you go in Mr. Packer's room?"

Betsy frowned. "His bell rang downstairs, and Mrs. Greer asked me to go up and see what he wanted." Her face crumpled. "But he couldn't've rung it! Why would somebody do something like that?"

"A very good question," I said grimly. Had the murderer rung the bell so that the body would be discovered right away? What kind of game was the killer playing?

Brett questioned me with a glance, and I nodded that it was okay for him to take the poor child downstairs. She went with him, gazing up adoringly into his handsome face. Poor child. She was going to be sadly disillusioned at some point with her newfound hero.

Miss McElroy stood up. Though her face was gray, she had had time to pull herself together, and she was once more in command of herself and the situation. "I believe we should await the sheriff's men downstairs. Russell, Alice, Lurleen, please come down with me, and we'll wait in my sitting room." Without argument they did what she said, preceding her down the stairs. She paused at the head of the steps and gave me a speaking look, nodding in the direction of Hamilton Packer's room, and I understood what she wanted.

Taking a deep breath and praying that I wouldn't disgrace myself, I went back to investigate the crime scene a little further.

Careful not to touch anything, I stood in the doorway of the room and looked around. Besides the clothes thrown across the bed, the only noticeably foreign object in the room was Packer's battered briefcase. There had obviously been no time yet to retrieve the luggage from his abandoned car, and I doubted whether he had attempted to lug it with him the two miles from where the vehicle had broken down. From what I could see, his briefcase no longer bulged, as if something bulky had been removed from it.

Like a manuscript.

I drew a sharp breath, then wished I hadn't. The man's odor persisted in the room. It was likely that the murderer had taken the manuscript and hidden it somewhere after having dispatched Hamilton Packer to his reward. I brightened. Surely the team from the sheriff's department would find it in short order, once they arrived. The killer wouldn't have had much time to hide it somewhere. Which made the ringing of the bell even more odd. Definitely something I would have to ponder, later.

With extreme care I walked back toward the door of the bathroom and stood just outside it, looking in. I forced myself not to look at the body for a moment, though the hideous sight almost compelled me to do so. For the first time, I noticed a companion door on the other side of the bathroom, which meant that the bedroom on the other side must share this room. Who was in that room?

Most likely it was Brett Doran. I'm sure Miss McElroy wouldn't have expected the Bertrams to share a bathroom with Packer. Since Lurleen Landry had the room directly across the hall from this one, the Bertrams must have the middle room across the hall, next to mine. Poor Brett wouldn't want to use this bathroom any longer. He'd have to move up to the third floor now.

I made myself look one last time at the body. The knife was buried, almost to the hilt, in Packer's back. I couldn't swear to it, not being able to examine it more closely, but I would be willing to bet that the knife used to kill him was the same one I had found earlier in my bedroom.

No doubt it still had my fingerprints all over it.

That was going to be interesting to explain to the sheriff's department investigators. Thank goodness I had an alibi! I had been with either Brett Doran or Morwell Phillips from the time Hamilton Packer had gone upstairs until we heard Betsy screaming.

There seemed to be nothing else to observe, so I made my way just as carefully back out into the hall. I regretted that I might have contaminated the crime scene by walking in there twice, but Betsy and probably Brett had already done so, as had the rest of the crew, when they crowded in after me the first time I came in here.

On my way downstairs I glanced at my watch. I figured about ten minutes had passed, at the most, since Phillips had gone downstairs to phone the sheriff's department. Though Idlewild wasn't that far outside Tullahoma, the county seat where the sheriff's department headquarters were located, it would take at least another five to ten minutes before anyone official arrived.

A heated argument was in progress when I walked into Miss McElroy's sitting room.

". . . can't seriously expect us to remain here, after this!" Alice Bertram's voice rose in shrill protest.

Miss McElroy was rubbing her forehead, as if it ached.

"I doubt you'll have much choice," I said.

Alice turned her hostile gaze on me. "And why not? Why should we have to remain here? Only to be murdered, like that idiot upstairs?"

"Oh, come off it, Alice," Lurleen said, her voice dripping with venom. "Even *you* can't be that stupid. Granted, you've done enough vicious things over the years to cause any one of us to want to kill you, but the chances of that happening now are slim to none. Whatever caused someone to kill poor Hamilton doesn't necessarily apply to you." She paused, as if struck by a new thought. "Unless, of course, you know something the killer thinks you shouldn't." An evil grin spread across her face.

"Don't be ridiculous," Alice snapped. "I know you'd like nothing better than to have me out of the way so you could hop into bed with my husband."

"Really, Alice, you're getting more tiresome by the minute," Brett said in disgust. "First you accuse Lurleen of being a lesbian, and now you make out that she's lusting after poor old Russ over there. Which is it?"

I didn't give her time to answer. "No matter what you might prefer, Mrs. Bertram," I said, "I doubt the sheriff's department is going to allow any one of us to get far from Idlewild until a suspect is in custody. So you might as well sit down and shut up, right now." I had no patience left to deal with her, and my voice gave ample proof of that.

"Good advice for all of us," Miss McElroy said, and Alice subsided. Though the look she shot me was full of acid, for once she must have decided to cut her losses and give in.

I sat down in a chair near Miss McElroy while the others got themselves situated. Once they were all sitting, I looked to Miss McElroy. She nodded.

"I don't know whether any of you have ever been involved in a homicide investigation." I waited a moment, but no one spoke. "Well, I have been, and it's not a pleasant experience. I urge you all to cooperate with the investigators, answer their questions, even if they don't seem pertinent. Let them decide what is important. If you think you know anything, however innocuous it might seem, tell them. The sooner this is resolved, the happier we'll all be. Trust me."

"Very sensible advice, Miss Carpenter," Miss McElroy said. "I urge you all to do as she says."

No one replied, and we sat in silence for a moment. Then came the sounds of cars arriving and doors opening and slamming shut, and the doorbell rang. Morwell Phillips must have answered it. Moments later he came to the door of the sitting room, accompanied by a young man in uniform. "I've sent them upstairs," he said. "The officer in charge asked that we all remain here, and he'll be down soon to talk to us."

I recognized the young man as one of my students who had graduated from the high school in Tullahoma about three years ago. His name was Robbie Davis. He nodded in recognition at me before announcing his name to us, then he requested us not to talk about what we had seen or heard until his superior came down to talk to us.

The result of that request was that no one said anything,

and we waited in silence for perhaps another fifteen or twenty minutes before the officer in charge of the case walked into the room.

"Afternoon, folks," he announced, "I'm Lieutenant Preston, and I'm in charge of this investigation." He took his time, getting a good look at each of us, and his lips twitched slightly when he saw me.

Maybe this wasn't going to be so difficult after all.

Dressed in street clothes, Jack Preston might at first have passed for a businessman. He had the easy assurance of a successful salesman, and after you were around him even for a few minutes, you'd be aware of his natural charm. Then maybe you'd notice the keen, intelligent, assessing gaze of his eyes, and soon you'd realize that here was a man who missed little and understood perhaps more than you wished he did. He had been my favorite student fifteen years ago, and I had watched his career in the sheriff's department with great interest.

Striding forward, Jack held out a hand to Miss McElroy. "Miss McElroy, though it's always a great pleasure to see you, I regret it had to be under circumstances like these."

She looked up into his face and returned his smile, though hers was considerably more strained. "Thank you, Jack," she said. "I'm pleased to know you'll be in charge. I know you'll sort this out very quickly."

He nodded. His smile betokened deference and respect, but Miss McElroy was no fool. Jack was a natural politician, and I fully expected to see him elected sheriff one day soon. But he had uncompromising views on justice, and he wouldn't let Miss McElroy's status sway him from carrying out his investigation however he deemed best. Even if Miss McElroy's distant cousin, his boss, disagreed.

The fact that he knew and respected me didn't hurt, either. I could talk to him about my own theories and impressions, and he wouldn't dismiss them out of hand. Thank heavens for small miracles, that he'd gotten the call and not someone else in the department.

"Miss Carpenter"—he inclined his head toward me and, I

swear, winked—"always a pleasure." He stood beside Miss McElroy and surveyed the rest of the group. "Folks, I know this is going to be an extremely difficult day for all of you, but I'm going to ask you to be as patient as you can and cooperate with me and my men to the fullest extent possible."

He waited a moment, as if expecting a protest from some quarter, then continued. "I need to talk to each of you in turn, and while I'm doing that, I have to ask you not to talk among yourselves about what you've seen upstairs. Or about anything to do with this whole situation, at least for now. Will you help me on this?"

Everyone nodded.

"Thank you," Jack said. He turned back to Miss McElroy. "If there's a room on this floor I could use for now?"

"I would suggest that you use the library. Morwell?"

"Yes, Mary Tucker." Morwell Phillips moved forward. "If you'll follow me."

"No need," Jack said. "I remember where it is. Miss Carpenter, I'd like to speak to you first."

"Certainly." I stood and followed him out of the room. He nodded in Robbie Davis's direction as we went out of the room, and Robbie stood even straighter than before. Behind us, the room was quiet.

In the library, Jack went to the desk and stood behind it, waiting for me to make myself comfortable in a chair across from him. "Quite a mess you're in the middle of," he said, grinning a little bit as he sat down and took a notebook out of his jacket pocket.

"You don't know the half of it," I said, my voice grim. "Where do you want to start?"

"How about you tell me why you're here in the first place. I never figured you for one of Miss McElroy's cronies."

I wasn't sure just what Jack Preston would think of my new sideline in problem-solving, so I stuck with the fiction that Miss McElroy had devised. "I'm assisting Miss McElroy with her memoirs."

He raised his eyebrows at that but didn't comment.

"The group you saw in there with Miss McElroy," I said,

"was all here at Idlewild at Christmas, when one of her guests, Sukey Lytton, was found dead on the grounds."

He nodded. "I remember. I was on leave at the time, but I know about the case."

I took the plunge. "Well, Miss McElroy doesn't think that death was suicide, or an accident. She thinks Sukey Lytton was murdered, and by one of the people in that room."

"What do you think?" His eyebrows rose again.

"I think she's right. Especially in light of what happened today."

He scribbled something on his notepad. "How are the two events connected?"

After taking a moment to organize my thoughts, I launched into a summary of the day's events, explaining briefly who each person was and his or her connection to Miss McElroy and to Sukey Lytton. I gave as thorough a recounting of what had happened at lunch as I could, and I prided myself on not leaving anything out. I even told him what I had said to Hamilton Packer, and Jack did his best not to laugh.

"You think the knife used on the victim is the same one you found in your bedroom?" he asked, making more notes.

"Unless the killer wiped it clean before he or she used it," I said, "you'll probably find my fingerprints on it."

"Maybe," he said. "Now, tell me why you and Miss McElroy think Miss Lytton was murdered."

I gave him a quick recital of the facts, and he nodded when I finished. "Sounds pretty plausible to me," he said. "Especially since this time the killer didn't take any trouble to make it look like an accident. Not a smart move." His grin was wolfish.

"No," I said. "But this time I think the killer was desperate. In a big hurry."

"And you think this manuscript is what they were after?"

"They had to be. It just doesn't make much sense otherwise, far as I can see."

"Right." He stood up. "Excuse me a moment."

I sat there, waiting—not very patiently—until he returned. I assumed he was giving orders for his team upstairs to start looking for the missing manuscript. The killer couldn't have had much time to hide it, so it had to be somewhere in the house. Finding it, and reading it, would help point the finger at the most likely suspect. Or so I was assuming.

Jack came back and sat down behind the desk.

"What's next?" I asked.

"I have to keep interviewing folks. And you," he said, grinning, "just keep your ears and eyes open and try not to end up with a knife in *your* back."

"Don't worry," I said, shivering a bit.

"Seriously," he said, his face darkening, "don't do anything that might put you in danger. Call me immediately if anything else happens." He pulled out his wallet, extracted a card, and scribbled a number on the back of it. "Here's my cell phone number. If you can't reach me through the department switchboard, try that."

"Thanks," I said, tucking the proffered card into my handbag. I stood up. "Where should I go now? Back in the room with the others?"

"No." Jack was firm. "I know I can trust you not to talk to them just yet, but I think it would be better for you not to see any of them until I've finished my preliminary questioning. But I'd also rather you didn't go upstairs to your room right now, either."

"I'll wait next door, then. It's another sitting room, and it has the only television set in the house."

"That's fine," he said. "The others can join you there as I'm finished with them. At least until my men have finished upstairs."

"Who's next?" I couldn't contain my curiosity.

"Cousin Betsy." Jack smiled.

I shook my head. "I should have guessed. There was something oddly familiar about the girl."

"She does have the Preston nose, doesn't she?"

I thought for a moment. "Let me guess. She's your uncle Cyrus's daughter, I expect?"

He laughed. "Got it in one."

"That explains why I hadn't taught her at the high school

then." Cyrus Preston lived on a farm in the edge of the neighboring county, and his children went to school there. No wonder, then, that I hadn't recognized Betsy, though she was of an age to have been one of my students, just before I retired from teaching last year.

Leaving Jack, I went next door. Closing the door behind me, I felt for a light switch and flipped it on. The room had a slightly musty, unused smell to it, which I had noticed earlier on my tour of the house. Evidently the residents of Idlewild didn't watch that much television.

Checking my watch, I saw that it was too early for the evening news, though it wouldn't be long now. What to do? A selection of magazines fanned out across the coffee table near a comfortable-looking sofa. I sat down and glanced through the available browsing material, various issues of *Architectural Digest, Southern Living,* and *National Geographic.* I settled for the old warhorse and started skimming an article on azaleas.

Somehow I didn't find the article particularly riveting reading, so I gave up trying and dropped the magazine back on the table. How I itched to be upstairs, watching what Jack's men were doing. I could imagine one of them, even now, finding the missing manuscript.

Aargh. This inactivity was giving me a headache. Such are the burdens of the truly nosy. I might as well cogitate on the problem and see where that might lead.

The timing of the murder intrigued me. There were a number of variables. Did the killer strike after he or she had swiped the manuscript? Or did Packer die first? The latter meant that someone had committed murder, then even more cold-bloodedly gone into Packer's bedroom and rifled through his things. I shivered. Either way, it was nasty.

As far as I knew at the moment, I was the only one who had an alibi. I had been with either Brett Doran or Morwell Phillips since Packer went upstairs to his room and got himself murdered. Brett could have done it after I left him; Phillips could have done it before he came to fetch me for the tour of the house.

Those thoughts creeped me out, as my former students might have said. But it was just as likely that Lurleen Landry or one of the Bertrams was the killer. I didn't think it could be Miss McElroy herself, though I couldn't really rule her out. Maybe Jack would be able to narrow down the list of suspects at some point, which would be a big help. But it would be a while before he could do that. If he could.

I sat and fumed—I wasn't making much progress trying to think this through. Occasionally I picked up a magazine and tried to interest myself in it, but to no avail. My mind kept going in circles, refusing to settle on anything. I checked my watch; nearly forty-five minutes had passed while I sat consumed by fruitless speculation. By now, I had expected someone else to join me here in the after-interview room.

Just when I was on the point of getting up and going in search of human contact, the door opened, and Jack walked in. The grim look on his face alarmed me.

"What's wrong?"

He rubbed his nose. "That blasted manuscript is nowhere to be found."

Chapter Nine

AFTER A RESTLESS NIGHT, I woke the next morning feeling sluggish and unrefreshed. Try though I might, I couldn't erase the image of Hamilton Packer's pathetic corpse from my visual memory bank. Unpleasant as the man had been, even in our brief acquaintance, I wouldn't have wished such an undignified death upon him. Maybe I could do something about figuring out who killed him, however, and help Mary Tucker McElroy sort out the whole messy situation.

I threw back the covers and crawled out of bed. Mornings like this I felt every second of my sixty years on this earth. Nothing that a brisk walk and a hot shower wouldn't help, of course. Not to mention a healthy dose of caffeine. I groaned. I really didn't want to have to face the rest of the household without having had at least two cups of coffee first.

Looking out the window at the storm clouds gathering, I decided to forego the walk and went for the hot shower instead. Twenty minutes later, dressed and in a slightly better frame of mind, I made my way downstairs as the heavens opened and the rains came down. Maybe the storm outside would pass soon; I doubted that the one inside would.

The dining room was empty, and I checked my watch. Just barely seven-thirty. The rest of the household didn't seem to be stirring yet. I hadn't heard any sounds of activity upstairs, and I wondered whether the staff would have reported for duty as usual this morning.

Opening the door to the kitchen, I discovered that even violent death didn't disrupt some of the routines of life at Idlewild. Mrs. Greer, Betsy, and Katie were busily involved in their preparations for breakfast.

Mrs. Greer looked up, a slight frown on her face. The frown creased into a smile when she saw who had invaded her domain. During a brief chat last night we had discovered that I had taught two of her grandsons, one of whom I had successfully talked out of a career as a petty larcenist. I had discovered the boy pilfering lockers at the high school. Instead of turning him over to the principal for the appropriate disciplinary measures, I marched him into an empty classroom and treated him to one of my patented "facts of life" lectures. My students had been known to refer to these lectures as "Doomsday 101," and most of them reformed quickly when threatened with a second dose of it. For showing this errant grandson the folly of his chosen course, I had the woman's undying gratitude. He was now a junior member of the State Legislature.

"Mrs. Greer, could I possibly have some coffee?" I offered a rueful grimace, and she laughed.

"Miss Carpenter, you can have anything you like out of this kitchen. Coffee we got aplenty, and breakfast'll be ready in two shakes of a lamb's tail, if you're hungry."

I looked at the plate of steaming biscuits she held and decided that I was indeed hungry. Good homemade biscuits are one of life's great pleasures, and I was imagining how one of these would taste, loaded down with butter and Mrs. Greer's no-doubt homemade jelly. My mouth watered.

"Bless you," I said. "But would it be an imposition if I ate here in the kitchen with y'all?" I indicated a small table over in the corner. "I don't think I can face that dining room this morning."

"Not a'tall," she beamed at me. "You just set yourself down right there, and Katie'll get you everything you need." Fixing Katie with a stern gaze, she continued, "Hop to it, girl, and don't keep Miss Carpenter waiting."

"Yes'm," Katie said, her eyes round. I imagined that Mrs. Greer was something of a benevolent tyrant in the kitchen. Katie didn't look especially fearful, but she also didn't waste time in following Mrs. Greer's orders. Moments later, I had a hot-to-the-touch mug of coffee and a plate full of scrambled eggs, bacon, grits, and biscuits.

With great contentment I enjoyed my breakfast while I watched Mrs. Greer and her two helpers finish their preparations for breakfast for the household. Once all the food was ready, Katie and Betsy took various chafing dishes out to the dining room, where they set the table and made sure everything was prepared to Mrs. Greer's exacting specifications.

I wondered why Morwell Phillips wasn't somewhere around, keeping an eye on things, because I thought that's what a butler was supposed to do. Obviously Mrs. Greer didn't need supervision, and the poor man had had such a hectic day yesterday he was probably taking a much deserved rest this morning.

Sipping at my second mug of coffee, I said, "Mrs. Greer, I hope you won't think I'm being ghoulish, but would you mind if I asked you and Katie and Betsy a few questions about yesterday?"

She wiped her hands on her apron and poured herself a cup of coffee before she answered. She came and sat down at the table across from me. Shrewd eyes in a deep brown face not much older than mine assessed me. "I know enough about you, Miss Carpenter, to know you got a good reason to want to ask questions. Not like that jackass of a reporter who came knocking at the front door at six-thirty this morning."

"Oh, dear, the press is already on the scene, are they?"

She snorted with laughter. "Yep, and so is old Herman Detweiler and his three big Dobermans. Those dogs are sweet as pie, but they can sure look mean enough. No reporter's going to tangle with them, you can bet on it. Sweet or not, those dogs aren't going to let no one who don't belong here get close enough to bother Miss McElroy or anyone in this house."

She went on to explain that Detweiler was the groundskeeper at Idlewild, and he doubled as the watchman when circumstances warranted. I hadn't seen a sign of him or the dogs while I'd been here, and I was relieved to know that Miss McElroy and the rest of us had some protection—from the outside world, at any rate.

"I can just imagine what the newspapers are going to make of all this," I said.

Her face tightened into a fierce expression. "Vultures is what they are! It was bad enough back at Christmas when that poor child killed herself out in the pond, but what in heaven's name are they going to be saying about us now, when that old gasbag done gone and got himself killed in the bathtub?"

"The more quickly the sheriff's men get this sorted out, the better."

Nodding, Mrs. Greer said, "That Jack Preston is a good man. He's like a terrier, and once he gets a hold of the rat that did this, we can all sleep a little easier."

I had to grin at the image of Jack as a dog, shaking a big rat in his mouth. "Yes, he'll sort this out as quickly as he can, I have no doubt."

"What did you want to ask me and the girls?" Mrs. Greer said, as Betsy and Katie returned to the kitchen. She motioned for them to join us at the table.

In the aftermath of Jack's surprising announcement the night before, I hadn't had time to ask him what he had learned from his questioning of Betsy or anyone else. He had been so caught up in the mechanics of his preliminary investigation and getting the corpse out of the house that I had kept quiet. By the time he and his men finally departed at around nine o'clock, Mrs. Greer and the girls had also settled in for the night in their quarters, and I hadn't been able to find out anything. I was too impatient now to wait until Jack showed up at Idlewild today to question him.

"I know this is pretty nasty for all of us," I said, looking at Katie and Betsy in turn. They were both pale and drawn, as if they hadn't slept well, either, and I didn't like to distress them with reminders of what had happened the day before. But if this thing was to be solved quickly, they were going to have to talk about it, over and over again.

The girls nodded at me. Encouraged, I continued. "It seems to me that one of the most important questions is where the weapon used on Mr. Packer came from." I grimaced. "To me it looked like the knife I brought downstairs yesterday, the knife I found in my room." Quickly I explained the circumstances.

"Well, I never!" Mrs. Greer said, plainly horrified. "Ruining your good silk like that, and not to mention my good pillow!"

I suspected that, if Mrs. Greer ever got her hands on whoever did it, that person would regret it mightily.

"Jack Preston showed us the knife," she said, "and I recognized it right off. It was one of a pair right from this kitchen, all right."

"Do you have any idea how one of the guests might have gotten it out of the kitchen?" I asked.

Mrs. Greer shrugged. "They all come in and out of the kitchen when they're here, because they feel at home here. They're always coming in to say hello to me and chew the fat a little. That Brett is always looking for something to eat." She chuckled. "Good thing that boy runs like he does, or he'd be as broad as the side of a barn. The way he eats!"

"So did they all come into the kitchen at some point yesterday, before lunch?"

"Yes," she said. "The girls and I were busy getting ready for lunch, and we didn't have much time to talk. Any of 'em could've taken that knife whiles we was running back and forth, and nobody would've paid no never-mind."

Katie had gone rather still, I noticed. "What is it, Katie?" I asked. "Did you see something?"

Startled, she gazed at me, her eyes wide with innocence. "No, ma'am. Betsy and me were way too busy. Somebody coulda carried the fridge outta here yesterday, and we wouldn't've seen it. It's always like that when Miss McElroy has a lotta company come in."

I thought she was lying, but I couldn't prove it. Just something about the shifty way her eyes darted away after the initial contact with mine.

Betsy snorted. "You sure had enough time to make goo-goo eyes at Brett, though."

"Yeah, and you woulda been rubbing yourself all over him if'n you'd had the chance!" Katie fired back.

"Girls!" Mrs. Greer's voice brooked no argument, and her

two chastened helpers shut up.

"So any one of them could have taken the knife from the kitchen yesterday before lunch," I said. "What about after lunch? When I left the dining room with Mr. Phillips—and we were the last ones out as far as I know—the knife was still on the table. When did you start clearing away?"

Mrs. Greer frowned. "Not for a while. I had the girls working on the vegetables for last night's dinner, and it wasn't till they was done with 'em that they went to clear the dining room."

"Yes'm," Betsy said. "It was a while before we did. It's like I told my cousin Jack, when we went to clear away, that knife wasn't on the table."

"Somebody came back and took it," I said, leaning back in my chair and sipping at my coffee, which by now had turned cold.

Again, Katie had that air of stillness about her. She wasn't old enough, or sophisticated enough, to hide it, though she was trying.

"I don't suppose either one of you saw something?" I asked.

Betsy shook her head, and so did Katie.

"Thank you for answering my questions," I said. "And thank you for a marvelous breakfast, Mrs. Greer. I don't know when I've ever had biscuits that light and fluffy. I could eat a dozen, and I'd still want more."

She beamed her thanks at me. I took one last sip of my coffee and set the mug down on the table. "Katie, Betsy," I said, slipping into my stern teacher voice without even thinking about it, "I want you both to be very careful. Someone in this house has killed a man in cold blood, and that person isn't someone to mess around with. If you've seen anything, anything at all, that strikes you as the least bit strange, you need to tell me or Jack Preston about it. Don't put yourselves in danger."

Betsy had a puzzled look on her face, while Katie assumed a mulish expression and said, "I can take care of myself."

I sighed. Maybe I could coax whatever it was she had seen out of her. If I couldn't, I was very much afraid that the girl's stupidity was going to cost her the ultimate price.

I decided there was no point, at the moment, in fretting over Katie's mulishness. I'd give her some time to think over what I had said, and then I'd tackle her again. If I couldn't get it out of her—whatever it was she knew or had seen—then I'd set Jack at her. Maybe he'd have better luck.

By the time I left the kitchen around eight-fifteen, I had settled on a course of action for the morning. First on my agenda was checking with Miss McElroy and informing her of my plans. We'd never had the chance for the chat that she had wanted yesterday afternoon, and I needed to consult her. From what she had already told me, I knew she didn't appear downstairs before nine. She had said I could come to her bedroom whenever I felt the need to talk with her; and though I hated to disturb her rest this morning, now was the best time.

As I passed the open door of the dining room, I glanced inside. Brett Doran, Lurleen Landry, and Russell Bertram were seated at the table, eating breakfast. No one was talking. Even with a brief glance I could see they all were as tired as I was.

Upstairs, I knocked on Miss McElroy's door, and after a moment I heard her call, "Come in."

I tried not to gawk once I was inside the room. Her bedroom was easily the most lavishly appointed chamber in the house. The richness of the materials in the drapes and the upholstery, the jewel-like hues of their colors, and the elegant solidity of the furniture bespoke money, pure and simple. This room had been tastefully and lovingly designed and maintained over the years, as had its sole occupant. Seated in a chair near the window which looked out over the back garden, and attired in a dressing gown of deep maroon velvet, Miss McElroy had the air of regal dignity which had not forsaken her, despite the events of the previous day.

Though her face had new lines etched into it this morning, she spoke in her usual vigorous tones. "Good morning, Miss Carpenter. I trust you didn't have as wretched a night as I did."

"I doubt anyone in this house slept very well last night," I responded, my tone as light as I could manage.

She nodded. "I take full responsibility."

For a moment, I thought she was confessing to the murder. The expression on my face must have amused her, because she laughed, a bitter sound.

"No, Miss Carpenter, I didn't thrust the knife into poor Hamilton's back, but I might as well have done it." Her hands gripped the arms of her chair so hard I could see her knuckles turn white. "If I hadn't brought everyone here on such a capricious notion, Hamilton would still be alive."

"You can't blame yourself for the man's death, Miss McElroy." My voice was mild and matter-of-fact. "Whatever little game Mr. Packer was attempting to play wasn't your fault. Neither was the outcome. He flung down the gauntlet, not you. He, and the person who killed him, bear the responsibility in this."

My words, chosen with care, did not appease the woman. "There is some truth to what you say," she said. "Nevertheless, Hamilton's blood is on my hands, just like poor Sukey's."

I had little patience with her determination to play the martyr, but there seemed little I could do, for the moment, to sway her from it. She was the one who, in our initial interview, said that she had to know the truth, whatever the cost. Instead of reminding her of this, I concentrated on more immediate concerns.

I briefed her on what I had learned from Mrs. Greer and her helpers, but I didn't voice my suspicions of Katie. I figured if I told Miss McElroy what I suspected, she would summon Katie immediately upstairs and demand that the girl cooperate. I didn't think those tactics would work, and I preferred to approach Katie on my own.

"Any one of us could have taken that knife, then."

I nodded. "I can't rule out anyone."

"Not even me." A ghost of a smile played on her lips.

I wouldn't have said so, though I appreciated her being direct. "Not even you."

"Good," she said. "We can't afford to overlook anything, or

— 83 —

anyone. What do you propose we do next?"

"I suggest that you follow your daily routine, as much as possible. I'm sure Jack Preston will be back this morning, with more questions, and he'll want to talk to both of us again. Right now, though, I'm going to drive into town to talk to someone at the library. One of my former students is the head of the reference department there, and I think she can help me with some questions I want answered."

Though her eyes narrowed, Miss McElroy didn't ask me about those questions. "I suppose I should count myself lucky you've got such a network of former students. Like Jack Preston."

"When you've taught at one school for over thirty years," I said, smiling, "you get to know a lot of students and their families. That can be very useful when there are problems to solve."

"Very well," she said. "Carry on, and if you need to inform me of anything, you'll do so."

Thus dismissed, I nodded and turned to leave the room. Glancing back over my shoulder as I opened the door, I saw her staring once again out into the back garden. For a moment, no more, she looked utterly defenseless and every second of her age. Then she realized I was still in the room, and her eyes burned with their accustomed fire as she commanded me with a glance to get moving. I made a strategic retreat, shutting the door quietly behind me.

I crossed the hall to my room to retrieve my handbag. Though my comfortable bed invited me to make up the sleep I'd missed last night, I grabbed the handbag and headed back into the hallway. As I approached the end of the hall, near the stairs, Brett Doran came down from the third floor with a laptop carrying case in his right hand. He was wearing a pair of well-worn jeans and a faded, collarless shirt. He could have graced the cover of *GQ*, despite the fact that his clothes were a bit on the threadbare side. No wonder both Katie and Betsy were making goo-goo eyes at him.

He wished me a good-morning as he accompanied me down to the first floor.

"Are you going to write?" I asked, a bit taken aback, I must admit.

He sighed. "Yes, though I'd rather not, right now. But you know how it is with deadlines. I'm already behind, as it is. And I might as well try to work, take my mind off all this mess."

"Where will you be?" I had thought he might just work in his bedroom. Where else could he get any peace in this house right now?

"I can't smoke in the house," he reminded me, "and I have a hard time writing if I can't smoke and walk around the room, telling myself I'm a complete idiot for thinking I have what it takes to write another book." He grinned at me as we stopped at the foot of the stairs. "So Mary Tucker lets me use that little summerhouse out back whenever I'm here. I can smoke as much as I like, and no one complains. They air out the place for a week after I leave."

"You might get interrupted today," I warned him.

He grimaced. "Until I *am* interrupted, I'll try to write, though it's going to be hard to get into the right frame of mind."

I had a number of questions I wanted to ask him, but they could wait until later. "I have some errands to run in town, but when I get back, maybe we can talk. By then you might be in a mood for some interruptions."

"Sure," he said. "Just come on out back and knock on the door. You should see that place, anyway, while you're here."

It wasn't until I was in my car and halfway down the drive that I felt myself begin to relax. I didn't see Mr. Detweiler or his Dobermans anywhere, but I supposed they'd made their presence felt. I didn't see any signs of the local press, either. Thank goodness we weren't being besieged by gawkers or thrill seekers. Yet.

The atmosphere in the house had been more oppressive than I realized. I scrunched up my shoulders to ease the knots in the back of my neck, and I began to feel better as the tension lessened. The farther from the house I drove, the lighter my mood seemed.

I raised a hand in greeting at a car approaching me. It didn't matter that I had no idea who was driving it; it was just one of those things we still did here. There wasn't much traffic on the highway this morning, or I'd have been waving a lot more.

In town, traffic was heavier and it took me about fifteen minutes to get to the library and find a place to park. A number of cars were already in the parking lot, even though it was about three minutes till the library's opening time of nine o'clock. I waited behind several mothers and fathers with young readers in tow, no doubt here for one of the summer reading programs. A high-school-age library assistant was unlocking the door of the library, and the small crowd surged inside with me in its wake as soon as the door was opened.

Like most voracious readers, I love libraries, and I had a great fondness for this one in particular, having seen it grow substantially over the years. It had outgrown its original building about a decade ago, and the county erected a wonderful new structure to house the collections and personnel which served a county population of about thirty-five thousand.

The smell of thousands and thousands of books is intoxicating, and I could stand there for quite some time, just inhaling the fragrance of my favorite addiction. I had an appointment, however, and I couldn't waste the time of someone who was doing me a favor. I headed through the stacks to the offices at the back of the library.

Farrah Lockett, a bright and promising student of mine at the high school about ten years ago, had gone off to college, gotten a degree in English literature, taught for two years, and then had gone off again, this time to graduate school. Once she had earned a master's degree in library science from the University of North Texas, she came home to Tullahoma and had been here the last three years. She was the chief reference librarian, and library patrons quickly learned that, if they had some bit of information they needed, no matter how arcane, she could track it down for them.

I had called her last night from Idlewild and given her a list of some of the things I wanted to know, and she had promised to come in early this morning and pull together whatever she could find in such a short amount of time.

Farrah was sitting at her desk, sipping something out of a mug and looking through a pile of papers, when I knocked on her open office door.

"Ernie!" Her elfin face lit with pleasure as she stood up. I had finally convinced her that it was okay for her to address me by the name my family and close friends used. "It's so good to see you! How've you been?"

"I'm doing just fine," I said, as I took a seat in the chair across from her. "I must say you're looking wonderfully well. That honeymoon in Spain sure did agree with you."

She laughed and blushed. I hadn't seen or talked with her since she'd come back from her honeymoon a couple of weeks ago, until our phone conversation last night. We spent a few minutes discussing her trip and her handsome new husband, another one of my former students who was now the coach of the football team at the high school.

"Now, enough of that," she said, "or else I'll drag out my pictures, and then we'll never get to what you really came here for."

"I'd love to see your pictures of Spain sometime, though. It's been about ten years since I've been there," I said. "But you're right, we'd better get to the business at hand. I really do appreciate your helping me like this, and at such short notice."

Farrah laughed again and shook her head. "When I think of all the times you went out of your way to help me! Don't you even think twice about asking me for help, Ernie. Besides, it's my job." She picked up a file folder of material and handed it across the desk to me. "I haven't quite finished searching some of the databases I wanted to get to, but I should have some time today to finish checking through them and see if there's anything else worth bothering with. I think, though, you'll find a lot of what you need there."

I looked at the pile of papers in my lap in amazement. "My goodness, Farrah. Were you up all night? This looks like a lot of work!"

"It's not if you know where to look. That's what librarians do. Besides, I had to get up early this morning to get Mitch up and out the door. He had to drive down to Jackson for a meeting, and he had to be there by eight-thirty. So I just came in early and got to work on your searches."

"No matter what you say," I told her, "I owe you for this. So some night soon, when you and Mitch are ready to spend time with someone besides each other, let me know, and I'm taking you both out to dinner."

She laughed and blushed again. "It's a deal. And the way Mitch eats, I think we'll be getting the best of it." Her husband was six-five and weighed about 275 pounds of solid muscle. I laughed with her.

"You're welcome to sit here in my office, if you like, and look through what I've dug up. And if you think of anything else you want me to look into, just make a note of it for me." She stood up.

"You go on and do what you need to do," I assured her. "I'll just sit here a few minutes, then, but I'll let you know before I leave." I declined an offer of coffee, though I wouldn't have minded another cup, truth be told. Time for that later, though.

Many of the pages in the folder were printouts from a computer; others had been copied from books. I decided I probably ought to send in a nice little donation to the Friends of the Library fund to help offset the cost of the paper Farrah had used in compiling all this information for me.

I skimmed through rapidly. She had found biographical information for me on every one of Miss McElroy's guests, including the late Sukey Lytton. There were also articles on them from various sources, like *Publishers Weekly*, *The Southern Review*, and a number of newspapers and literary journals. Somewhere in all of this there might be information which would help sort out what had happened at Idlewild, but it would take me some time to work my way through all of it.

Toward the bottom of the folder, I found pages devoted to Miss McElroy herself. I really knew very little about her, except the meager stuff of local folklore, and I had thought I might as well know as much as I could about my enigmatic employer. Almost as an afterthought I had asked Farrah to find out what she could about Morwell Phillips, too, and at the very bottom of the pile of papers in the folder, I found several pages devoted to him. One page had been xeroxed from *Who's Who in the South*, and I scanned the rather lengthy entry with some surprise.

I had had no idea that Phillips was a lawyer of some repute, nor that he had spent several years at Ole Miss as a professor at the law school. But what really threw me for a loop was the fact that he had been—and still was—married.

To Mary Tucker McElroy.

Chapter Ten

TO SAY I WAS STUNNED would be a gross understatement. I thought it a bit odd that Morwell Phillips always addressed Miss McElroy casually and familiarly as "Mary Tucker," rather than as "Miss McElroy," but I had dismissed it as simply the familiarity of a long mistress-servant relationship. Now I knew better, but that didn't make the relationship any less strange, at least to my way of thinking.

According to the biographical information I held in my hand, they had been married nearly fifty years. I would have been too young at the time they married to have paid any attention to what passed for a society column in our local paper; and later on, if I had ever run across a reference to them as a couple, I had no memory of it. Miss McElroy had always kept a rather low profile here in her hometown, so perhaps the knowledge of the marriage wasn't all that common.

Phillips had grown up in Mobile, according to one article. As I read further, I figured out, by what the article carefully skirted around, that he also came from a poor family. The Phillipses of Mobile were not in the same socioeconomic category as the McElroys of Tullahoma. That could explain a few things about their relationship.

Still, I felt like a fool. Either Miss McElroy had assumed I already knew, or else she didn't think it any of my business. Or anyone else's, for that matter.

What bearing did their marriage have on the two murders at Idlewild? It might have none at all, or it might be important. I felt like thumping my head against the wall to clear it.

Instead of denting the walls of Farrah's office with my thick skull, I thumbed back through the collection of papers in my lap. I found an interview with Sukey Lytton that had appeared in a poetry magazine a few years ago and began to read.

The girl's beginning in life had been nearly as tragic as her end, or so it would seem from the tale of woe she had spun for her interviewer. She had been born in Itta Bena, a small town in the Mississippi Delta, the only child of parents who scratched out a living on a small farm. Her parents had died in a house fire when she was only three, and no relatives could be found who would accept responsibility for the orphaned girl.

She went into foster care, an experience which had scarred her irreparably, or so she had claimed. She hinted at abuse, both psychological and sexual, all before she was twelve years old, when she finally found a home with a family in Oxford who took better care of her, if more by neglect than by design. At least no one had molested her, even if nothing much had been done to nurture her. She was nothing if not bitter, this Sukey Lytton.

An intelligent child, she had attracted the notice of a couple of her teachers who encouraged her intellectual aspirations. Between the scholarships she had earned and student jobs on campus, in various places like the English department and the law school library, she got through four years at Ole Miss with a degree in English.

She had been hopeless at teaching, she said, so she gave up on the idea of graduate school or a career as a high school English teacher. Instead, she had failed her way through a succession of jobs on newspapers and in restaurants and libraries.

Through it all she wrote—mostly poetry, but the occasional short story as well. She got enough encouragement through publication to continue, despite the fact that being a poet is a hard way to go. Eventually she was able to get enough grants and sponsorship to eke out a meager living. The generosity of patrons like Mary Tucker McElroy and a few others whose names I didn't recognize had made all the difference, she asserted.

She was able to concentrate on her art, as she put it, and

she didn't need a lot of material goods to make her happy, anyway. Writing was her life.

Writing was also her death, if her alleged manuscript was what the crew at Idlewild said it was.

I felt a headache coming on—whether from lack of sleep or sheer annoyance, I wasn't sure. Late last night, tossing and turning in my bed, I had given up trying to figure out where the blasted manuscript had gotten to. The murderer surely hadn't had time to get it out of the house or destroy it, so it had to be there, somewhere. But where?

When questioned by Jack Preston, Miss McElroy hadn't mentioned any secret passages in the house. There was no evidence of burning, or burying, as far as any member of the sheriff's department could discern. So where the flaming hell was it?

I gave up the fruitless speculation and bundled together the papers Farrah had collected for me. I might as well head back to Idlewild. I was tempted to drive home, just to check on things, but one of my cousins had promised to keep an eye on my house while I was at Idlewild. He was also looking after the mischievous dog I had inherited from a friend, and seeing me would only cause Gemma, a Patterdale terrier, to misbehave even more than usual. I realized I was actually beginning to miss the Devil Dog, as I called her in more affectionate moments.

Back to the task at hand. I found Farrah assisting a harried father who couldn't figure out how to use the library's on-line catalog, though his eight-year-old twin daughters didn't seem to be at all puzzled by it. I nodded my thanks at Farrah over the man's bitter complaints about the retirement of the old card catalog, and she smiled before turning back to her fretful patron.

During the hour I had spent inside the library, the temperature had risen outside and the interior of my car was even warmer. I sat for a few minutes, letting the air-conditioning play catch-up and hoping my head would clear. Then I put the car in gear and drove back to Idlewild.

The missing manuscript continued to occupy my thoughts.

Where would I hide a manuscript so that no one else could find it? The problem was, I didn't know the house well enough to pinpoint potential hiding places. The library was an obvious choice, but the killer would know that. I doubted he or she would have chosen such a place, unless the killer was playing a game out of "The Purloined Letter."

Fretting over it did me no good, except to make my headache worse. Maybe all I needed was more caffeine and two aspirin. I stopped at a gas station on the way and got a cold Diet Coke from the cooler. Fishing aspirin out of my purse, I popped two in my mouth and downed them with a cold swig of the cola. I swear my head felt better in two minutes.

When I drove up to Idlewild I saw a couple of strange cars parked in front of the house. One was clearly a sheriff's department car, the other a nondescript sedan. The latter must be Jack's car. As a plainclothes investigator, he drove an unmarked vehicle. I drove on around the side of the house to the old stables, where I parked my car. I locked the Jeep, then I stood outside. Scanning the area behind the house, I zeroed in on the summerhouse Brett Doran had mentioned.

There it nestled, off to my left, on the edge of the lawn, just under a stand of old oak trees. I hadn't paid it much attention before, because in the mornings it would be covered by the deep shade of the trees. I thought about going to talk to Brett, to ask the questions I wanted him to answer, but I decided they could wait a while longer. I felt diffident about interrupting his work.

I let myself in the back door and headed up the rear stairs to the second floor. I wanted to put away my folder of materials before anyone spotted me with them. It would be just as well that no one else knew I had them, except perhaps Miss McElroy. I hadn't yet decided whether to ask her about her marriage to Morwell Phillips. The situation disconcerted me, not a feeling I tend to enjoy.

There was no one about in the second-floor hallway, though I could hear the sounds of some activity from down the hall. Probably the investigators continuing their search for clues, I guessed, in the victim's bedroom. In my room, I looked about, trying to decide the best place to stow my folder. There was a desk underneath the window on the back wall of the house. That would do. I dropped my handbag on the bed, then went and sat down at the desk.

Period furniture is not one of my fortes, and I wasn't sure just how old this desk was. It certainly looked antique. The wood had the glow that comes from years of polishing. I thought it might be maple. I pulled open the top drawer on the side. The drawer was shallow, and it was filled with blank typing paper.

That was a bit odd. I might have expected to find some kind of stationery there, but not plain typing paper that was slightly crinkled about the edges.

I shut the drawer and opened the next one. It was empty, so I shoved my file folder into it. I thought for a moment, then I pulled open the top drawer again and lifted out about half of the large stack of blank paper. Shutting the top drawer, I deposited the paper on top of my folder and spread it out a bit so that it concealed the folder. Anything more than a casual search would reveal my stuff, of course, but that would do for now.

I closed the drawer and sat back in the chair. Staring out the window, I drank in the view of the tranquil back garden of Idlewild. From my vantage point on this side of the house, I could see the old stables off to my left and the summerhouse under the trees to my right. Everything looked so peaceful at the moment, I had to force myself to remember that a violent death had occurred just down the hall from where I sat.

As I watched, a figure came into view from the direction of the back door of the house. Her head was bent and her face was turned slightly away from me, but I recognized Katie, one of the two housemaids. Where was she going? At this time of the morning, I figured she ought to be busy either helping with preparations for lunch or cleaning the bedrooms. The latter activity was probably suspended for a while, thanks to the investigation, I realized.

Maybe the girl was just taking a brief break to get outside the house for a few minutes. I could understand that impulse.

While I watched, she continued walking, and I realized she was headed for the summerhouse. She stepped up onto the small porch across the front of the summerhouse and knocked. Moments later, the door opened in response to her knock. I couldn't see who stood inside the door because of the shadows cast by the trees around the summerhouse, but I assumed it was Brett Doran. After a brief conversation, Katie went inside the house and the door closed behind her.

Curious, I thought. Perhaps she had gone to try her luck with Brett, not realizing that she most emphatically wasn't his type.

Or maybe it was something a bit more sinister. I still had that gut feeling she knew something she wasn't telling. Moreover I was afraid she might try to make use of that knowledge and get herself in serious trouble—if she didn't get herself killed, that is. I recognized her type. Secretive, sly, looking for some way to work a situation to her advantage.

I was concerned for Katie's welfare if she tried something so stupid as blackmail, but the fact she had approached Brett alarmed me. I had taken quite a shine to that young man, and I was going to be horribly disappointed if I found out he was the killer. I knew I couldn't afford to let my emotions be engaged in a situation as dangerous as this one, but sometimes you just can't help liking someone. The head knows better, but the heart won't listen.

I decided I'd better tackle Katie straightaway, so I watched for her to leave the summerhouse. The door opened after only a few minutes, and she came strolling back out into the sunshine of the lawn. I was too far away to be able to read the expression on her face, but her body language didn't lead me to believe she was upset.

By the time she came into the house through the back door, I was waiting for her, having hustled myself down to the first floor via the back stairs. I startled her when she came inside. Her smile, when she realized who it was, wasn't exactly warm and friendly, but she paused when I spoke to her.

"Katie, I'd really like to talk to you for a minute," I said.

"Yes'm," she said. "I'm afraid Mrs. Greer needs me back

in the kitchen right now. I could maybe talk to you after lunch is done."

I shook my head. "No, this really can't wait. I'm sure Mrs. Greer won't mind if I delay you for a few minutes more. I'll explain to her, so you won't be in trouble."

She rolled her eyes and sighed heavily, but she didn't argue with me. The door to the kitchen was shut, so I figured here by the back door was as good a place as any to question her. I didn't intend to keep her very long, anyway.

"Do you remember what I said this morning, Katie? About telling the sheriff's department investigator anything you might have seen?"

She nodded, but I could feel her withdraw from me.

"This is a dangerous situation, Katie, and more bad things could happen, if we're not very, very careful. Do you understand what I'm talking about?"

She tossed her head, causing one stray curl of her blonde hair to bob on her forehead. "I been taking care of myself for years now, and I don't need no advice on how to do it. I can watch out for myself, don't you be worrying about that." She shot me a hard look. "Besides, I'm just a maid here. Nobody pays no attention to me, noways."

The bitterness in her voice told me a lot more than she realized. She was desperate for attention, and I suspected she was going about getting some the worst possible way.

I decided there was no point in pussyfooting around with her. "A man was murdered here yesterday. You didn't see the body, like Betsy did. I saw it, too, and it was a nasty sight. The man who died was taunting people because of something he knew and they didn't. He ended up dead in the bathtub, with a knife sticking out of his back. Do you want to end up that way?"

Katie paled, but she remained as obstinate as before. "I done told you, I don't know nothing. And even if I did, why should I tell a nosy old bitch like you?" She whirled away and opened the door to the kitchen, letting it shut with a firm click behind her.

That flew all over me, and I had to work hard to keep

myself from following her and slapping her stupid little face. Short of holding her down and poking her with a stick until she told me what she knew, however, I couldn't see any way of making her talk. I just prayed she wouldn't pay the ultimate price for being such a little jackass.

I sighed in frustration. I might as well tell Jack Preston what I suspected. Maybe he could get something out of her.

Where would he most likely be? I decided to try the library first.

The first floor appeared deserted as I pushed through the door into the main part of the house. I walked around the stairs to the other side of the hall and knocked on the door of the library.

After a brief delay, the door opened, and the young deputy, Robbie Davis, stuck his head out. "Yes, ma'am? Oh, hello, Miss Carpenter. What can I do for you?"

"I'm looking for Jack Preston, Robbie," I said.

"He's busy at the moment, Miss Carpenter," he said. "If you don't mind waiting a few minutes, he can prob'ly see you before too long, though."

"Fine," I said. "I'll just wait out here, if that's okay."

"Not a problem," he said. "Just a few minutes." The door closed.

I sat down in a chair against the wall and waited. I discovered that if I leaned my head back and turned my ear to the wall I could hear the rumble of voices from inside the library. I couldn't hear what was being said, but I could discern different pitches. Jack was talking to a woman; that much was clear from the higher pitch of the second voice.

Suddenly, the sounds from within the library grew louder. The female voice hit an even higher pitch, and the next thing I knew, the door to the library opened and crashed back against the inside wall with a resounding thump. I jumped in my chair, wincing and rubbing my ear.

"I will personally complain to the sheriff about this, you can count on that!" Alice Bertram was in full tirade as she came hobbling out into the hall, leaning heavily on her walker. "I'm not one of the hillbillies you're used to dealing with, and you're going to find out that you can't treat me in that disgraceful and disrespectful manner."

She stormed past me, moving at a faster clip than I had thought her capable of, barely missing my toes with her walker. She paid no attention to me, however, being intent only on getting away from Jack Preston. He had come to the door of the library and stood watching her, a bemused smile on his face.

"What was all that about?" I asked him as I stood up and motioned him back inside the library.

Robbie closed the door behind us, and I sat down in a chair across from the desk.

Attired more formally today in a suit and tie, Jack shook his head in bewilderment. "All I did was ask her a few questions about the nature of her physical problems. I was trying to rule her out as having the physical strength to stab the victim with the amount of force that was used, and you would have thought I had asked her for some intimate details of her relations with her husband. She flew off the handle at me, and, well, you heard what she said."

"She certainly overreacted." I grinned.

"Yeah," Jack said, his mouth twisted in disgust.

"But it does make you wonder, though," I said.

He nodded. "Yeah, from what I could see, the way she used that walker of hers, her upper body strength is pretty darned good. She could have done it, alright."

I found I rather liked the idea of Alice Bertram as the killer. The woman was so thoroughly unpleasant, I wouldn't mind seeing her hauled off to jail. Awfully petty of me, I know.

"But that's not why you came to see me," Jack said.

I shook my head. "No, there's something I think you should know about." I sketched for him my two conversations with Katie, but I didn't tell him I suspected she had gone to talk to Brett Doran. I wasn't ready to do that until I had talked to Brett first, on my own.

"You think she knows something she's not telling?"

"I'm almost positive of it, now."

Jack groaned. "So now I have a potential little blackmailer

on my hands." He sighed. "I'll try talking to her. Maybe if I lean on her a little bit, I'll get her to confide in me."

"I hope so." I grinned at him. "A handsome cop might stand a better chance getting her to crack than a nosy old-maid schoolteacher."

He guffawed, and I heard a muffled snort from somewhere behind me. I had forgotten that Robbie was still in the room with us.

"I wonder what it was she saw?" Jack said after he stopped laughing. "Or who?"

"I've been thinking about it, and the best guess I have is that she must have seen someone coming in or out of the dining room after lunch. Someone with an opportunity to have taken the knife. The girls had to clear away from lunch, and she might have seen something when she went into the dining room."

"Surely whoever it was, if there was anybody, would have seen her," Jack objected.

I shook my head. "Not necessarily. As she was coming into the dining room from the kitchen, she could have glimpsed someone leaving through the main door. That person probably wouldn't have seen her. Katie might not have given it much thought until later on, when she found out the murder weapon had been on the dining room table. She would know it wasn't there when she came in to clear away, and she would figure whoever she had seen leaving the room had taken it. And why."

"Makes sense." Jack nodded. "But it's almost too good to be true."

"And it may be too good to be true," I said, having an attack of conscience. "I may be reading more into this than there really is. She may not have seen anything, and I may have been badgering her for no reason."

"Possibly," Jack said, unconvinced. "I'll still talk to her and hope for something. I could use a break like that, if only she'll talk to me."

"Getting leaned on from above?" I asked. His boss, the sheriff, was always sensitive to public opinion, and this case must be giving him heartburn, because of the family connection. Frankly I was surprised he hadn't been here himself to reassure Miss McElroy that he'd take personal charge of the case. Evidently he had more sense than I'd given him credit for, because Jack was the best man for the job.

"And how! The sheriff and the chief deputy have already let me know they want this solved yesterday." He grimaced. "Nothing less than I'd expect, given who's involved. She may stay out of the public eye around here, but Miss McElroy is still what passes for royalty in this county."

"Or should we be saying 'Mrs. Phillips,'" I said, half-mockingly.

"What do you mean?" Jack was puzzled.

I told him what I had discovered about the relationship between Mary Tucker McElroy and Morwell Phillips.

"Holy shit!" he said, then immediately looked embarrassed.

"It's okay, Jack, I've heard worse," I assured him. No matter how old they get, they never forget you were their teacher, once upon a time. I almost laughed at the expression on his face.

"Nobody's mentioned that little fact to me before," he said. "Not even the sheriff, and I'd think he knows."

"Maybe he assumed everybody knows."

Jack shrugged. "Maybe, but it's downright peculiar, don't you think?"

"Yes, but the more I've thought about it, I can understand why Miss McElroy continues to use her own name. After all, it's a famous one in Mississippi. And, even though she comes from a generation for which it would have been scandalous not to take a husband's name, I can see her doing it and letting the rest of the world think what it wanted to."

"Uh-huh," he said, "now that you mention it, so can I." We shared a conspiratorial grin.

"Are you going to talk to Katie now?"

Jack shook his head. "She can wait a while. She's not in any danger at the moment. As much as I'd like to find out what she knows, I've got a few other things on my plate at the moment. The chief deputy expects another report, so I'll be heading back to town soon to check in with him. I can't put him off because he and the sheriff have called a press conference for noon. The papers from Memphis and Jackson have sent reporters to cover this, and I think there's even one from Atlanta. We've got to have something to tell them that'll keep them off our backs for another day or two." He sighed. "In the meantime, I've got a couple men here searching, trying to find that blasted manuscript."

I felt a momentary twinge of guilt for not telling him about the scene I had witnessed at the summerhouse, but I still wanted to talk to Brett first. I'd do it while Jack was gone to town to talk to his superiors, and by the time he returned, I would have decided what to do, depending on what Brett had to say to me. I was hoping Brett would talk to Jack himself, if his conversation with Katie had something to do with the murder.

"I'll see you later on, then," I said, standing up. "You'll be coming back here after the press conference?"

"Yep," he said, standing with me. "The folks here are going to get sick of the sight of my face before this is all over with."

I preceded him out of the room. He moved up the hall toward the front door, giving instructions to Robbie. I ducked through the door into the back of the house and outside.

The heat was stifling in the late morning sun. Not a breath of air moved as I walked across the lawn toward the summerhouse. With some relief I stepped into the shade of the trees and onto the porch. I knocked at the door and listened.

"Just a minute!" a voice called—a voice sounding thoroughly annoyed.

"Oh," Brett said blankly as he opened the door. "It's you." He offered a halfhearted smile of greeting.

"Sorry to intrude on you when you're busy," I said, "but I really do need to talk to you." I sniffed at the air coming from inside the summerhouse. He wasn't kidding when he said they'd have to air the place out for a week. The haze of cigar smoke was thick in the room behind him.

He shrugged. "It's okay. I'm not really getting that much done anyway. Come on in."

He stood aside for me to enter. As he shut the door, he flipped a switch, and two large ceiling fans whirred to life. In moments, the smoke began to dissipate, though the aroma lingered.

I examined the main room of the summerhouse with great interest. It was about twenty-five by twenty-five, a nice big space with lots of windows. Two of those windows held air-conditioning units, and the temperature was comfortable. There were couches and chairs spaced around the room, and off to one side stood a desk with a modern-looking office chair in front of it. On top of the desk sat Brett's laptop and an ashtray with a smoking cigar in it. Bookshelves lined two walls, and I resisted the urge to examine them.

Brett retrieved his cigar and the ashtray from the desk and wandered over to a couch. "Do you mind if I finish this?" he asked.

"Not at all," I said, making myself comfortable on the other end of the couch. "Not a bad place to work."

"I can usually work pretty well here," he said, emitting a plume of smoke into the air above his head. He motioned over the back of the couch with the hand holding his cigar. "See those doors back there? Through the left one is a tiny kitchen, and through the one on the right is a bedroom with a full bath."

"It's more like a guest cottage than a summerhouse," I commented.

He nodded, waiting.

I decided I'd work my way up to the real purpose of my visit. "We haven't had much chance to talk since last night," I said. "I didn't know Mr. Packer very well, and frankly I don't think I would have wanted to. But for those of you who knew him, this must be a terrible shock."

One eyebrow arched as Brett drew again on his cigar. He expelled the smoke before replying. "It's a shock, all right, but it's more of a shock that someone hadn't killed the old bastard before now, frankly."

"Why is that?" I refused to be offended by his tough-guy talk.

"He was a shark, pure and simple."

"That's in line with what you told me yesterday. Why don't you elaborate a little more."

"He preyed upon anyone he perceived as weak."

"Including you?"

Brett nodded. "Including me. He was my first agent. He signed me when I was fresh out of college, convinced I was going to write the Great American Novel and win the Pulitzer, the National Book Award, and the Nobel Prize at one fell swoop. He saw me coming a mile away."

"But you're obviously very talented," I said.

"Yeah, and that and a nickel won't buy you a cup of coffee. Or one of these." He brandished his cigar.

"He can't have done all that badly by you, because you've been very successful. Hitting the best-seller list, a movie deal, articles in *People* magazine, the works."

"I didn't say he wasn't a good agent, like I told you yesterday," Brett said, a touch of humor in his voice. "He knew what he was doing when it came to negotiating a contract. He just counted on a first-time author's inexperience with contracts, and he took advantage of that fact."

"How did he do that, if you don't mind my asking?"

"I feel pretty stupid, now, telling anybody about it, but you might as well know." He looked disgusted with himself as he contemplated the ash on the end of his cigar. He deposited the ash in the ashtray before he continued. "I was completely naive about publishing. I'd never seen a publishing contract, and I had sure never seen an agency contract. He spoke to a group I belonged to, and he agreed to look over any manuscript that a member of the group submitted to him. I sent him mine, and after about three months, I got a letter from him, asking me to come to New York to see him. I had to hock something to get the plane fare, but I went."

"Wasn't that a bit odd, asking you to come all the way to New York?"

"Yeah, I realized that later. But what he wanted was to get me hooked, and I thought that if he wanted me to come all the way to New York to see him, I must be pretty darn special. He had a way of making you feel like that, that you were the most talented writer to come along in years. And I fell for it, like the idiot I was."

"So what did he do?"

"He got me in his office in New York and presented me with an agency contract. He said he wanted to sign me because he was convinced that I was going to be the next Tom Wolfe and John Irving, all in one. He offered me expensive cigars and expensive liquor, and I had signed the contract before I knew what hit me."

"Was it a bad contract?"

Brett shrugged. "It was standard, I found out later, with one exception. Most agents take a ten-percent commission, some fifteen, but then they don't charge you for a lot of incidentals, like making copies of manuscripts, basic office expenses, things like that. Packer charged twenty percent, which he told me up front, but he said it was because he always got such large advances for his authors that he was worth it. Hell, what did I know? It sounded impressive to me, because he could be charming and persuasive when he wanted to be. Plus I was more than a bit drunk by the time we got to that part."

"Couldn't you have fired him?"

"I did, eventually," he said. "But at first he really was doing a great job for me. He didn't sell that first manuscript, but he sold the second one, and he got me a shitload of money for it." He thought about what he had just said. "Sorry. Anyway, he got me so much money, at first I didn't care that he was getting a hefty percentage of it."

"But eventually you got tired of it and fired him."

"Yeah," he said as he stubbed out his cigar. "Like I told you yesterday."

"I guess that means you didn't have to deal with him at all, after that?"

Brett cocked his head to one side. "Not exactly."

"What do you mean?"

"He would still get income on the books he sold for me, as long as the books remained in print. If they went out of print, and the rights reverted to me, he was out of the picture."

"But that hadn't happened, had it?" Thinking of the phenomenal success of his first book, I could see that it galled him to know Packer had continued to reap the benefits from it.

"Nope."

"But what about now that he's dead? Does someone else inherit the agency?"

"Nope." He almost bit off the word.

"Then that probably means your rights revert back to you."

He nodded.

That was a pretty darn good motive for murder, if he'd been angry enough with Packer and his shady dealings.

As if he'd read my mind, Brett said, albeit not very robustly, "It's not worth murdering someone over."

"Maybe not," I said, "but it's suggestive."

"Are you going to tell your buddy the cop about this?" He almost sounded jealous.

I tried not to smile as I replied. "No, I think you should be the one to tell him, if it's necessary."

"So you think I didn't do it." Was that a look of relief in his eyes?

"It may not have anything to do with the case. At least, not directly."

"Thanks for the vote of confidence. I think." He got up from the couch and walked over to the desk. He picked up his cigar case, opened it, and selected another cigar. I watched in silence while he clipped off the end and lit it, after pulling a lighter from his pocket.

He turned back to me, smoke billowing around his head. "Would you like something to drink?"

"What are my choices?"

"Water, soft drinks, coffee if you'd like me to make some."

"How about a Diet Coke?"

He nodded before he stalked off in the direction of the kitchen. He was back in less than a minute with two cans of Diet Coke.

"Thanks," I said as I accepted mine. I popped the top and took a nice long sip. Eyeing Brett speculatively, I chose my next words with care. "An investigation into a crime like this can be rougher on the innocent than it is on the person who committed the crime."

"Meaning?"

"The investigators have to ask questions about matters that may have nothing to do, ultimately, with the outcome of the case. They have to know a lot in order to be able to rule out what's extraneous and zero in on what's pertinent."

"Basically you're telling me I should cooperate with the cops and tell them whatever they want to know. And if I'm innocent, I have nothing to worry about." He snorted.

"Jack Preston is a good man. Not only is he good at his job, he's a good man, period. He's not going to arrest someone just because he's under pressure to solve the case and he spots someone who looks like a convenient answer."

Brett sighed, spewing forth smoke. "I hope you're right."

"In this case, I believe I am," I said.

He laughed. "I'll have to take your word for that."

He was more relaxed, at least for the moment, which was all to the good. The next bit was going to be tricky.

"The fact that you were in the room next to Packer's is going to be of interest, naturally. Because of the connecting door."

Brett nodded. "I didn't see or hear anything. I was in my room the whole time, reading. I've got a book I'm reviewing for the *New York Times*, and I've got to get it in soon. Plus I had the radio on, listening to the local station. I didn't hear anything until that poor girl started screaming."

"What did you do then?"

"I could tell it was coming from the bathroom, because it was so loud and so close. I tried opening the door, but it was locked from the inside." He grimaced and looked away, taking a draw from his cigar before he continued. "So I went out into the hall and into the bedroom. When I got there, Betsy was still standing in the edge of the bathroom, shrieking, and I could see what was wrong." He looked sick at the memory. "I got us both out of there, and that's when everyone else showed up."

"Then whoever did it had to go in and out through Packer's bedroom."

"Provided that I didn't do it myself." Brett offered this in a bitter tone.

"Provided that you didn't do it, naturally." But I smiled to take the sting out of the words. I really didn't think he was the killer, but I had to try to keep an open mind. He was in a difficult position because he would certainly have had the best opportunity. The killer had taken some risks, going in and out of Packer's bedroom. The risks were even greater if the person had gone back, after taking the manuscript away and hiding it, to ring the bell and summon someone to discover the corpse.

"Now, you didn't see anyone in the hall when you came out of your room?" I asked.

Brett shook his head. "Nobody."

"If only you had seen something," I sighed. "But of course, sometimes people see things and don't understand exactly what they've seen. Or else they do know and won't talk about it, for reasons of their own."

"I suppose," Brett said, puzzled, not sure where I was going with these remarks.

"For example," I said, looking straight at him, "I happened to be looking out the window of my room not long ago, and I saw Katie come and knock on the door here. She stayed for a few minutes, and then she left."

"Maybe she was just coming to tell me when lunch would be ready," Brett said, stone-faced all of a sudden.

"Maybe," I said. "But it certainly took her a few minutes to pass along such a simple message." I waited.

He tried to stare me down, but he didn't have the years of practice that I do. Finally his eyes fell, and he muttered something under his breath.

"What was that? I didn't quite catch it," I said, trying not to smile.

"I said," Brett talked through clenched teeth, "that it was too damn embarrassing to talk about."

"Don't worry about being embarrassed in front of me. Just

tell me what it is."

He drew deeply on his cigar, then watched the exhaled smoke for a moment before replying. He stared at the far wall, refusing to look at me.

"The silly girl thinks I'll hop into bed with her, just because she thinks she's in love with me. She came out here to ask me to meet her here tonight, in the summerhouse, so she can show me just how she feels about me."

Truly, he did look embarrassed, because he had blushed dark red. But I think the embarrassment came from the fact that he was lying to me.

Chapter Eleven

I WAS A BIT HURT that Brett wouldn't confide in me. I thought we had established a good rapport, even on such a brief acquaintance, and it bothered me that he wouldn't tell me the truth. His refusal to meet my eyes now convinced me I was right about his lying. For the moment, I'd pretend I believed him, and later maybe I could get the truth out of him. In the meantime, I'd be speculating, furiously and fruitlessly perhaps, on what it was he didn't want to tell me.

"You must have let her down gently," I said, pretending that I saw nothing amiss in what he had told me. "She sure didn't look upset when she left here."

Brett shrugged. "There was no point in pissing her off, or I'd have to make my own bed." He rolled his eyes at me. "Sorry, that sounded incredibly patronizing. I didn't want to hurt her feelings, and I wasn't sure she could handle the complete truth, so I told her she was pretty, but that I was seeing someone back in Memphis. Someone I had no intention of cheating on."

As lies go, it was pretty good. After all, he was someone who lied for a living, if you subscribe to the theory that all fiction is lies.

"Well, I guess they'll be calling us for lunch soon," I said. "I hope so, because I'm more than ready for one of Mrs. Greer's fabulous meals."

Brett laughed, relieved at the change of subject. "Whenever I go home from staying here, I have to work out twice as long every day for a month to get rid of the extra pounds I put on."

"Guess I'll see you back at the big house," I said, smiling

as I stood. "Don't bother to see me out. I'm sure you'd like to get back to work."

Casting a look of loathing at his laptop, he shook his head. "I might as well pack it in for the morning. I can't seem to get into anything today." He got to his feet. "I'll just close everything down, and I'll be along in a few minutes."

When I shut the door behind me, he was sitting at the desk, tapping at the keyboard with one finger.

I peered at my watch through the dazzling sunlight. I had to squint to make out the hands. Only a quarter past twelve; it seemed later. Lunch wouldn't be served for another forty-five minutes. How would I occupy myself until then? Might as well go back to my room and continue going through the materials that Farrah Lockett had compiled for me. I might come across something promising.

I encountered no one as I entered the house and trudged up the back stairs to the second floor. The hallway upstairs was deserted, and I opened the door of my room. I stopped in the doorway, appalled.

My red silk dress, the one I had found impaled on the bed, had been cut into long swathes of fabric, which were strewn around the floor of the room.

I don't take blood pressure medicine, but in that moment I thought I might need some, to keep me from having a stroke on the spot. The malice behind this second attack—I couldn't think of a better or more appropriate word—made me even angrier than the first. If whoever did this thought I was going to be put off the chase by these antics, he or she definitely had another think coming! Some of my students used to joke—behind my back, they thought—that I'm one-third bulldog and two-thirds mule, because I'm so tenacious. This old mule still had a lot of kick, not to mention bite, in her yet, as some idiot was going to learn, at great cost.

Grieving slightly for my dress, I gathered up the scraps. I'd give them to a quilting friend of mine, and she'd sew them into one of her creations that regularly won prizes at quilting shows.

I stowed the dismembered dress in my suitcase in the bottom of the wardrobe, then I made myself comfortable at the desk, forcing my thoughts away from the mutilated dress. Opening the drawer where I had put my papers, I pulled them out, along with the blank paper I had placed on top of them for camouflage. Then I sat there for a long moment, staring at the empty pages, struck by a wild idea.

Opening the top drawer, I picked up the rest of the blank paper I had found and laid it to the left beside the other bit. Then I picked up the stack on the right side and placed it atop the other. There was about a ream of paper on my desk.

I examined the top sheet. Along both sides, about halfway down each, there were small rents, as if something had rubbed the paper until it had torn. Like a rubber band, perhaps.

What if this might be the missing "manuscript" which Hamilton Packer had been carrying in his briefcase? There was enough paper here to have made the briefcase bulge, if it were stuck inside. Maybe Packer had been bluffing, but the killer hadn't known that.

Continuing with this train of thought, I wondered who had hidden the supposed manuscript in the desk in my room. Had Packer done it himself, before he was killed? Or had the killer done it, after having killed Packer and having discovered that there was no manuscript?

Good questions, all of them. If no other manuscript turned up, then I'd guess I was right about at least part of my little theory. Unless each of the guest rooms had similar paper available in the desks, I figured I had located what Jack and his men had been seeking since yesterday.

I put my own papers back in the desk and placed the blank typing paper back in the top drawer, where I had first found it. Time to let Jack know what I was thinking—he could be the one to sort out the truth, if possible. Just suppose, I thought, if Packer's fingerprints could be found on this paper, or some kind of trace of him, that would clinch things. Jack and his men had fingerprinted all of us last night, so they would be able to identify mine right away. I just hoped they would find Packer's prints on some of this paper.

As I closed the bedroom door behind me, I thought about asking Morwell Phillips for a key. I should have considered it before now, especially after the first incident involving my dress, but I had let other matters take precedence. I doubted that guests at Idlewild had had much need of locking their doors before this week.

Downstairs I went to the library, looking for Jack or one of his men. The room was empty. I looked at my watch again. Only about fifteen minutes had elapsed since I'd last checked it. Then I remembered the press conference Jack said he had to attend. He wouldn't be back at Idlewild for another hour or two, most likely. I might as well try to find Phillips and ask about that key.

In the kitchen, Katie shot me a glance full of resentment, and I guessed our little chat earlier still rankled. "Hello, Mrs. Greer," I said, then nodded at Betsy and Katie both. "Is Mr. Phillips around somewhere? There's something I'd like to ask him."

"He's probably in the sitting room with Miss McElroy," Mrs. Greer said, peering into the oven. "We'll be ready to serve y'all lunch soon."

I sniffed at the banquet of appetizing aromas in the kitchen. "Everything smells wonderful. If I had your gift, Mrs. Greer, I'd be wide as the side of a barn."

She smiled her thanks. "The Good Lord saw fit to make me a good cook, and I treasure the fact He found me such a good place to work, with folks that appreciate my food."

"I'm glad to know they appreciate you here," I said.

"There's some that'd do good to remember we've got good jobs in this house," she said, looking pointedly in Katie's direction. When Mrs. Greer turned back to the oven, Katie stuck out her tongue at her. Betsy, who saw it all, just rolled her eyes and continued with her work. I offered Katie a repressive glance of my own, but she remained undaunted.

"I guess I'll go see if I can talk to Mr. Phillips before we eat this delicious lunch," I said, then turned and walked away. I didn't envy Mrs. Greer, having to deal with the rebellious Katie, but I also didn't have much doubt as to who would get the upper hand in that contest.

Moments later, I knocked on the door of Miss McElroy's sitting room. Her voice bade me enter, and I opened the door and walked in. She was seated in her usual place, and her husband sat in a chair near her.

"Miss Carpenter. I do trust that you've had a productive morning?" The tone of her voice indicated that I had better have found out something useful. She had relaxed her guard with me a bit yesterday and earlier this morning, but the martinet seemed to be back in full force now.

"Yes, I do have some things to tell you. But first, if you don't mind, I'd like to ask Mr. Phillips for something."

He stood. "Certainly, Miss Carpenter. What can I do for you?"

"Could I have a key to my bedroom door?"

If either of them was startled or dismayed by my request, neither manifested it. "I'll find one for you. That's not a problem." He frowned.

"Did you find something else in your room?" Miss McElroy asked.

"The shreds of my best dress."

The shock on her face was not feigned. "My goodness! What on earth?"

"Obviously someone has figured out that Miss Carpenter isn't here merely to assist with your memoirs, Mary Tucker." Phillips's voice was dry, almost amused.

"I shall certainly reimburse you for the dress, Miss Carpenter," Miss McElroy said. "The very idea! I trust that this hasn't intimidated you?"

"Not in the least," I assured her. "It would take more than that to get rid of me. Somebody miscalculated very badly. The only way I'd leave now is if you told me to leave." I grinned. "And even then, I'm not sure I'd go."

Miss McElroy smiled. "That's the kind of determination I admire. I chose well, Miss Carpenter, I am more and more convinced." She looked up at her husband. "Why don't you see about that key, Morwell?"

Taking this for the dismissal it was, he inclined his head.

"You'll have it right away, Miss Carpenter." Nodding at me, he departed the room.

"Now, come sit down here by me"—with a wave of her hand, Miss McElroy indicated the chair her husband had vacated—"and tell me what you've learned."

I had debated how to broach the point of her marriage. I decided that head-on was the best way. "I had no idea that you and Mr. Phillips are married, Miss McElroy."

"Ancient history, Miss Carpenter." She shrugged. "We've been married so long, neither one of us thinks twice about it. I kept my maiden name, and Morwell didn't want to change his, despite my father's wishes and very forceful attempts to persuade him to do so. It caused a bit of a scandal when we were much younger, but I've never let a little bit of talk stop me from doing what I think is best."

I didn't doubt that for a moment, but I also thought, somewhat cynically, that it hadn't hurt her to have her family's money and their background behind her. A poor woman of lesser social standing couldn't have carried it off, at least not fifty years ago.

"All the same, I do wish I had known. It was a bit of a surprise, having to find it out from someone else."

Miss McElroy looked affronted. "I can't imagine that it should make any difference to the situation here. If I had even thought about it, I would have presumed that you knew before you ever walked through the door."

"It doesn't really matter," I said, withdrawing a bit in the face of her vehemence. "I just thought it curious."

She took umbrage at that. "My relationship with my husband is my own business, and no one else's. It has nothing to do with the matter at hand, and I'll thank you to remember that."

"Certainly," I said, in as pacific a tone as I could manage. All the same, her defensiveness piqued my curiosity. There was something, some story, behind all this. If it was pertinent to the current situation, I'd have to winkle it out somehow.

I reported as much of my morning's activities as I thought necessary for her to hear at this juncture. I held back on telling her about Katie's visit to Brett Doran, my subsequent visit to the summerhouse, and my own speculations about the typing paper I had found in the desk in my bedroom. Since I hadn't seen them on my tour of the house, I did ask her whether all of the guest rooms had desks, and she replied in the affirmative.

"What kind of supplies do they generally contain?"

Miss McElroy frowned, obviously puzzled at the point of my question. "A few pens, some stationery bearing the name and address of this house, that's about it."

Before she could say anything more, I interposed, "I was just wondering if I could get some ordinary paper. I'd like to make some notes, and I hate to use that expensive-looking stationery." I gave a self-deprecating smile as I lied to her. "I forgot to pack a notebook, and I didn't think about getting one when I was in town this morning."

"I'm sure Morwell can find you what you need. Just ask."

Morwell Phillips saved me from further inquisition by reappearing then to announce that lunch was ready to be served. He handed me a key, then offered his arm to his wife. He escorted her to the dining room, and I trailed behind.

The others were all assembled in the dining room, waiting for us. Alice Bertram and Lurleen Landry had sat down, but the two men had waited, standing, for Miss McElroy to be seated. Brett pulled out my chair for me, and I smiled my thanks up at him. He still wouldn't quite meet my eyes, and I vowed to myself that I would get him sorted out soon.

Miss McElroy said grace, then Phillips summoned Katie and Betsy. The menu today consisted of pork chops, biscuits and redeye gravy, and an assortment of vegetables. This was cooking like my mother and grandmother knew, passed down from one generation to another of Southern women for well over a century. There's nothing like it. I sighed in happy anticipation.

Conversation at first was desultory. No one seemed much in the mood to talk, and with the pall of violent death hanging over us, I wasn't surprised. Alice Bertram was uncharacteristically silent. I found it hard to believe she didn't have something to complain about, but even she was subdued today. Her face was haggard, and I doubted she had slept well last night. Then again, I could say the same for each and every one of us, as I made a quick survey around the table. No one looked well-rested.

But which one of them had sneaked into my room and shredded my dress? Brett I could rule out, since he had been with me the entire time; but any of the rest of them could have done it, even Miss McElroy. I couldn't imagine why she would do such a thing, when she had employed me in the first place. But you never knew. I couldn't rule her out completely, just in case.

I was still debating how to proceed with my investigation after lunch, when Miss McElroy solved the dilemma for me. Without warning, she tapped her spoon on the side of her iced-tea glass. Everyone looked at her expectantly.

"In view of what has happened here," she began, "I have decided to tell you all the real reason that I invited you here this week. I am working on my memoirs, true enough, but that wasn't why I asked you here. The murder which occurred in this house last night wasn't the first one to take place at Idlewild. Sukey Lytton was murdered, I am firmly convinced, and that is why you are all here."

She paused, taking time to look for a long moment at each of her guests, except for me.

Her survey completed, she spoke. "One of you murdered Sukey, and I am determined to find out which one of you did it."

Chapter Twelve

I THINK I WAS AS TAKEN ABACK as everyone else at Miss McElroy's little speech. The last thing I'd expected was for her to offer such a direct challenge to her guests. I sat back and waited for the fireworks.

Alice Bertram was first out of the starting block, as I might have predicted. "Mary Tucker, the Good Lord knows you have always had enough nerve for any three people, but I cannot believe the colossal effrontery of what you just said! How *dare* you say something like that to Russell and me? Heaven knows, I'm glad the little bitch is dead and gone, but I sure as hell didn't have anything to do with getting rid of her, and neither did Russell." Her glance at her husband spoke volumes. "He doesn't have the nerve to do something like that."

"Your wifely loyalty does you credit, Alice dear," Lurleen said. She looked ready to spit nails, but whether at Alice Bertram or Miss McElroy, I couldn't tell. "Mary Tucker, you've always had an *unusual* sense of humor, and I expect you think this is some kind of macabre joke. But for once I have to agree with Alice, though it pains me mightily to do so. Are you out of your cotton-pickin' mind, my dear?"

"Holy mother of. . . ." Brett choked out. "Just how dumb can y'all be? Hasn't it occurred to you yet that one of us sitting here at this table, with the possible exception of Ernie, stabbed ol' Hamilton in the back yesterday?" He snorted in disgust. "Who the hell do you think did it? It has to be one of us! And if one of us killed Hamilton to get their hands on Sukey's manuscript, the odds are the same person probably killed Sukey too. She was too self-involved to kill herself."

"Brett's right," Russell said, surprising us all. He spoke

so seldom that I tended to forget he was there or capable of speech. "We have to look at this logically; and logically, one of us who knew both Sukey and Hamilton well has to be the killer."

His wife emitted such a shriek of rage I thought she'd keel over from a stroke. "Russell! There are other people in this house. What about the cook? You know those blacks know all about using knives. And those two little tarts who call themselves maids! They're both sly and probably no better than they should be. No telling what either of them might take a mind to do."

"Alice!" Miss McElroy's voice lashed out like a bullwhip. "You will apologize *at once* for that insult to Mrs. Greer, or, the Good Lord give me strength, I will slap your face seven ways from Sunday. I will not abide such trash talk in this house!"

Alice realized she'd gone too far. Her eyes wide with shock, she began mumbling an incoherent apology.

Miss McElroy let her babble for a moment, then cut her off. "Don't forget yourself again, Alice, or you won't ever be welcome in this house. You will not speak about Mrs. Greer, or any member of my staff, like that."

"If I might just interject a note of sanity here," Phillips said, his voice dry and detached, "I don't think anyone need worry about either Katie or Betsy. They're good girls—I chose them myself. They only started working here last fall, just before Christmas. Neither one of them knew Sukey long enough to want to harm her, and the same goes for Hamilton. They would have seen him only twice in their lives."

"And no matter how obnoxious he could be," Lurleen added, "even he couldn't have offended them badly enough to earn a knife in the back! You're even stupider than I realized, Alice."

"That's quite enough," Miss McElroy said, her patience clearly worn thin. "I don't want to hear any more of this sniping and name-calling, do you hear me?"

A chorus of "yes, Mary Tucker" followed her declaration. The viciousness of the exchange had made me uncomfortable, but it hadn't surprised me. Emotions were high, and resentments and prejudices were bound to expose themselves. I just hoped Miss McElroy hadn't chastened them all to the point that they wouldn't talk. I wanted them all feeling a bit raw and edgy in order to get what I needed. Otherwise I wouldn't be much use in trying to sort out this mess. Nor would Jack Preston, come to think of it.

"Mr. Preston of the sheriff's department will be back sometime this afternoon," Miss McElroy said, "after the press conference the sheriff is holding in town. I expect he has more questions to ask each of us, so you will make yourselves available to him." She spoke with her accustomed air of command, and no one said a word in response. "I will also be speaking with each of you, at some point today or tomorrow, to clarify points about what I'm writing in my memoirs. I also expect you to make yourselves available to me, when you are not needed by the investigators."

After mulling it over for a few minutes, while I continued to eat my lunch, I concluded that Miss McElroy was playing some kind of mind game with her guests. Surely as we were all sitting here, they must know she intended to interrogate them about the events surrounding Sukey Lytton's death, under the guise of writing her memoirs. Yet not a single one of them, at least at this point, offered any kind of refusal or rebellion. I didn't know enough of the history of any of their relationships with Miss McElroy to understand precisely why they would allow her to dictate to them in this manner. I had seen evidence of her powerful personality, but there were other reasons, deeper and more compelling, most likely, which allowed this elderly woman to ride roughshod over them in this fashion.

Perhaps it stemmed in some ways from the fact that they were all Southerners, born and bred. Though they came from different parts of the South and from different backgrounds, they had that indefinable link that being a child of the South creates in all of us who are born here. I sometimes think that we imbibe, along with our mothers' milk, a respect for tradition and certain kinds of authority that we find difficult to cast aside or to overthrow. Miss McElroy embodied both tradition and authority; moreover, she had bound these people to her with a deep sense of obligation for her patronage over the years. Such ties would be difficult for them to ignore, no matter how they might chafe at the restrictions imposed by them.

Yet one of them had violated, in the most ugly way possible, the bonds which linked them all together. By striking not once, but twice, the killer had treated the sanctity of Miss McElroy's home, her generosity and hospitality, as nothing. I understood the outrage Miss McElroy undoubtedly felt, the same way I understood the ruthlessness which now drove her to identify the person responsible.

The rest of them, who knew her better and longer than I, must have understood it, too. They would do as she said, and only the killer would try to outwit her. I didn't doubt that Miss McElroy would emerge victorious at the end, though I didn't want to estimate the cost.

Conversation after Miss McElroy's royal decree was desultory, at best. No doubt every one of us at the table wished to leave the room as soon as possible, but good manners held everyone in place until the dessert course had been served and eaten. I must confess that Mrs. Greer's homemade peach ice cream was well worth the delay.

As we were leaving the dining room en masse, Jack Preston appeared in the hallway from the back of the house. Miss McElroy moved forward to greet him.

"We have just finished our meal, Mr. Preston," she said, after they had exchanged the niceties, "and we are all at your disposal. What would you like for us to do?"

If Jack was startled by her pronouncements, he didn't show it. Years of experience had schooled his features into a polite, uncommunicative mask. "Thank you, Miss McElroy," he said. "My men and I will be continuing to examine the crime scene, and I do have more questions to ask all of you, I'm afraid." He glanced at his watch. "If I could have about fifteen minutes or so with my men, I'll start talking to y'all then."

"Certainly," Miss McElroy said. "I'll be in my sitting room, and anyone who cares to join me there is welcome." She turned to face us. "If anyone wishes to wait somewhere else, you will inform Morwell where you will be, and he will summon you when Mr. Preston requires you."

With that she swept by us on her way to her sitting room. The Bertrams and Lurleen Landry followed her, while Brett Doran paused to speak with Morwell Phillips. Brett probably intended to go back to the summerhouse, where he could smoke and write, if his muse called. I hung back until they disappeared; and Jack waited, having caught my signal that I wanted to speak to him.

"How was the press conference?" I asked.

He grimaced. "The usual. The sheriff said a lot, without saying anything, other than that the investigation was well in hand. Same old same old."

"Figures," I said. "But I think I may have good news for you."

"What?" he said, instantly alert. His eyes probed my face.

"Come upstairs with me, and I'll show you." I turned toward the stairs. "I think I've found the missing manuscript."

He whistled. "Be right with you. Let me just tell my guys to come with us, if that's okay."

"Fine," I said, pausing at the foot of the stairs. "Bring them along."

Moments later I led him and two of his men up the stairs and down the hallway to my bedroom. Jack was burning with impatience to know where I had found the manuscript, but I wanted to show, rather than tell, him.

Once we were all inside my room, I pointed to the desk and told Jack to open the top drawer. Before doing so, he got a pair of cotton gloves from one of his men and slipped them on. He pulled open the drawer and stood staring down at the pile of blank paper. He shot me a swift glance, then picked up a few of the pages and fanned them in his fingers. "What is this? There's nothing here!" The disappointment on his face made me think of a child who finds his stocking empty at Christmas.

"I think this bundle of paper may be what Hamilton Packer

had in his briefcase. There's no reason for such a large stack of blank typing paper to be here in the desk. Miss McElroy told me there should be a bit of Idlewild stationery in each room, but that's it. There's no stationery in this desk. Probably because guests are seldom put in this room, according to what Morwell Phillips told me."

"But why would Packer be carrying around blank paper, telling people he had an actual manuscript?" Jack was still skeptical, and I couldn't blame him.

"I know it sounds ludicrous, but maybe Packer was intending to play some kind of blackmail game. He might actually have had—somewhere at home, or maybe in his office—an actual copy of a manuscript like the one he said he brought with him. But he might have anticipated someone would try to steal the manuscript, so he just made it look like he had one. After all, he wouldn't have had to show it to anyone, at least not in the preliminary stages."

"Someone wasn't willing to let the game progress that far, however." Jack was beginning to believe me, as his mind ran through the possibilities.

"The killer got a rude shock, then, when what was in Packer's briefcase turned out to be blank pages."

"Then why hide it?" Jack asked. "Why not just leave it where it was?"

I shrugged. "I'm not sure. Maybe the killer wanted to confuse the issue as much as possible. Delay things until he— or she—could get his hands on the real thing, if it exists."

He motioned to one of the deputies, who moved forward with a large plastic bag. Jack put the blank pages inside and handed the sealed bag back to the deputy.

"Can you get fingerprints off that paper?" I asked.

"Oh, yes," Jack said, grinning wolfishly. "That kind of paper is excellent for fingerprints. Unless someone handled it with gloves, their fingers will have left various kinds of deposits that should yield us some good, usable prints. We can at least tell whether Packer himself handled the paper, but the killer might have been smart enough to be wearing gloves."

"At least if you can find Packer's prints on the paper," I said, "you'll know that part of my theory is correct."

He peeled off the gloves and handed them to one of his men. "As weird as this whole situation is, I'm beginning to think you could be right about the so-called manuscript. It's just nutty enough to be true." He paused long enough to give his men orders to fingerprint the desk. "Just in case," he said.

Jack and his men had gone back downstairs, and I was in the bathroom, cleaning my hands, when someone knocked on the bedroom door about five minutes later.

Calling "just a minute," I finished drying my hands on one of the fluffy towels. I checked my reflection in the mirror, and everything seemed to be in its accustomed place. Satisfied, I went to open the door.

Lurleen Landry stood there, arms folded across her chest, the fingers of her right hand tapping out a rapid tattoo on her left arm.

"Miss Landry, what can I do for you?"

"I'd like to talk to you, if you don't mind," she said, her fingers slowing down their rhythm. "May I come in?"

"Please do," I said, stepping aside, then shutting the door behind her.

There was an old, but sturdy-looking armchair near the desk, and I motioned her toward it while I took the desk chair. "What can I do for you?"

"I know why you're really here," she said.

"Oh, and why is that?" I should have thought it was obvious to anyone by now, but she was the first to say it to my face.

She fluttered a hand impatiently. "Mary Tucker may be working on her memoirs. I wouldn't doubt it. But she doesn't need anyone to help her with them, except maybe somebody to take dictation and type, that kind of thing. Frankly, you don't impress me as someone who'd be very happy listening to an old woman ramble on and on about her life, taking notes and so on. Unless you were in desperate need of money, and I can tell by your clothes you're not here because you need a job."

I nodded. There was no point in lying to her.

"Mary Tucker wanted another pair of eyes and ears," she said. "Someone who was an outsider, to come in here and observe. Someone who would take a fresh look at everything. Someone not bound by old loyalties who could cut through all that to the truth."

"And you think I am that person?" I asked.

She laughed, a bitter sound, with nothing of amusement about it. "Just because we're of a certain age doesn't mean women like us are stupid. The rest of the world may be content to ignore us or to push us to one side, but we know better. We have experience and intelligence on our side. We can see and understand things the younger ones might not notice or grasp, even if they do take the time to see them."

"I can't argue with you there," I said, intrigued by the passion with which she spoke. I thought about the reviews I'd read of some of her more recent books. Critics sometimes lambasted her for what they saw as an outmoded gentility in her heroines, women they considered out of step with the world as it now is.

I had to admit that her later work lacked the fire of her first books. I thought she had become complacent with success and refused to tamper with her "formula," turning out variations of the same book over and over, year after year. They still sold in impressive numbers, no matter what the critics said about them.

Yet underneath all that, she still had a keen eye for detail, for understanding what made people tick. That's what made me continue to read them, though I regretted her inability to take risks and try something fresher. She had once had the talent, if no longer the will, to do so.

"You seem to know the investigating officer rather well," she said, off on another tack.

"Yes," I said, wondering where she was heading. "He was once a student of mine, at the local high school."

"Would you say that he's a perceptive man? An understanding man?"

"I'd say so, yes."

"Is he prejudiced, do you think?"

This was getting stranger and stranger. I knew Jack reasonably well, but I didn't think I could answer her question with any kind of authority. "In what way?"

"Is he a racist?" she said, scowling at my obtuseness. "Is he a misogynist? Is he homophobic? That should about cover it."

"As far as I am aware," I said, choosing my words with care, "he is none of those things. But you have to realize I don't see him on a daily, or even weekly or monthly basis. I know the boy he was, and something of the man he has become, but other than telling you, without reservation, that he is intelligent and fair-minded, I don't know how to answer you."

"You're like me," she said, once again changing tack. "You've never married."

"No," I said. "I've never married." I began to have an inkling where this was leading, remembering one of the nasty things Alice Bertram had said to her.

"Women like us can sometimes be put into a difficult position, because we're older and unattached to a man," she continued, her eyes gazing into mine with great earnestness. "Sometimes our actions can be misinterpreted, and people can do damaging things in response. And there's nothing you can do about it afterwards. Nothing at all."

I thought it was time to cut through all this shilly-shallying. "Did Sukey Lytton accuse you of making advances toward her? Did she tell people you were a lesbian?"

Lurleen's face crumpled, and slow tears began to slide down her cheeks. Her distress moved me, but I wasn't sure what to say or do to comfort her.

"Why don't you tell me what happened?" I found some tissues in my handbag and gave them to her. She accepted them with a tremulous smile and began dabbing at her eyes.

"I know you must think I'm being ridiculous," she said, her voice raw with emotion. "I was just so hurt by the way she turned on me. She was such a vicious little cat when she wanted to be."

"I'm beginning to think I wouldn't have cared for her very much, if I had known her," I said.

She smiled at that. "Probably not. She could be charming, when she wanted something. Otherwise, she didn't have much use for you."

"What happened?" I asked her again.

"We first met, about six years ago, at a writers conference. I was one of the invited speakers, and I did a workshop for beginning writers." She waved a hand in the air. "I don't know why I still do these things. Heaven knows I don't need the publicity, but I like to feel that I'm giving something back. They're a lot of work, but I remember those who helped me, and I try to return the favor."

"A very admirable attitude," I said with utmost sincerity.

"Thank you," she replied. "Anyway, I was at this conference, and Mary Tucker was there, as always. She came up to me after my workshop with this starved-looking creature in tow, and she introduced Sukey as her latest protégée. Mary Tucker had that gleam in her eyes, and I knew she wanted something from me." She sighed. "I was Mary Tucker's first pet project, more years ago than either of us cares to remember, and I've always felt an enormous debt of gratitude to her. She introduced me to my first, and only, agent; and right after that, I sold my first novel, *Down on the River Road*. I can never forget what Mary Tucker did for me then, nor in all the years since."

"I can understand your sense of obligation," I said. "What did she want you to do in this instance?"

"She thought Sukey needed a mentor, one who was more directly involved in the writing process. Mary Tucker has the kind of connections to get someone attention from editors and agents, but she knows her limitations." Lurleen was calmer now, more authoritative. "Mary Tucker thought Sukey needed the guidance and advice of a successful writer, and she assumed, wrongly as it happened, I could offer all that to Sukey."

"A reasonable assumption, I would have thought."

She nodded. "On the face of things, yes. But Mary Tucker didn't know Sukey all that well then, even though she had been acquainted with her for a year or two, and she had no idea what the girl was capable of. None of us did. At first she was so pathetically eager to be part of what she called the 'in crowd,' she was practically licking Mary Tucker's shoes." She laughed in derision. "That girl's nose was so brown! Well, I'm sure you know the type."

"Quite well."

"Anyway, I talked with her at the conference, and I agreed to read some of her poetry and one of her stories. I knew, if Mary Tucker had taken her up, she must have talent, but I had no idea how extensive, or how limited, it might be. Mary Tucker has had the occasional lapse in judgment over the years."

I nodded, encouraging her to continue.

"After we met at the conference, Sukey sent me some things. I read them, offered suggestions and criticisms, which she seemed to take well. I saw potential in her writing, and I did my best to encourage her. We continued to correspond, about twice a month, I guess. When she wrote to me, about nine months after we first met at the conference, and said she was worried about being able to make ends meet, I foolishly offered to let her come and stay with me for a couple of months. It was spring, and I had moved to my beach house down near Mobile, where I spend the spring and summer every year. It's a big house, with plenty of room, and I thought she could use the time to write and not worry about her finances. I still remember what it was like, in those early days."

"Again, very admirable of you to take an interest in her," I said, wondering when we were going to get to the point.

"Yes, well," she said, her mouth turning down in a grimace of distaste, "the worm soon turned. Two months passed. Then three, then four, and she showed no signs of budging. That house began to get smaller and smaller by the day. I was getting ready to close it up and move back to my house in Atlanta, and I didn't want to take her with me."

She paused for a steadying breath. "I had no idea what an encroaching little creature she could be! She hadn't been there a month before she was telling my staff what to do—the housekeeper, who's been with me for nearly thirty years, and her husband—and they were threatening to quit." Still appalled by the memories, she shook her head. "I couldn't believe the way she was behaving. When I finally worked up enough nerve to confront her about it, to tell her she was going to have to leave, she turned on me. I flat-out lied and told her I had some guests coming, and I was going to need her room."

She paused; her momentary calm had fled, to be replaced by considerable agitation. "That's when she accused me of making improper advances and threatened to tell everyone about it. She said she'd see to it that every newspaper and magazine in the country knew about it, and I'd become the laughingstock of the publishing world. I can't bring myself to repeat all the nastiness that spewed out of her mouth." Her voice trailed off.

"What did you do?" I figured there were probably aspects of the story she had edited out, to present herself in the most favorable light, but I had no way of knowing for certain.

"At first I was so flabbergasted I didn't know what to do or what to say." Her hand trembled as she touched her fingers to her lips in a gesture of distress. She drew a deep breath, and her hand fluttered back down to her lap. "Then I got mad. I used language that probably had my mother rolling in her grave, but I told her to get the hell out of my house. I also told her I was going to call Mary Tucker and a couple of the other people I knew who had befriended her, like Russell and Alice, and tell them how she'd repaid my kindnesses to her. I'd see to it, I said, that she never got another handout from anyone who could help her career."

"Did that rattle her?"

"You bet your grits it did!" Her smile indicated her feelings of vindictive triumph. "She couldn't start backpedaling fast enough, but by then it was too late. She didn't expect me to fight back, and when I did, she had sense enough to back down. But it was too late," she repeated. "I wanted her out of my house, and she was gone within the hour."

"And she never made good on her threats?" If Sukey Lytton was as vicious as Lurleen Landry claimed, she must have somehow tried to get back at her erstwhile mentor.

"I heard the odd bit of gossip, relayed back to me by very well-meaning friends." She grimaced, and I understood just what kind of "friends" she was talking about, the kind who can't wait to see your reaction to something nasty or ugly. Not that they believe it themselves, of course.

"But essentially nothing really came of it," I said.

"No," Lurleen said, almost with reluctance. "She really wasn't in a position to do much. I went ahead and called Mary Tucker anyway, so she'd know what was going on. She promised to talk to Sukey, and she must have, because the next time I saw the girl, she acted like nothing had ever happened. She even had the nerve to thank me for my hospitality and tell me, in public, how sorry she was she'd had to leave when she did, although I had practically begged her to stay!"

"I can certainly understand your feelings of outrage," I said. I was also very curious to know what Sukey's side of the story had been, although her version might have been unreliable. She sounded completely self-serving. "But that was all over and done with, wasn't it? Surely you didn't have anything more to worry about?" I wasn't as naive as I sounded, but I wanted to hear her explanation.

"I thought so, myself, but when I heard about that damn manuscript of hers yesterday, I just about had a heart attack! I'm terrified of what she might have written. And if it appears in print, she could have the last laugh after all." Lurleen looked as if she might start crying again.

"If the manuscript doesn't turn up, I don't think you'll have much to worry about," I said.

"That's a big *if*," she said. "How could it just vanish? Unless someone shredded it or burned it." Her eyes lit up with hope at the thought. "That would be wonderful."

"It could still turn up," I told her, though I didn't intend to be deliberately cruel. The light in her eyes died, and she slumped back in the chair.

"Yes," she said, "and that's why it's important that your Mr. Preston doesn't assume the worst of me, if he reads it."

I didn't correct her by asserting that he wasn't *my* Mr.

Preston, but I did try to point out the gaps in her thinking. "You're forgetting something. You probably aren't the only one who might have been maligned by that manuscript."

"That's true," she said slowly. "The others have as much, if not more, to lose if it should be found and published."

"Like what?" I asked, though I doubted she would answer.

"I really couldn't say," she replied, standing up. "I won't carry tales." She had withdrawn from me, just that quickly, and I knew it wouldn't do any good to press. She might already have begun to regret telling me what she had, though she would have to talk to Jack if the manuscript ever reappeared. If it existed in the first place!

I admired her for her refusal to gossip, even though it was frustrating. I got to my feet and stared down into her face. "I don't know whether you want my advice on this, but if I were you, I'd tell all this to Jack Preston as soon as you have the chance to talk to him. Like I said before, he's intelligent and fair-minded, and he will treat what you have to say appropriately. I have every faith in that."

"Thank you," she said. "I'll think about it." She moved past me and headed for the door.

"Before you go," I said, recalling what I had overheard between her and Miss McElroy just before I met her for the first time, "I have a question for you. About something else."

She paused, her hand on the doorknob. "What is it?"

There was no point in trying to appear disingenuous. "The day I arrived, I overheard the last part of your conversation with Miss McElroy."

Her face turned to stone. "What about it?"

"It sounded to me like you were threatening Miss McElroy."

She frowned at me. "Just a difference of opinion, that was all. About something that has nothing to do with what's going on here."

"Are you entirely certain of that?"

"Yes, I am! If you must know, I had recommended someone for one of the scholarships that Mary Tucker sponsors at Ole Miss. She has someone else in mind. Someone I don't think is as qualified or deserving, frankly. But she has the final say. Not me."

"It still sounded like you were threatening her."

"You can interpret it any way you like." With that, she opened the door and stalked out. Frankly, I was surprised she didn't slam it behind her.

I guess if I wanted to know any more about it, I'd have to ask Miss McElroy herself. I wasn't sure it had anything to do with the murders, but I'd have to follow it up at some point.

Dismissing that for the moment, I speculated instead on Lurleen Landry's motives for seeking me out and confiding in me. She had made a point of referring to our mutual unmarried state. Had she been expecting me to say, "Honey, it's okay, I'm a lesbian, too, and I understand completely?" She is a few years older than I am, and I could understand her reluctance to be open about her sexuality, if she were indeed a lesbian. Women of our generation and upbringing often find it difficult to be open about such matters. I was unmarried, largely by choice, though I enjoyed the company of men and could even boast, discreetly, of a couple of mutually satisfactory love affairs over the years. I pitied her inability to say and be who she was openly, and I despised the way the world around us would react if she did, at this time in her life.

I told myself that I might be reading way too much into her words and her actions, but she reminded me of others I had known in the past, deeply closeted and unable to come to terms with their sexuality. I only hoped she would feel comfortable in confiding in Jack, if the need arose.

I wasn't eager to play the role of confessor again, yet I realized that, before this investigation had run its course, I would know more than I really wanted to about the lives of the people involved. Though I find people in general enormously interesting, I'm not prurient or prying by nature, though it might appear so.

I had a job to do, and my employer expected me to do some poking and prying. Best get on with it, I told myself. Before I went any further, I needed to finish reading through the pile of documents that Farrah Lockett had compiled for me.

Somewhere in all those pages, among the many details of the lives of Miss McElroy's current guests and the two murder victims, there might lie the one bit of information which could help unlock the whole puzzle.

I went to the desk and opened the drawer where I had placed the folder of papers. Retrieving them, I made myself comfortable in the armchair and began to read. Five minutes into reading, I realized I needed something on which to make notes, so I found my handbag and pulled out a small notebook and a pen. Thus armed, I bent once again to my task.

Nearly two hours later, I had a headache and about three pages of scribbled notes and questions. I put the last page aside and leaned back in the armchair. My neck and shoulder muscles were tensed up, and I made an effort to relax them. I rolled my head around several times, each direction, then I flexed my shoulders up and down a few times, until the muscles began to loosen a bit.

Farrah had done an amazing job of collecting information for me in a very short period of time. She had even found a copy of an article from the local paper, reporting on the wedding of Miss Mary Tucker McElroy, forty-eight years ago, to Mr. Morwell Martin Phillips. There was a grainy picture of the bride and groom, both looking imposing but stiff in their wedding regalia. Even in the badly reproduced copy I held in my hands, Miss McElroy at thirty had that same air of regal command I had come to know in the last few days.

I studied the likeness of Morwell Phillips with great interest. For one thing, I hadn't realized that he was nearly ten years younger than his wife. He had just turned twenty-one when they married. From his appearance now, I had assumed he was a few years older than Miss McElroy, but obviously the years had not worn well on him. In the photograph he was robust, even verging on the pudgy, with a fleshily handsome face. It was hard to associate the gaunt visage and frail frame I knew with this strapping young buck who looked ready to burst out of his formalwear.

According to the newspaper article, the bride and groom were going to honeymoon in Europe for two months, before they returned home to Idlewild. The groom would then take up his place as a student at Ole Miss law school while the bride continued her charitable works and her involvement in various literary activities around the South. Little was said about the bridegroom's antecedents, though there was a brief mention of his parents. Since no occupation was mentioned, I figured that Phillips Senior had the kind of job that was beneath notice, at least in the society pages.

Other articles in the stack chronicled Miss McElroy's rise to fame as a hostess and patroness of the literary arts, while little was said of her husband's legal career. He was mentioned here and there as an adjunct to his wife, but he seemed never to have had much employment as a lawyer, other than looking after his wife's estate.

Then, about fifteen years ago, he had begun teaching at the law school at his alma mater. For eight years he was the McElroy Professor of Law at Ole Miss, then he retired. A brief career, it seemed. For the most part, he apparently went through life in his wife's shadow.

Interesting, I supposed, as a bit of insight into the life of my employer, but not much use that I could see in the present situation.

I had found more potentially useful information in the clutch of articles Farrah had gathered on Russell and Alice Bertram. One of the bits of information I had gleaned was that Russell had endowed a scholarship at Ole Miss for creative writing students. One of the recipients of this scholarship had been Sukey Lytton. I had found the connection by cross-checking the information which Farrah had compiled on Sukey: the scholarship was mentioned in one of the articles on her from a southern literary magazine.

The connection was interesting, because apparently Russell Bertram was actively involved in the scholarship process. According to the information Farrah had found, he was part of the committee which each year read the applicants' work and then interviewed the short list of candidates. Thus he and Sukey Lytton had met while she was still a student at Ole Miss. He would have met her again as a protégée of Miss

McElroy's a few years later, but the fact that he had known her earlier could be significant. Was he the one who had introduced her to Miss McElroy? I'd have to remember to ask her at some point.

I had already heard from Brett Doran and Lurleen Landry the stories of their own connections to, and problems with, Sukey Lytton. I found nothing more in the stack of papers now resting in my lap to add to that.

The other information that I had learned was that each of them also had a connection to Hamilton Packer. He had never been Lurleen's agent; but at one time, he had served in that capacity for both Brett Doran and Russell Bertram. Lurleen had obviously known him through her connection to Miss McElroy, and perhaps in the general way that a best-selling author might know a high-profile, successful agent. There was no other connection between the two of them that I could discern at the moment.

The key to it all seemed to me to be the murder of Sukey Lytton. If I could determine which of them had the most compelling motive to kill her, then the rest should fall into place. I was assuming, of course, that the murder of Hamilton Packer was a corollary to the first murder. If not for the alleged manuscript of Sukey Lytton's, then Hamilton Packer might still be alive and breathing and polluting the atmosphere with his fetid-smelling self.

Hoisting myself up out of the chair, I placed the papers back in the desk drawer. I stretched some more, relieving the tension in my back and neck further while I thought about what to do next. My next move, I figured, would be to try to talk to Russell Bertram alone. Thus far I hadn't seen him without his wife somewhere nearby, but at some point, the two had to spend time apart.

I glanced at my watch. Nearly four o'clock. I bent over the desk and looked out the window, toward the summerhouse. I couldn't tell whether it was occupied at the moment. The encroaching afternoon shadows from the trees around it had obscured the porch and the front windows from view.

Nothing ventured, nothing gained. I'd go down to the summerhouse and see if Brett might still be there. If so, I'd get him to find Russell Bertram for me and bring him to the summerhouse so I could talk to him there, away from the baleful influence of his wife.

I slipped down the back stairs without encountering anyone and stepped out onto the back verandah. The moist heat enveloped me, and I could hear the rumble of thunder in the distance. Watching the sky for a moment, I could see some dark clouds moving in from the south-southwest. We might have more rainfall before too much longer. This morning's downpour hadn't lasted very long. The atmosphere was oppressive enough to foretell a good thunderstorm.

I reached the welcoming shade of the summerhouse porch and rapped on the door. No one answered, so I twisted the doorknob, pushed open the door, and walked in.

A moment later, I stumbled back out, trying not to throw up my lunch.

Chapter Thirteen

I STOOD IN THE SUN and gulped in deep breaths of humid, hot air, trying to steady my stomach. What I had seen inside the summerhouse was seared into my visual memory banks. I couldn't erase it, but at least here in the sunlight it was receding a bit. I knew I should probably go back inside and check for signs of life, on the faint chance that life wasn't completely extinguished. But I realized that it was a faint hope. No one could sustain that kind of damage and still be alive.

As I stumbled my way back to the house, still shaken by what I had seen, clouds diluted the sunlight. Shadows gathered about me, and I felt cold. The viciousness of this death was even more horrifying than that of Hamilton Packer's, and I feared the killer was losing whatever tenuous grip on sanity that he or she had.

Once inside the house, I could feel my equilibrium beginning to return, and my steps were far less shaky as I made my way to the library. Surely, by now, Jack Preston or one of his men would be available.

I opened the library door without knocking, and Jack looked up at me from the desk, annoyance in his expression. One glance at my face, however, and any rebuke faded away, unspoken.

"Ernie! What's wrong?" Faster than I could have believed possible, he was around the desk and at my side.

I took a deep breath. "In the summerhouse. Katie. She's dead. Someone's beaten her face in."

Saying the words brought that terrible image back, and I could see the poor, misguided girl all over again. Her body lay sprawled drunkenly across the sofa where I had sat talking to Brett earlier in the day. Her uniform had been hiked up over her waist, and her panties—red silk, no less—hung off one leg. Her head had been turned into a pulpy mass. The only way I recognized her was her hair, the long blonde tresses now streaked with blood and brain matter.

Jack swore under his breath. "Here, sit down." He guided me to a chair, and I sank gratefully into it. My knees wouldn't have held me up much longer. He crouched in front of me. "Did you see anyone else in there?"

I shook my head. "I should have gone in to check on her, but I couldn't. It was too horrible, and I don't think she could still be alive."

"Right." Jack stood up. "I hate to leave you like this, but I'd better get out there." He motioned for one of his men, whom in my distress I hadn't noticed lurking in the background, to accompany him.

"I'll be okay. Just go," I said. My voice sounded almost normal, which surprised me.

Jack had pulled a cell phone from his pocket as he strode out the door. He would be summoning the crime-scene investigative team back to Idlewild. I prayed they would find something to link the killer to the crime scene, something that would help resolve this horrible situation as quickly as possible.

As I was trying to summon the strength to get myself out of the chair, Mrs. Greer came into the room. "Miss Carpenter. What's going on? Mr. Preston popped his head in the kitchen and asked me to come check on you in here, then he disappeared like a tornado out the back door. Is something wrong out there in the summerhouse?" She held out a hand to me, and I clasped it in mine, taking comfort from the warmth and sturdiness of her work-roughened fingers.

"I'm afraid," I said, "that I have some really bad news, Mrs. Greer. I went out to the summerhouse just now, and I found Katie there." I breathed deeply. "She's dead." I couldn't tell her how, I just couldn't describe that scene again for anyone.

Mrs. Greer went completely still, and I could feel the sudden tension in her hand. She closed her eyes and said a brief prayer. "That poor girl," she said when she had finished and opened her eyes. "Always trying to reach for something she couldn't get, and now someone's done gone and stopped her forever." Her drawl was even more pronounced.

The compassion in her voice made me want to cry. She was obviously shaken by the news, but as usual, her first thoughts were for other people. She got me to my feet and held my hand as she led me to the kitchen, where she sat me down at the table. Within minutes she had presented me with a hot, sweet cup of coffee, and I sipped at it gratefully. In the bright and warmly cheerful kitchen, the horror of what I had seen finally began to recede a little.

Mrs. Greer joined me at the table, her face still a bit ashen from the shock, and drank from her own mug of coffee. "Lawsy me, there's wickedness in this ol' world," she said, shaking her head dolefully. "I thought that child was doing better, now, but I guess she just couldn't get above her raising."

"How do you mean?" I asked, wondering what she meant by that remark. Surely she wasn't blaming Katie for her own death, saying she deserved it.

"That pore girl didn't deserve getting something like this done to her, no how, no way," Mrs. Greer said shrewdly, as if she'd read my mind. "But if there was a way of inviting trouble to the table, that child and her family knew how to do it. Her granddaddy made his living with 'shine, and her daddy and big brothers been running dope 'tween here and Memphis for years. They done spent more time over at Parchman than any family in this county."

"Katie took after her family, then? You mean she'd been in jail?"

She sighed deeply. "No, she hadn't been in jail. She had some troubles when she was younger, 'bout thirteen or so. But her mama did her best to get that girl out of trouble and keep her there. She was doing some better, I thought, by working here, keeping a steady job, the last year. But sometimes you just can't get away from your family and their bad ways."

"What do you think Katie did? Do you think she did something that led her to . . . this?" I couldn't bring myself to say it.

"She was acting awful sly and secret the last two days. She musta seen something, and I reckon she thought she could make something out of it." Mrs. Greer shook her head again. "Ever' one of that family always thought they was smarter than they was, else they wouldn't've kept getting caught so much. I was praying to the Good Lord that Katie might have more on the ball than the rest of 'em, but I guess I was wrong. I surely was wrong."

"I'm sure you did what you could to help her," I said sympathetically.

"Me and Miss Mary Tucker both. I known that girl's mother since she was a baby, and she was desperate to find Katie a good job. So I talked to Miss Mary Tucker, and she was willing to give Katie a chance. She didn't always want to work too hard, and I'd have to push her along, but she was doing pretty good. Until now." A few tears trickled down her face, and she used her apron to wipe them away.

"Speaking of working," I said, as something occurred to me, "what was Katie supposed to be doing this afternoon? Hadn't anyone noticed that she wasn't working?"

Mrs. Greer shook her head. "Miss Mary Tucker gave each of the girls one afternoon off each week, so's they could go to town and do stuff. This was Katie's afternoon, and I would've reckoned that's where she was."

"When would she have left for town? Normally, I mean?"

"Oh, just as soon's she could get away after lunch. 'Bout one-thirty, most likely."

"She would have changed clothes before she went into town, wouldn't she?"

"Oh, my, yes," Mrs. Greer laughed, sadly. "She wouldn't've wanted any of her friends to see her in no maid's uniform. She always wore her blue jeans with those rips in the knees and some kinda skimpy little ol' top."

My hands clutched my mug of coffee, seeking to absorb some of the ebbing warmth. "She never changed clothes to go into town," I said, my voice sounding strained. "She was still wearing her uniform."

We both sat there, quiet, for a few minutes. I had no doubt that Mrs. Greer was again saying prayers for Katie's soul, which was probably what I should have been doing as well. Instead, though, I was buzzing from one thought to another, trying to sort out the implications of what I had seen and where it had taken place.

Had Katie been sexually assaulted? The way the body was left, you could sure get the notion she had been. Her uniform pulled up like that, over her thighs, her panties dangling off one leg, down around her ankle. My stomach ached at the thought of it.

Maybe she had been willing to have intercourse with her killer, and that was how she had been taken unawares. That made me even sicker to contemplate. Which of the men in this house could have done that to the girl? Calmly had sex with her, then beaten her face in?

Then again, maybe it was all an illusion, trying to misdirect us. The problem with that, of course, was that the autopsy would soon reveal whether Katie had had sex with someone, willingly or not. Maybe the preliminary crime-scene investigation would yield enough information to answer those questions. I wasn't sure, and I didn't want to dwell on those details.

Finally I forced myself to ask the question that had been lurking in the back of my mind ever since I had discovered Katie's body. "Mrs. Greer," I said, trying to make my voice as casual as possible, "have you seen Brett this afternoon?"

"He stuck his head in here right after lunch," she said, not noticing how tense I was, waiting for her response. "He was going into town, he said. He'd run out of them cigars he smokes, and he was going to pick up some in town."

I drew a shaky breath of relief. At first, I had feared that Brett, too, might be dead in the summerhouse, though I hadn't had the stomach to go in and see for myself. Then I had been afraid he might have killed Katie and fled the scene. The latter case might still hold true, I reasoned, but I was praying it wouldn't and that Brett would soon appear, innocently unaware of what had happened to Katie.

"Well, he won't have anywhere to smoke them now," I said, with a faint attempt at humor, black though it was.

"No, I reckon not," Mrs. Greer said, her composure cracking for a moment. I held out my hand, and she grasped it, taking comfort from me this time.

From where we sat, we could now hear sounds of activity from outside. More personnel from the sheriff's department must have arrived.

I got up and looked out a window, toward the summerhouse. As I watched men going inside, a jaunty black BMW convertible drove around the side of the house and came to an abrupt halt. Brett Doran got out of the car and ran up to the summerhouse. I ran for the back door, to try to head him off before he could walk in on that horrifying scene.

By the time I had the door open and was calling his name urgently, one of Jack's men had come out onto the porch of the summerhouse and was talking to him. Brett heard me calling and turned toward me. He turned back and nodded at the officer, then loped across the grass, his long stride covering the ground between us in a matter of seconds.

"What the hell's going on in there?" he demanded. In one hand he clutched a large plastic bag, emblazoned with the logo of Tullahoma's only cigar and pipe shop.

Impulsively, I threw my arms around him and gave him a huge hug. "You don't know how glad I am to see you," I told him as I released him.

"I'm glad to see you, too," he said, "but would you please tell me what's going on back there?" His head jerked back in the direction of the summerhouse.

"Come inside with me," I said, taking his hand. For a moment, he thought about resisting, but the look on my face warned him against it. I got him inside and sat him down at the table, where Mrs. Greer had more coffee waiting for us.

"There's been another murder," I said.

Brett paled, and he reached with a shaky hand for the mug of coffee. "Who?" His voice squeaked.

"Katie," I said, my voice terse. "I found her, about half an hour ago. Someone had beaten her to death."

He shuddered. "What the hell is going on here?" He had to set down the mug, his hands were shaking so badly.

Footsteps sounded behind us as someone came into the kitchen. "Mr. Doran," Jack Preston said. "I'd like to speak with you, if you don't mind. Could you join me in the library?"

Brett stared at me, his eyes wide with fear.

I wanted to say, *Brett, what have you done?* Surely the boy wouldn't have looked so terrified if he hadn't done something, just because Jack Preston wanted to talk to him. But if Brett had gone into Tullahoma to buy cigars, and had been in town for any length of time, he ought to have an alibi for Katie's death. Or so I told myself as I watched him follow Jack, with great reluctance, out of the kitchen.

"That boy is some scared," Mrs. Greer said.

"You saw it, too," I replied. "Why on earth do you think he is? Surely he didn't do this."

She shook her head. "That boy's no killer. He's got a good heart, you can tell. But he be a bit misguided sometimes. He just a country boy with some education who made good, and he don't always know how to handle himself."

"I like him a lot," I said, and Mrs. Greer smiled, gently. "I think you're right, he is a good boy, but right now I'm worried about him."

She sighed, staring down at the mug in her hands. "He didn't kill that poor girl, but I 'spect I know what's worrying him." She sighed again, more heavily this time. "If it was someone else, Miss Carpenter, I wouldn't be saying this, but I know you won't be carrying tales where they ain't no business going."

I nodded, encouraging her to continue.

"I 'spect it was drugs," Mrs. Greer said. "That boy was living the high life for a while, and a time or two when he came here, he was flying so high, he didn't need no jet plane. Miss Mary Tucker was terrified for him, 'cause she lost a young cousin to drugs, so she set him right down here, at this table, and gave him a talking to like you wouldn't believe. She put the fear of the Good Lord into that boy, and when she was done with him, I would've sworn he'd never touch drugs again in his life."

"When was this?"

"Back just before Christmas. He came here a few days ahead of the other guests, and Katie was working here then. 'Course, he didn't go off 'em right then; he couldn't, 'cause he needed some help to do it, and I 'spect Katie might've helped supply him while he was here." She shook her head. "I never could catch her for sure, but I found her a-talking to him a few times when she should've been working. They both looked awful guilty. If I hadn't've known better, I'd've sworn they was sleeping together. But Mr. Brett being like he is, I knew that wasn't it. So it had to be them drugs."

"So you know that Brett is gay?" I asked, a bit stunned by the casual way in which she referred to it.

Mrs. Greer treated me to a look that made me feel about three inches tall. "Miss Carpenter, I been too long in this world not to know when somebody's different, and it makes no nevermind to me who that boy wants to be with. I just hope he finds someone who'll be good to him, because he's a good boy himself, and he deserves that much. You know his folks won't talk to him a'cause of that?" She shook her head at the folly of such behavior.

"That's very sad," I said. "I had no idea."

"That boy's got a lotta hurt inside of him, and he don't quite know what to do with it," she said. "I reckon that's why he was taking those damn drugs for a while."

I was shocked, momentarily, at Mrs. Greer's use of even a mild profanity, but the depth of her emotion was such that it slipped out without her even realizing what she'd said.

"Do you think he's off them now?" I asked.

"Yeah, he is. I can generally tell. I seen too much of it, I tell you, and you can see the signs, if you know what you're looking for. He went off from here—after all that mess at Christmastime—and checked himself into one of them fancy clinics and got himself clean. He's been more at peace with himself since then, I reckon, and he hasn't needed them anymore."

"That's good news," I said, vastly relieved. I hadn't noticed any signs of drug use in Brett; and like Mrs. Greer, I had way too much experience, thanks to years of teaching, not to recognize some of them. "But you think he's afraid that Jack will find out about the drugs?"

She nodded. "Most likely. Just 'cause he might've bought drugs from the girl last year don't mean he killed her now, though."

"You're right," I said in a firm tone, to convince myself as much as her, "and I'm sure Jack will see that."

A lingering doubt remained, nevertheless. What if Brett had killed Hamilton Packer, and Katie knew something about it? Then if she'd tried to blackmail him, he might have panicked and killed her. The fact that Katie was killed in the summerhouse was important. Either Brett had done it, or the killer was attempting to make it look like Brett had done it.

I glanced at Mrs. Greer, and she nodded. It was almost eerie, the way the woman was following my thought processes. "It's a good thing that boy has you on his side," she said, smiling slightly.

"I was just about to say the same thing to you," I said, grinning back at her. "I don't think he killed anybody, but it doesn't look very good for him at the moment."

"Then somebody's gotta figure out who did do it, Miss Carpenter." Mrs. Greer made a simple statement of fact. "Mr. Jack will do it, I've got that much faith in him. But it don't mean someone can't help him along to finding the truth."

"My thoughts exactly," I said. "I know I can count on you, Mrs. Greer." I stuck my hand out impulsively, and she took it. "And please call me Ernie. All my friends do."

A broad grin lit her face. "And I'm Selma." She squeezed my hand, then released it. She stood. "I'd better get Betsy down here and tell her what's going on. She's gonna be terrified, and we'll be lucky if she don't quit, right straight."

"Where has she been?" I had forgotten all about Betsy, and now I was worried that some harm might have befallen her, too.

Selma gestured with her head. "She's supposed to be upstairs, straightening up the bedrooms and making the beds. She's probably listening to that Walkman of hers, even though I told her not to, else she would've noticed some of this commotion going on." She carried her mug to the sink and rinsed it out, leaving it there. "You gonna be okay now?"

Standing, I acknowledged that I would. "If someone hasn't done so already, I suppose I ought to go and let Miss McElroy know what's going on."

"And I'm going upstairs to find Betsy," she said.

"Do you think Miss McElroy will be in her sitting room?"

Selma consulted the kitchen clock; it was a bit after four. "She ought to be by now," she said. "And let her know that dinner's gonna be a mite late tonight." She left the kitchen, and moments later I could hear her climbing the back stairs.

Taking a deep breath, I went out the door into the hall and into the front of the house. Before I got to the sitting room, however, the door to the library opened, and Jack walked out. Seeing me, he called out my name, and I halted.

"Can I talk to you now?" he asked.

"Sure," I said. "But has anyone informed Miss McElroy about what's happened?" I was feeling a bit guilty I hadn't done so already.

He nodded. "She's with her husband and the Bertrams in the sitting room. I've asked them to wait there until I can talk to them. Right now, though, I'd like to talk to you."

"Where's Brett?" I asked, fearing the answer.

"He's gone up to his room with one of my men," Jack said. He then gestured toward the library. "Let's talk."

"Certainly," I said, preceding him into the room. I sat down in the same chair I had occupied earlier in the day, and Jack went around behind the desk and plopped down.

Deep lines had appeared in his forehead, and I could see that the strain of this second murder was eating away at him. His posture bespoke his tiredness; and as I watched, waiting for him to say something, he rubbed a hand across his face.

Taking a chance, I said, "There was nothing you could have done to prevent this."

Startled, he dropped the pen he had started to pick up. "I didn't realize mind reading was one of your talents." His grin was rueful, full of regret.

I shook my head. "It's the same thing I've been telling myself, that's all. I don't think either one of us could have forestalled it."

Jack's mouth compressed into a grim line. "Maybe. But if I had gotten to the girl sooner and made her talk to me, then I might have prevented this." He threw his hands up in the air. "If she even knew anything. But now we'll never know for sure."

"She probably knew something, or else she pretended she did," I said. "I can't imagine why else someone would have done this to her."

"You're right," Jack said, "and I should have made more of an effort to talk to her and get her to tell me what she knew, or what she thought she knew. Poor girl." He suddenly struck the top of the desk with the flat of his hand, and the sound made me jump. "Damn it! This shouldn't have happened!"

I could see the grief and frustration in his face. I wanted to offer him some kind of comfort, but for the moment, I couldn't think of anything else to say, anything that would convince him. He'd have to work through it on his own. Just like I would, I thought. I didn't know if I could ever forget the sight of that poor girl, beaten so savagely. She would haunt me for years to come.

Time to move on. Dwelling on it at this moment wasn't helping her or me. "What did you need to ask me?" I said.

Jack collected himself, stopped staring broodingly off into space. "Right. Tell me again how you came to find her, and what you saw."

I sat back in the chair and drew a deep breath, willing my voice not to shake. Slowly, and as clinically as possible, I related what I had seen. "I'm afraid I didn't have time to notice very much. I was so horrified by . . . her that I couldn't take in anything else."

Jack nodded. "It was grim, one of the worst I've ever seen."

"One thing which occurs to me," I said, wondering whether he would, or could, answer me. "How could someone do that to her and not"—I searched for a way to describe it that wouldn't sicken me—"show the signs of it?"

He stared at something I couldn't see, as if weighing what to say. "We found a sheet that the killer must have draped around himself—or herself."

I took a moment to consider that, then risked asking another question. "But why would Katie have just waited, passively, to be attacked, while someone wound a sheet around himself? Or herself?"

"We don't know for sure," Jack said, after another long pause. "But we suspect she was already unconscious before she was beaten so severely."

The horror of it all came back to me with such immediacy that I felt I was once again standing on the threshold of that room. I could see the poor girl all over again, could smell the stench of the blood, feel the sweltering heat around me. I fought for control, willing myself not to vomit.

Jack, lost in his own torments, didn't appear to notice that it took me a couple of minutes to regain some semblance of composure. My voice was shaky when I could speak again.

"What about the murder weapon?" I asked. "Did you find it."

"Oh, yes. There was no mistaking it." He rubbed a hand across his face again.

"Can you tell me what it was?"

He looked at me, his eyes cold and distant. "You'll know soon enough. It was Brett Doran's laptop computer."

I sagged in my chair. I thought about seeing Brett that morning, fiddling with his laptop. I couldn't, wouldn't, believe that he had done this horrible thing. Illogical as it sounded, even to me, the weapon used convinced me of Brett's innocence. Someone had deliberately used the computer in order to frame him.

When I could speak again, I asked, "Does Brett know yet?"

He shook his head. "No, and I shouldn't have told you, but I know you won't tell him." He fixed me with a steely glare. "Will you?"

"No, you have my word on that."

"Thank you," he said. "If my boss ever finds out about any of this"—he waved a hand back and forth between us—"I'd be in deep doo-doo for sure."

"He won't hear it from me," I said fervently. "I know this is highly irregular, and I appreciate your trust. I won't violate it."

"I know," he said.

"I think someone is trying to implicate Brett," I said. "I just don't believe he would have done this thing. And if he had, which I don't think he did, he certainly wouldn't have used his computer as a weapon!"

"Luckily for him, he may have a good alibi," Jack said. "We won't know for sure until after the autopsy, of course, but at a guess, she'd been dead for about an hour when you found her. According to Doran, he left about thirty minutes after lunch. He went into town to buy cigars, went straight there, and he says he hung around the shop, smoking and talking to the owner, for over an hour. If the owner corroborates that, then he's probably in the clear."

"Lucky for Brett, but not so lucky for the killer."

"If someone is trying to implicate Doran, of course," Jack said.

"Or at least really trying to muddy the waters." I frowned. "I don't suppose there's any chance someone saw Katie going out to the summerhouse?"

He shook his head. "I haven't had much chance to ask questions yet, but from what I can tell so far, everyone was either busy working or taking naps. No one saw anything. For sure, no one has told me that they saw anyone, Katie included, going into that summerhouse."

"Frustrating," I said. "So what do you do?"

"Keep digging," he said, "and hope that we turn up something on the scene that gives us a link to someone in the house."

"How long is all that going to take?"

Jack shrugged. "We have to send most of it to the state crime lab in Jackson, and normally it could take several weeks. But I'm sure the sheriff will ask for a rush to be put on it, and we might get something back in a week, if we're lucky. And if there's anything to find."

"Let's pray that there is."

"Yeah, I want this over with, and fast." His face was as grim and determined as I had ever seen it.

I shivered, as if the proverbial goose had just walked over my grave. "You think there's a chance the killer might strike again?"

"I sure as hell hope not," Jack said, "but it looks to me like someone's unraveling. The other two murders were much cleaner, more clinical. This one, well, it was nasty, full of rage. I don't think it's a good sign."

"Surely the same person is responsible?" The thought that we might be dealing with more than one killer was mighty unsettling.

"Most likely," Jack said. "The likelihood of having two different killers at work here is about nil, I'd say." He threw up his hands. "I could be wrong, but I don't think I am. This whole mess doesn't make a whole lot of sense to me. A nice, clean domestic, where you know immediately what's going on—that's what I'm used to. We don't get many cases like this, at least not in our county."

"Thank goodness for that," I said. "But any murder is one too many."

"Yeah." The strain in his face suddenly made him look years older. *Poor boy,* I thought, *he really is taking this hard.*

"Is there anything else you need from me right now?" I asked.

"No, thanks," he said, standing up. "I need to get on with things, check in on my men, see what they've found out. Plus I need to keep asking questions."

"And I'd better go check in with Miss McElroy. She's probably been wondering where I am." I got out of the chair and followed Jack to the door. He motioned for me to precede him, ever courtly.

He headed for the kitchen, to talk to Selma and Betsy, I figured, or else to go back out to the summerhouse. I shuddered. I stood and watched his retreating back for a moment, then turned toward Miss McElroy's sitting room.

As I approached, I could see that the door stood the tiniest bit ajar. I lightened my footsteps, almost by instinct, wondering what—or whom—I might observe through the crack in the door.

Mindful of Miss McElroy's warning yesterday, I cautiously stuck my eye to the crack and peered in. Not much of a view, although I could see Miss McElroy's chair from my vantage point.

Empty. That was strange, since Jack told me he'd asked for Miss McElroy, her husband, and the Bertrams to wait for him in here.

As I waited and listened, I couldn't hear any signs of conversation. Then there was a bit of movement. I recognized Alice Bertram. She had come just within my line of vision, and she appeared to be alone. Then she walked fully into view, her back toward me.

I pushed the door lightly, and it swung open a few inches on silent hinges. She didn't appear to have heard anything. Now I could see better, and as I waited and watched, she continued walking around the room.

I drew in a breath of surprise. I realized what was strange about what I was seeing.

Alice was moving about without the assistance of her walker, which I noticed several feet away, abandoned. In fact, she was walking upright, moving without any evidence of stiffness or pain.

I must have made another, more audible sound of surprise. She whirled around, and her face blanched upon seeing me.

She stumbled, with a cry, and sank down into a chair. Miss McElroy's chair.

But it was too late. I had caught her, and by the look on her face, she knew it.

Chapter Fourteen

"HOW LONG HAVE YOU BEEN FAKING?" I asked as I strode into the room, thrusting the door shut behind me.

"You startled me!" Alice said, her voice hostile.

"And you've been lying to everyone," I said, trying real hard to hold on to my temper. "How long have you been faking?"

She tossed her head. "I don't know what you're talking about."

I laughed in derision. "Don't put on that fake innocent act with me, sister! I just caught you, walking around this room. You weren't using your walker or being assisted by anyone. Your back is straight, you don't seem to be in pain. So, I'll ask you one more time, how long have you been faking?"

"Bitch," she responded, almost spitting the word at me.

"Maybe," I said, "but I think Jack Preston is going to be very interested in the fact that you can get around a lot better than anyone realized."

Her nostrils flared, and her eyes grew wild. "You wouldn't! You can't tell him!" She was almost wailing.

"Like hell I won't," I said, my voice rough. "I hadn't given you much thought as a possible murderer, I'll admit, despite the fact that you're a vicious, unpleasant cow. I figured it had to be someone more mobile, someone who could get up and down stairs quickly and easily. Or out to the summerhouse and back without anyone noticing." I grinned, making it as evil as I knew how. "But now I know the truth about you, and I figure you're as good a suspect as anybody in this house."

"You're insane," Alice said, affecting a hauteur that was laughable in the circumstances. "What possible reason would I have for killing any of these people?"

I snorted. "Please. Every chance you've had, you've said something nasty about each and every one of them. You can't possibly imagine that anyone is going to buy this Little Miss Innocent act. You can't possibly be that naive, though you might be that stupid."

I'll admit I was doing my best to provoke her. Cajoling her wouldn't work, but I figured getting her dander up was the best strategy for making her talk.

"You have some kind of nerve talking to me like that!" Evidently I had laid the final straw, because she cut loose with a flood of invective that would have done a sailor proud.

When she paused for breath, I interjected a comment. "You know they say that reliance on an excessive use of profanity is a sign of a severely limited imagination." I couldn't help myself. This was turning into a catfight, largely instigated by me, but there was something about this woman that just brought out the worst in me.

Abruptly, she became calmer. "Who the hell are you to sit in judgment on me? You don't know the first thing about my life. You haven't had to put up with what I've endured for the last thirty-five years."

"Oh, my, I'm sure you've had such a tough life," I said, my voice oozing false sympathy. "The wife of a best-selling novelist, a man who is considered one of the great American writers of the century. You've been invited to dinner at the White House by two or three presidents, you have a nice big house in Memphis, with servants to take care of you, so you never have to lift a finger for yourself. At least, according to *Southern Living* magazine. I could go on, but I think you get the picture. You live a life of such deprivation, it's cruel."

"Can you possibly be as naive as that?" Alice turned my words back upon me. "Or maybe you're just that damn stupid, yourself." She laughed bitterly. "Yes, I'm married to one of the outstanding men of American letters. I'm also married to a first-class shit who can't keep his pants zipped, whenever there's a young woman around making eyes at him, just begging him to read her work, to tell her that she's going to be the next Joyce Carol Oates or Ellen Gilchrist."

"So he's an adulterer," I said, unimpressed. "Ever heard of divorce?"

She laughed again. "Oh, that's a good one. You think I'd let him off the hook that easily, after all he's done to me?"

"Just what has he done, besides cheat on you?"

"He killed our only child," she said. The stark simplicity of that statement took my breath away, and I collapsed onto the sofa nearest me.

"Good heavens," I said, when I finally found my voice. "What happened?" I now dimly recalled having read, in the pile of documents my librarian friend had compiled for me, something about a tragic accident involving the Bertrams' only son, but the article had been skimpy on details.

"Bobby was only three," Alice said, her voice soft and sad, the force of her anger dulled. "He was a beautiful child, bright, loving. Busy, active—you couldn't take your eyes off him for a minute because he was into everything. I left him with his father for a few days because I had to go down to Florida to check on my mother. She'd had a stroke, and she needed some help. I didn't take Bobby with me, of course. We didn't have servants in those days, and I thought he'd be safe with his father." She stopped, her face deathly pale.

After a moment, she went on. "Russell was screwing around again. Some bimbo in one of his classes. He was still teaching then. He invited her to our house for a little fun. He put Bobby down for a nap while they were carrying on in our bedroom, but Bobby woke up and somehow got out of the house. He loved to go 'sploring, as he called it." The pain in her face was so intense it was like a knife through my heart.

"He wandered out into the street. He was fearless, and impulsive. He was hit by a car. He died right there, on the street in front of our house." She looked at me. "He would have been twenty-six last month."

I did the only thing I could think of to do, to answer the naked pain in her voice and in her face. I got up from the sofa, walked over to her, and knelt on the floor. I wrapped my arms around her, and she clutched at me as the sobs racked her body.

I have no idea how long we stayed that way, but my knees were aching by the time the storm of grief had begun to pass. The sobs diminished into quiet tears, and I gently disengaged myself and stood up. I went to the drinks tray and poured a tot of brandy for each of us. I handed her the glass, and she took it without protest. We sipped at the warming, restorative liquor, and I examined her with newly aware eyes.

"I'm sorry," I said, knowing how vastly inadequate those two words were in the face of such soul-wrenching pain, the likes of which I could only imagine.

"Thank you," she said. The episode had left her drained, but somehow more at peace. She held out the glass, now empty, and I poured her more brandy. As she continued to sip at it, the color slowly seeped back into her tearstained face.

"Maybe if we'd been able to have other children, I could have forgiven him," she said eventually. "But I suffered complications from Bobby's birth that left me barren. I could never forgive him for what happened. He couldn't forgive himself either. I went a little crazy for a while, and Russell never left my side. He was attentive, loving, more like the man I had married. But eventually he began to drift again. That's when I discovered that the only thing that would keep him in line was my being ill. The more I suffered, the more he paid attention to me, the less liable he was to wander."

She said it simply, with no hint of irony or self-accusation. The nature of their unhealthy relationship revolted me, but at the same time I couldn't help but feel enormous sympathy for her. The loss of a child is the most horrifying thing a mother can endure, it seems to me, and I couldn't find it in my heart to judge her any longer for what she had done to herself and her husband in the time since her son's tragic death.

Though I could now see her in an entirely different light, that didn't change some of the facts. *But how*, I asked myself, *can I possibly badger her now, in the face of what she's just revealed to me?*

She saved me the trouble. "I hated Sukey Lytton," she

said, her voice hardening. She looked me square in the face as she said it. "She was one more of Russ's little conquests. But for the first time in his whole miserable career as a philanderer, he hit on a girl who actually had some talent outside the bedroom. He was going through a rough patch when he was involved with her. Hadn't been able to write anything decent for nearly three years, and she suggested that they work on something together."

Alice laughed. "Sukey did all the work, probably. Then Russ had the nerve to submit it as entirely his own. That was before Sukey had any reputation to speak of. I'm surprised the grasping little bitch didn't try to sue him, but he talked her out of it somehow, when she found out about it." She laughed again. "She was fit to be tied, like one of the Furies raging, right there in our house. I left them to it, so I don't know exactly how he got her calmed down."

Russell Bertram a plagiarist. That thought didn't sit well with me. Intellectual theft was as abhorrent to me as material theft, and I could never look at the man with any kind of respect after this.

"Do you think she wrote about all that in this mysterious novel of hers?" I asked.

"I'd be willing to bet on it," Alice said. "She was vicious, and conniving, and downright nasty. I'm not saying that Russ doesn't deserve it for what he did to her, but if that novel is ever published, he'll become a laughingstock. She's dead, and there's no way now he could ever prove that he wrote that story himself."

"You realize that this gives him a very strong motive for murder," I said.

She nodded, her face bleak. "I tell myself that he isn't really capable of it. He's a shell of the man he used to be. I don't think he has the guts to be a multiple murderer." She shuddered as she said the words. "But the hell of it is, I just don't know."

"You can't give him an alibi for any of the murders?"

She shrugged. "Maybe when we're told more about when they occurred. It's just possible he might have been with me, but most of the time, I've been alone in our room. He goes off somewhere in the house to write, or so he says. Up on the third floor, in one of the unused bedrooms. Frankly, I think he was trying to get his hands up the skirt of that girl who was murdered." The thought of it sickened her. Her face twisted in loathing. "She was the type he liked. Young, pretty, not too bright. Impressed by an older man who was so famous."

I hesitated to fracture the curious rapport that now existed between us, but I felt I had to be straight with her. "Alice, you need to talk to Jack Preston about all of this. He has to know."

She drew a deep, ragged breath. "I know." She got up from her chair and went to stand by her walker. She stared at it for a long moment. "I can't hide any longer. And I can't protect him. If he's responsible for these murders, he's going to have to pay for them."

She came back toward me. She held out a hand, and I grasped it. Her fingers were ice-cold and trembling. "Would you get rid of that thing for me?" She jerked her head in the direction of her abandoned walker. "There's no point in using it anymore."

I nodded.

"Thank you," she said. Without looking back, she walked out of the room. I hoped she was going to talk to Jack. The sooner she did so, the better.

Closing my eyes, feeling completely drained, I sat there for a while, trying to gather my thoughts. I had no idea what had happened to Miss McElroy or Morwell Phillips. They were supposed to be in this room with Alice and her husband, or so I had been told. I had never even thought to ask Alice where the others might be.

Russell Bertram now loomed large as my favorite suspect for the murders. He had cheated on his wife with the first victim, Sukey Lytton, with disastrous results. Because of that, and his plagiarism, he had a powerful motive to murder Sukey. The other two murders stemmed from that first one, surely. Hamilton Packer claimed possession of a manuscript that, if published, could damage the lives and reputations of almost everyone in this house. And poor, silly, none-too-bright Katie had perhaps seen something, and an attempt at blackmail had ensured her fate.

But does that manuscript really exist? I wondered, not for the first time. I had the nagging sense that I was overlooking something. Was the pile of blank paper that I had found in my room simply a blind? Or even a mistake on my part? What if the manuscript was still here, somewhere in the house?

That didn't seem likely, however. Jack and his men had searched pretty thoroughly. Surely, if it was still here, they would have found it by now.

Maybe I needed to go hibernate in my room for a while. Sit at the desk and jot down things. Make lists. That kind of thing. Maybe it would make me feel like I was doing something to earn the fee that Miss McElroy was paying me. Sitting here staring at Miss McElroy's chair wasn't accomplishing anything.

Then it hit me. What I was overlooking. When I had first peeked inside this room, I saw Alice Bertram moving around without her walker. That revelation had stunned me so that I had forgotten what she was doing while she was moving around the room.

She had been searching the room. Picking up things, looking underneath and behind them.

But what had she been looking for?

Maybe she had lost an earring or some other piece of jewelry. I thought about that, but I couldn't remember her wearing earrings, and the one ring I had seen her wear had been on her finger when she left the room just minutes ago.

I'd be willing to bet she was looking for that blasted manuscript. Did she know something about it that she hadn't told anyone? Or maybe she knew something about hiding places in the house that no one had told Jack or his men about. Surely a house this old had some hidey-holes.

I decided I'd better ask Jack about that, before I went off, half-cocked, doing a Nancy Drew routine, searching for hidden staircases and the like. If such things existed in this house, Miss McElroy or Morwell Phillips would have told him.

The next thought chilled my blood.

They would have told Jack—unless one of them was the murderer and they were protecting each other.

No, I decided. That's too fanciful. I couldn't see Miss McElroy doing such a thing. Her husband was still a bit of a cipher to me. He was such a dignified, Old-South gentlemanly type that I had a hard time seeing him doing such a thing either.

I sighed. This wasn't a very scientific approach to solving the murders. Which was why, I reminded myself sharply, Jack Preston was in charge of the investigation. I might nudge things along here and there, but it would be Jack who'd probably crack the case first.

I was just getting to my feet when the door to the sitting room opened and in walked Morwell Phillips.

"Miss Carpenter," he said, his voice clipped. "Mary Tucker would like to speak with you, if you wouldn't mind going up to her room. I'm afraid this latest . . . incident"—his face twisted in distaste—"has upset her considerably, and I've put her to bed, per her doctor's instructions."

"I'll go to her at once," I said. I wondered whether he shouldn't be in bed himself, his face was so gray. He moved more slowly than usual as he stood aside to let me precede him from the room.

"Thank you," he said.

I almost ran up the stairs, and for some reason, when I reached the top, I paused, turned, and looked back down. Phillips stood there, staring up after me. His expression was fleeting, gone so quickly that I probably imagined it, because he moved away the moment he realized I was watching him.

But I would have sworn that what I saw on his face was fear.

I couldn't afford to puzzle too long over the strange expression on Morwell Phillips's face because I felt a sense of urgency behind his request for me to talk to Miss McElroy. Perhaps what I had seen on his face was simply his fear for the well-being of his wife. Surely he wasn't afraid of me. Unless, of course, he was the murderer, and he knew that his wife and I were closing in on him.

I shook my head at the absurdity of it. I couldn't see Miss McElroy's husband as the person who had murdered poor Katie so violently.

I tapped at Miss McElroy's door but didn't wait for a summons to enter. Pushing open the door, I beheld her lying like a wax effigy in state on her bed. My heart almost stopped for a moment, then she moved, blinked her eyes, and said, "Come in."

As I hesitated, she said, "Don't stand there gawking, Miss Carpenter. I'm not ready for the boneyard just yet."

Relieved, I did as she bade me, shutting the door behind me and advancing toward her bed. She gestured weakly for me to sit in a chair which had been pulled near the bed. I sat.

"How are you doing?" I said. Her pallor alarmed me, though I was a bit reassured by the tart tone of her voice.

"I'll do," she said, her voice gruff. "The strain seems to have gotten to me a bit, but I'll be better by tomorrow morning. Just some rest, and I'll be up and about as usual."

I thought she might need more than one night's rest, judging by the look of her at the moment, but I wasn't going to argue with her. She had an indomitable will, from what I had seen, and she might well be up and bustling around tomorrow, leaving me eating the dust in her wake. I fervently hoped so.

"Mr. Phillips said you wanted to see me," I prompted her gently. She had fallen silent, while her hands pleated and unpleated the bedspread at her chest.

"Yes," she sighed. "No one will tell me exactly what has happened to that poor, misguided girl. Nor will they tell me anything else that's going on, simply because I had a moment of weakness and nearly fainted." She fixed her eyes upon mine and gave as good a glare as she could, daring me to contradict or deny her. "You, however, will tell me everything, and don't leave anything out, no matter how trivial."

I resisted the impulse to salute, though I thought it might actually make her smile. "Of course, because I know how irksome it is, not knowing."

"Exactly!" she said, before I could continue.

I took a deep breath, then launched into a brief, dispassionate description of what I had seen when I walked into the summerhouse earlier in the day. Miss McElroy's mouth twisted in pain suddenly, and I paused to ask her if she needed anything.

"No," she said, her eyes closed. I feared she was seeing all too clearly the image that others had tried to protect her against, of Katie, brutalized and dead. "Go on."

Not completely reassured, I complied. I told her of my talk with Selma Greer and the subsequent discussion with Jack Preston. She appeared alarmed when she realized that Brett Doran might be implicated in Katie's murder because of where it had occurred and the possible drug connection, but I hastened to reassure her Brett most likely had a good alibi for it. I couldn't tell her about the murder weapon, not without Jack's permission. Fortunately she seemed not to have noticed my omission of that fact.

She smiled faintly. "Brett and his cigars! For once, they may have saved him."

"I certainly hope so," I said.

"At least it's better than his smoking pot, or ingesting something worse," she went on.

Before I revealed the most sensational information I had discovered—the fact of Alice Bertram's malingering—I thought I had better tell her about the conversation I'd had with Lurleen Landry.

Miss McElroy already knew about Lurleen's experiences with Sukey Lytton—or at least Lurleen claimed she did—so I doubted I was telling her anything new or startling. I truly feared how she would react when I revealed to her the depth of Alice Bertram's deception. But I wondered how much Miss McElroy really knew about the dynamics of that marriage. Did she know the truth, I wondered, about what had happened the day the Bertrams' son was killed?

I pushed those thoughts away for the moment and concentrated on recounting my conversation with Lurleen. As I was nearing the end, I heard a gentle snore. I hadn't been watching Miss McElroy closely as I talked, and now I could see that she had fallen asleep. Just as well, because she needed rest now more than she needed to hear me babble out my report.

I extricated myself quietly from my chair and tiptoed across the room. Praying that the door wouldn't squeak, I eased it open. Hovering outside was Morwell Phillips, an expression of anxiety stamped across his face.

"How is she?" he asked, his voice low.

"Asleep," I said, shutting the door with great care behind me.

"Good," he said, and his whole body seemed to slump, all of a sudden, as if he had been holding himself at rigid attention, bracing for the worst.

With a hand on his elbow, I guided him across the hall toward the door of my bedroom. "What happened to her?"

He rubbed a weary hand across his face. "When Jack Preston came to tell us what had happened, she fainted. Fortunately, she was seated at the time. I'm afraid the strain of all that's happened has been too much for her. Ordinarily, she's got the fortitude of any ten women, but for the last year or so, she's been having these 'little spells,' as she calls them." He smiled weakly. "To Mary Tucker, they're 'little spells,' but to anyone else they'd be cause to rush to the doctor for all kinds of tests, I suppose."

"Is she in any danger?" I asked, alarmed all over again.

He shrugged. "Her doctor thinks she'll be fine, as long as she doesn't let herself get too upset." He threw up his hands. "But how on earth I'm supposed to keep her from getting upset, in the middle of all this mess, I surely don't know." His voice had risen sharply in frustration, and he made an effort to control himself. "She's very obstinate, as I'm sure you've noticed by now. She won't listen to what anyone says."

I detected more than a faint trace of bitterness in that last remark. I could only imagine what it must be like to be married to such a woman, one used to having her own way in all things. Especially since, in our limited contact, Morwell Phillips hadn't impressed me as a particularly forceful man. He was the perfect foil, I supposed, for a strong woman like

Mary Tucker McElroy.

"I'm sure Jack Preston and his men will get this all sorted out very soon," I said, as soothingly as possible. "Once the investigation is over and someone has been charged, Miss McElroy will be fine."

He stared at me, one eyebrow raised. "Perhaps" was all he said.

I hoped my face hadn't betrayed me by flushing. He wasn't to be mollified by platitudes, and I felt foolish.

"Would you like me to sit with her?" I said. "I don't think she should be alone tonight."

He shook his head. "No, I'll stay with her, and if necessary, Mrs. Greer will relieve me. She's used to Mary Tucker's little ways and her medicines. I do appreciate your kindness in offering."

He was turning away, when on impulse I asked him, "Do you have any idea who's responsible for all this?"

He swung back to me, frowning. "No, but if I did, I'd strangle the bastard with my own two hands. And if Sukey weren't already dead, I think I'd kill her all over again for the mess she's caused. I wish I had never laid eyes on that damn girl!" He stalked off, leaving me staring after him, openmouthed.

Miss McElroy's bedroom door opened and shut, quietly and quickly, and there I stood, alone in the hallway, gaping after Morwell Phillips.

I shut my mouth and unlocked my own bedroom door. Now that I wasn't engrossed in conversation, I realized that I needed to do something, rather soon, about all that coffee I had drunk earlier. I headed for the bathroom.

In due course, I stood at the sink, washing my hands and staring into the mirror. I had been pondering several questions, and I realized I needed more information. With luck, I could catch Farrah Lockett still at the library and ask her to do a bit more research for me.

I dried my hands and went to the telephone in my bedroom. I plopped myself down on the bed after I had punched in the number. As I sat, waiting to be connected to Farrah's voice mail, I glanced toward the door. A small envelope lay on the floor, just inches from the door. I frowned. Who was slipping notes under my door?

Farrah's voice came on the line, asking me to leave a message. Hastily gathering my distracted wits, I did that. I knew that, if the information was available, she could find it for me. If she found nothing, that in itself would be an answer, a confirmation of sorts. But just in case, to make sure people were telling me the truth, I thought it best to find out as much as possible.

Placing the telephone receiver back in its cradle, I sat and stared at the envelope on my floor. Something about it spooked me, though for the life of me I couldn't have said why. It was just odd, and I was probably overreacting. But in view of what had happened today, anything out of the ordinary bothered me.

I got up from the bed and approached the envelope slowly, as if it were going to explode. Wondering whether I should be wearing gloves, I picked it up, very carefully, by one corner.

Gingerly, I carried it over to the desk, where I placed it on the blotter. I opened the drawer and rummaged inside for a pencil and a letter opener. Using the letter opener, I flipped the envelope over. There was nothing written on the outside, and the flap hadn't been glued down. Using the pencil in my left hand to hold down one corner of the envelope, I took the letter opener in my right hand and worked open the flap.

There was a card inside, and I could see the initials *BD* emblazoned across the top in dark blue ink. Below the initials were hand-printed words, in block capitals. Catching one corner of the card between thumb and finger, I eased the card out so that I could read the message.

"Ernie: can you meet me ASAP out by the summerhouse?" Below that was a scrawled signature which looked like it could be "Brett."

I stared down at the card on my desk. Very odd, I thought. Why didn't he simply knock at my door and talk to me here? Or at least ask me to accompany him to the summerhouse?

Maybe I was making too much of this. Brett was probably just rattled by what had happened today. After all, he had to be aware that it was his computer that the killer had used as a murder weapon. That would be enough to make me a bit scatterbrained, I supposed.

I looked out the window and down toward the summerhouse. I couldn't see anyone. Brett couldn't be inside because the sheriff's department had sealed it. Where was he?

Enough dithering, I told myself. *Just go down there and see if he's there!*

I started to leave the note where it was, on the desk, but at the last moment I got a handkerchief out of my purse, picked up the card and envelope, and took them out into the hall with me. The hall was empty, and I walked a few paces to my left and hid the card and envelope under the cushion of a chair there. It wasn't a great hiding place, but it was the best I could do at the moment.

Tucking my handkerchief in my pocket, I walked down the hall toward the back staircase. I paused at the top, staring down. The stairs were a bit darker than usual because the door at the bottom was shut. Frowning, I started down the stairs, moving with care as I continued to think about the oddity of Brett's having left that note for me. I was a little over halfway down the stairs when I nearly stumbled and went headlong down the rest of the way. I managed to steady myself, thankful that I hadn't been going down the steps as fast as I normally would have taken them.

I sat down, the impact of my rump making the stair creak. I leaned over and stared down.

Someone had arranged for me to have a very nasty accident.

Chapter Fifteen

I'M NOT SURE HOW LONG I sat and stared down at the neat little trap someone had laid for me.

What looked like fishing line had been stretched across the length of the step, fixed at either end around a small nail in the boards along the sides of the staircase. If I had been going down the stairs any faster, I would have tripped and probably not been able to stop myself from falling down the rest of the way.

I shuddered. I could have broken my neck, at the very least, not to mention any number of other bones. I could even have died as the result of such a fall.

It's a good thing I have such a suspicious nature, I guess. I had known all along there was something odd about that note. The killer had read the same mystery novels I had, but he or she expected me not to catch on to the little game being played for my benefit.

If I had fallen for it (and I groaned at my own bad pun), my injuries or even death could have been dismissed as an accident. "Elderly woman dies in tragic fall"—I could see the headlines now in the local paper.

Was the killer lurking downstairs right this very moment, waiting to hear me plunging headlong down? I shuddered again at that pesky little question.

Probably not, I decided. I had made enough noise walking down the stairs, moments before. Surely if someone had been waiting, he or she realized when I stopped so suddenly and didn't make a huge amount of noise, that I hadn't fallen, nor was I about to fall.

As the saying goes, that dog won't hunt.

I couldn't just keep on sitting here like this. Either I had to continue downstairs or go back upstairs. I couldn't scream for help, because I didn't want to alarm Miss McElroy and risk causing her to have another "little spell," one which might do considerably more damage than the one she'd had already today. But I wasn't too eager to rush downstairs into the potentially waiting arms of someone who intended to do me grievous bodily harm.

I wanted to get Jack Preston here, so he could see what someone had done; and I was afraid that if I left the stairs, by the time I got back with someone to act as a witness, the evidence would be gone. Mostly, that is. The nail holes might still be there, but everything else could be removed fairly quickly, if someone was prepared.

But was the killer behind me, somewhere on the second floor? Or was he or she waiting down at the bottom of the stairs? That was the crux of my dilemma. Which way?

I needed to make a decision—fast—because I also didn't want to be a sitting duck in case the killer got tired of waiting and decided to come after me with a big, blunt object or something sharp, like another butcher knife from the kitchen.

With that thought, I was on my feet and moving back up the stairs—with caution, mind you.

I almost wished the killer had been there, on the second floor. At least a confrontation might have resolved things, one way or another, but the hallway was empty when I got there.

Stopping only to retrieve the envelope from its hiding place, I went down the hallway to the front stairs, then stopped. I peered down but could see no one lurking in the hall below.

I figured the front stairs couldn't be booby-trapped too, so I almost ran down them. Not slowing my hectic pace, I went through the hall and on into the back of the house, thrusting open the kitchen door and nearly causing Selma Greer to drop the roast she was carving.

"Can you come with me immediately?" I asked, not stopping to think that I might be scaring the living daylights out of her.

Carving knife still in hand, she came toward me. "What's wrong?" she said.

"I want you to witness something," I said, whirling and moving quickly back into the hallway and across to the door to the back stairs. Such was my faith in the woman that I never even thought about the foolishness of turning my back on someone with a big knife until later that evening. Sometimes you just have to go with your instincts.

I pulled open the door to the back stairs and flipped on the light switch. I started up the stairs, going slowly. I could hear Selma behind me.

I had gone nearly halfway up the staircase before I conceded defeat. Whoever had laid the trap for me had, in the time it took me to get back here, removed the fishing line. It took me a couple more minutes of patient searching—though my patience was in extremely short supply right then—but I did find the two small nails which had been used to secure the line. The killer hadn't had time to remove those.

Selma waited, a few steps below me, a patient frown on her face. Sighing, I explained to her what had almost happened to me, though I didn't tell her about the note I had, tucked inside my blouse. I would give that to Jack Preston and no one else.

"Did you see anyone or hear anyone come through the back part of the hallway or the back stairs in the last five or ten minutes?" I asked.

She relaxed her grip on the knife a bit while she thought. "Betsy was in the kitchen just before you came, getting some dishes to set the table with, and Miz Alice was there right after, asking for something cold to drink." She shook her head. "I just couldn't believe her walking upright like that, without her walker. She didn't say nothing about it, but she sure looked different, I can tell you."

"Anyone else?"

She started to shake her head, then stopped. "I did see Mr. Brett out the window, coming toward the house. I reckon he came in the back door, though he didn't stop by in the kitchen, like he usually does. He almost always stops to speak to me, even if he's in a hurry. But this time he didn't."

Brett Doran! I was stunned, to put it mildly. Surely Brett wasn't responsible for this.

No, he couldn't be, I reasoned with myself. He wouldn't have given himself away so clumsily by using his own note card to entice me into the trap. It simply didn't make sense.

"Anything, or anybody, else?" I said, a note of desperation creeping into my voice.

"People's always coming and going out in that hall," Selma replied. "Mr. Morwell, he be in and out of the kitchen three hundred times a day, though I hadn't seen him much this afternoon. Except when he come to ask me to sit with Miss Mary Tucker later on. And then to get Miss Mary Tucker some cold juice." She thought for a moment. "Half the time I don't pay no attention to what's going on, with the door shut and all; and if someone's making an effort to be quiet, then I wouldn't hear 'em no way. So I reckon just about anybody could've been up and down the stairs, doing what you say they did, and I wouldn't ever've known about it." Seeing the frustration plainly in my face, she added, "I sure am sorry, Ernie."

My shoulders slumped in defeat. "It's not your fault, Selma," I assured her. "With everything else you have to do, you certainly can't play watchdog for me." I paused for a moment. "The more I think about it, I'm reckoning that whoever set that little trap for me must have been upstairs the whole time. Then, as soon as I started down the front stairs, he or she nipped over to the back stairs and removed the fishing line and disappeared back up the stairs."

"Mrs. Greer, is something the matter?" Betsy came out of the kitchen, wringing a towel in her hands. The poor girl looked terrified. If someone said "boo" to her about now, she'd hit the back door running and never look back, I'd be willing to bet.

"No, no, Betsy," Selma said, trying her best to appear like the knife she was carrying was simply a utensil and not a weapon.

"We were just talking about something," I chimed in.

"Nothing you need worry about."

Betsy didn't appear to be very much relieved by our assurances. "The reason I'm asking is that I came into the kitchen just now, and the gravy was bubbling over on the stove and making a mess." By the tone of awe in her voice, I knew such an occurrence was rare in Selma Greer's kitchen.

Mumbling under her breath, Selma strode past Betsy, back into the kitchen. Betsy shrugged in my direction, then turned and followed.

I thought I might as well see whether Jack was anywhere nearby. He couldn't do much, after the fact, about the thwarted attempt at making me break my neck, but he ought to know about it.

There was no sign of him, however. When no one answered my knock, I tried the knob of the library door, but it refused to turn. Jack and his men were off somewhere, working on the case. Surely they'd be back before the night was over, and then I could tell him what had almost happened.

What to do next? I asked myself. I thought of two things I should do, but I wasn't overly inclined to do one of them. I needed to talk to Brett, just to verify my suspicions that someone else had written that note, pretending to be from him. But as far as I knew, he had moved up to the third floor after Hamilton Packer's murder, and I didn't relish the thought of going up to there in search of him. This house, so eerily silent at the moment, made me twitchy.

The second thing I had thought about, I could accomplish more easily. Ever since I had caught Alice Bertram *in flagrante delicto*, as it were, I had been wondering what it was she was searching for in Miss McElroy's sitting room. I had interrupted her, that much I was sure of, but what was she looking for? And why was she looking for it in that room?

I figured she must have been looking for the missing manuscript. But why in that room, in particular?

Time to ask her some more questions, so up to the second floor I went. The first bedroom to my right on the second floor belonged to Lurleen Landry, and I had seen one or the other of the Bertrams coming out of the door of the second bedroom on this side. To that door I marched, and then I knocked lightly upon it.

After a moment, I heard footsteps approaching the door, but the door didn't open. "Who is it?" A muffled voice came to me through the burnished wood.

"Ernestine Carpenter, Mr. Bertram," I responded. "I'd like to talk to your wife for a moment, if I might."

I heard a key turning in the lock, and the door opened a few inches.

Russell Bertram, looking more washed out than usual, regarded me with hostile eyes. "What do you want now?"

What had his wife told him, I wondered, to make him change his demeanor toward me in this way? Then I realized that, more than likely, he was deeply ashamed for me to know the part he had played in the death of his only child. Perhaps he was expecting me to say something nasty to him.

I could only pity him. I couldn't imagine what it was like for him to bear such a terrible responsibility, but he probably paid for his negligence every day of his life.

Because of that I was gentler in my response to him than ordinarily I would have been, confronted by such rudeness. "I apologize for disturbing you," I said, "but I really must talk to Mrs. Bertram. Would you ask her if I might come in and see her?"

With a sudden, violent motion, he threw open the door. "You might as well come in. I'm going down for a drink, Alice." He nearly careened into me, and I got a strong whiff of his breath as he passed. The drink he sought downstairs would not be his first of the day, nor likely his fifth or sixth. I was afraid he might fall down the stairs. I listened for a moment, but I heard no crash.

I shut the door behind me. Gazing across the room toward the window, I could see Alice Bertram regarding me balefully from an armchair.

"I really can't think of anything else I have to say to you," she said, her voice icy with disdain.

Sighing, I walked at a slow pace toward her. I was familiar with this reaction. I had seen it many times in my years as a teacher. Often, once someone confides a dark and shameful secret, that person harbors resentment toward the recipient of the confidence. Alice now deeply resented me for having heard her tale of misery. I couldn't let that deter me now, however.

"If this weren't important," I told her, my voice calm but firm, "I wouldn't disturb you. Would you mind if I sat down?" I gestured toward the chair which stood as companion to her own.

She shrugged. "You might as well."

"Thank you," I said, sitting down. Before I could say anything further, she began speaking, her anger pouring forth.

"Russ is convinced that as soon as Mary Tucker knows what happened, she'll throw us out of the house. He says she won't have any more to do with him if she finds out he was responsible for our son's death. I daresay he might be right, because Mary Tucker is such a pious old bitch sometimes. But she has a nerve, I can tell you that, if she thinks she's just going to throw Russell Bertram out of this house! Why, that woman wouldn't be anybody if Russ hadn't become friendly with her and given her entrée to all the fancy publishing folk that she was trying to cozy up to! If it hadn't been for Russ, she wouldn't be anybody."

The best defense is a vitriolic offense—that must be the Bertram strategy in deflecting criticism or blame. I still had a lot of sympathy for Alice Bertram and the ordeal she had faced in losing a child in such a senseless, brutal fashion. Nevertheless I wasn't going to sit here and indulge her by listening to such foolishness.

"That's between you and Miss McElroy," I said, staring her straight in the eye. "It's nothing to do with me, but you'd better wait until Miss McElroy has recovered a bit before you go blasting away at her."

Alice had the grace to look somewhat abashed at that, but her patience with me had worn thin. "So what is it that you want from me?"

"Earlier today, when I found you in Miss McElroy's study, you were searching for something when I interrupted you. I should have asked you about it then, but I got distracted. Now I want to know what it was you were looking for and whether you found it."

For a moment I thought she might try to deny it, or to bluff her way out of it, but the look of determination on my face must have convinced her it wouldn't do much good.

"If you must know, I was looking for that damn manuscript of Sukey's. I wanted to find it and destroy it. That piece of trash can't ever be published, and if I get my hands on it first, there won't be anything left of it for anyone to see."

"I figured that's what you were looking for," I said. "Did you find it?"

"You're not blind," she said. "Did you see me with it?"

"No, but that doesn't mean you didn't go back afterwards and keep looking."

"Well, I didn't," she said. "I've been in this room ever since I left you, talking to Russ."

I decided not to press her any further on that point. It sounded like the truth, and it very well might be. But I had another question.

"Why were you looking in Miss McElroy's sitting room? Why would you think the manuscript would be in there?"

She laughed. "Because I saw Mary Tucker go in there with it."

Chapter Sixteen

FOR A MOMENT I forgot to breathe, I was so stunned by Alice Bertram's statement. "Miss McElroy?" I croaked out at last. "Surely you can't be serious!"

In response, she snorted derisively. "You don't have to believe me if you don't want to. By now you probably think that sainted Mary Tucker McElroy walks on water, just like the rest of the freaking world, but that woman has a few secrets of her own to hide. There're things she doesn't want anyone to know, just like the rest of us."

Despite the obvious malice behind her words, Alice's tone carried conviction. She had known Miss McElroy far longer and far better than I, and I had to admit the possibility that Miss McElroy did indeed have secrets she wanted to keep hidden. The thought rankled me, because I had come to admire Miss McElroy, after some initial hostility toward what I had perceived as her high-handedness and downright snobbery.

I wasn't going to give Alice Bertram the satisfaction, however, of asking her what Miss McElroy's secrets were. That she was itching to tell me some of them was perfectly obvious. If they were germane to the murders, I'd find them out, but in some other way. If the queries I had directed Farrah Lockett to make for me bore any fruit, I'd know soon enough. And, I reasoned, I'd get the information from a far less malicious—and less biased—source.

"Just what did you see?" I asked, trying to keep my voice cool.

That ruffled her, because she was expecting another question. "It was the other day, after lunch. After everyone had left the dining room. Russ went off to the third floor, to pretend to write, and I came up here. I knew Hamilton had come upstairs as well, and I decided I might go across the hall and talk to him. Try to reason with him about the manuscript and get him to see what kind of damage it could cause."

"You mean you talked to him not long before he was murdered?" My voice rose in disbelief, despite my attempts to remain nonchalant.

She shook her head impatiently. "Of course not. I had pulled my door open, just a fraction, when I heard another door opening. I peeked out into the hall, and that's when I saw Mary Tucker coming out of Hamilton's room."

"Did she see you?"

"No, I'm sure she didn't," Alice said. "She was in too much of a hurry."

"And you saw her with the manuscript?"

"Yes, I did." Alice's tone was a purr of triumph. "She had it clutched to her chest, though she was trying to hide it underneath her shawl. She went down the stairs so fast I thought she might trip and break her neck. But she didn't." Alice sounded almost regretful.

"What then?" I said, prompting her.

"I went out into the hall and looked downstairs to see where she was going with the manuscript. She went right straight into her sitting room and shut the door behind her."

"Then what did you do?"

"I came back in here."

"Why didn't you follow her downstairs and confront her? Ask her to let you see the manuscript?"

Alice shrugged. "What was the point? By the time I'd've gotten downstairs, she probably would've had it hidden away. She would've denied the whole thing anyway."

"And all this happened right after you came upstairs."

She pondered that for a moment. "Maybe about ten minutes after I came upstairs."

Time enough for her to get to her room and for Miss McElroy to come along behind her and go into Hamilton Packer's room.

"How long was all this before the body was discovered? Can you remember?"

"I'm not sure," Alice said. "It was probably another twenty minutes, maybe twenty-five, before I heard that girl screaming out in the hall."

"Was today the first time you had looked for the manuscript?" I asked.

"No, I had a brief look last night, but I didn't find anything. There haven't been many opportunities. People have been in and out of that room a lot ever since yesterday. I could've gone down last night, after everyone was in bed, but I didn't much care for the thought of being downstairs by myself with a murderer in the house."

Unless you're the murderer yourself, I thought.

"Are you going to look for it?" Alice asked me.

"I don't see why not." If I had said that I wasn't, she wouldn't have believed me anyway.

"And just what would you plan on doing with it?"

"I'd turn it over to the sheriff's department, of course. Why, what did you think I'd do with it?"

"You might be willing to sell it."

I didn't like the expression on her face. "Does this mean you're buying?"

"If you find it and don't tell anyone else you've found it, I am."

I had had enough. I stood up. "If I do find it, I'll turn it over to the proper authorities. Because it's the ethical thing to do. It's evidence which will help put an end to these murders. More than likely, that is. None of us really knows what's in the manuscript. It could be completely harmless."

"You can't do that," Alice said, as if she hadn't heard the tail end of what I'd just said. "You could ruin us all if the sheriff's department—or anyone else, for that matter—gets a hold of that piece of trash." Her eyes begged me, and I felt sorry for her, but not enough to comply with what she wanted.

"This is going to have to run its course," I said as gently as I knew how. "If I find the manuscript, I have to turn it over to the sheriff's department. We can't allow anyone else to be murdered. Do you understand me?"

With great reluctance, she nodded. Her face had turned gray with exhaustion, and she made no effort to stop me as I left the room.

Once out in the hall, I stopped for a moment, my back against the Bertrams' bedroom door, trying to gather my wits. My first instinct was to barge into Miss McElroy's room and confront her with what Alice had told me. But I couldn't do that, I knew. I couldn't risk causing Miss McElroy to have a stroke or a heart attack, for goodness' sake!

Had Miss McElroy stabbed Hamilton Packer to death before she took the manuscript from his room? It was possible, though it was also just possible that Packer had either given her the manuscript or she had sneaked into his room and taken it while he was in the bathroom. Or maybe he was already dead when she went in there, and she just took the manuscript and left the discovery of the body to someone else.

I shook my head. Too much speculation, and not enough cold hard facts.

First, I had to determine whether Miss McElroy really had taken the manuscript and hidden it in her sitting room downstairs. Alice could be inventing the whole story, for spiteful reasons of her own, but somehow it had the ring of truth to me.

I glanced at my watch. There was still time before dinner would be served for me to do some ferreting around downstairs. I headed to my room to retrieve something.

In my room I dug around in the huge wardrobe and pulled my suitcase out onto the floor. Stuffed inside was a knitting bag which would be large enough to conceal a manuscript, if I found one. It might not really fool the rest of the household, but it could at least confuse them for a moment. The bag actually contained some knitting. Not very good knitting, mind you, but respectable enough for my cover as a Miss Silver impersonator.

Knitting bag in hand, I walked briskly back down the hall and down the stairs to Miss McElroy's sitting room. I opened the door without knocking, and I found no one inside, to my great relief. I had no way of locking the door, since there was no key in the lock, so I found a suitable chair and wedged it underneath the doorknob. It wasn't a failsafe, but at least it would give me a warning, should someone try to enter the room. I could always pretend I was nervous about being alone in the room as an explanation for doing such a thing. And, truth to tell, it wouldn't be much of a pretense.

Setting my bag down on the sofa, I surveyed the room. If I were a manuscript, where would I be stashed? I smiled at the whimsical thought. There was always the possibility that a house like this would have some secret hiding places, like a secret passageway or some other such thrilling device. Without a floor plan, I couldn't tell if any of the interior walls were set too far in to match the outer walls of the house. I'd have to do this the hard way and start tapping, hoping to hear a hollow sound somewhere.

The problem with this plan was soon apparent. The room was stuffed to overflowing with all kinds of tables, pictures, shelves, and knickknacks; thus, getting close enough to a wall to tap on it was quite a bit of work. I must have spent nearly a half hour trying to find a secret panel, while nervously looking at the door every three seconds, before I gave up in disgust. If the room had a secret panel, I just wasn't going to find it this way.

Time to try a different approach. I thought for a moment. There was always the old "Purloined Letter" gambit—i.e., hide it in plain sight. The trouble with that method, however, was that a manuscript was much bulkier than a mere letter and, therefore, not as easy to secrete. There were a few books, here and there throughout the room, which looked big enough, if they were hollowed out, to hold a manuscript. An examination of them revealed that they were all whole. Musty smelling, in some cases, but whole.

There was always the furniture. The room held numerous chairs, one big sofa, and several tables of varying sizes, some of them with drawers. Perhaps that old desk in the corner had a secret compartment. I spent nearly another half hour, crawling in and around the desk, the tables, and finally the sofa, before concluding that none of them had any secret compartments.

On to the chairs. Might as well start with Miss McElroy's chair. I sat down in it, to rest for a moment.

I sat, then I squirmed. It wasn't a very comfortable chair. The cushion was a bit thin for my taste, and it almost felt like there was something underneath it.

Bingo! I thought, a broad smile creasing my face.

I stood up and pulled the cushion up from the bottom of the chair. At first I thought I was doomed to disappointment, because it looked to me like the fabric beneath the cushion was whole. I put the cushion on the floor, then knelt on it, the better to examine the seat of the chair at a close angle.

Pinching a bit of the fabric at the front of the chair, I tugged at the covering. For a moment, it held against the firm pressure I was applying. Then, without warning, it pulled free. Resting in a hollow in the bottom of the chair was a pile of paper, tied together with a purple ribbon.

Chapter Seventeen

WITH GREAT SATISFACTION, I stared down at the manuscript in the bottom of Miss McElroy's chair. I had been half-inclined to believe the whole story of the manuscript was a hoax, intended by the late and mostly unlamented Hamilton Packer to extort money or power from the group assembled in this house.

But there it lay, the cause, so it would seem, of the multiple murders which had taken place here at Idlewild. For a few moments longer I gazed at it without touching it.

The title was intriguing. "*Closer Than the Bones*," I read, "a novel by Sukey Lytton." A vague memory stirred. Where had I read that phrase, or something similar to it, before? A quotation from a poem, perhaps, or a line from a novel, no doubt. There was one way to find out. I reached for the manuscript.

Then I stayed my hand, albeit reluctantly. Should I remove it from its hiding place? I had planned to, but now I was doubtful. Perhaps I should leave it, in situ, so that I could show it to Jack Preston just as I had found it. Would it be safer here than in my knitting bag, until I could locate him?

No, I decided, I'd much rather carry the manuscript with me, even though Alice Bertram might suspect I had it. I doubted she would confront me in the presence of others, anyway.

I dumped the contents of my knitting bag on the floor, then reached into my skirt pocket for my handkerchief. Gingerly, with the handkerchief wrapped around my hand, I lifted the manuscript from its hiding place and slid it into the empty bag. Then I stuffed bundles of yarn, several knitting needles, and my latest project, an afghan for my cousin Maggie, into the bag on top of the manuscript.

With as much care as possible, I put the chair back together and got up from the floor. Moments later I had restored the chair I had been using to block the door to its accustomed place, and I opened the door and sailed out into the hall, as if I hadn't been doing anything more important than knitting in a quiet place for an hour or two.

Brett Doran was coming down the stairs, two at a time. "Ernie!" he said. "Where have you been?" He eyed my bag. "What's this?" He halted at the bottom of the stairs, a few paces away from me. "Don't tell me you've been doing your Miss Marple routine? Knitting calmly and pondering the guilt of all assembled." He grinned.

I bit back the retort I wanted to make. "Well, actually, I have been doing just that. I find that having something for my hands to do helps free my mind to do its work."

He laughed. "Idle hands make the devil's work, and all that, huh? How positively Victorian of you, Ernie!"

"Very funny, Brett," I said, my tone purposely a bit sour. I didn't want him to suspect that I was lying, but by the calculating glances he kept directing at my bag, I wasn't sure I had fooled him in the least.

"Time to put your knitting aside," he said, taking my arm and beginning to guide me toward the dining room. "Time to eat instead."

I muttered something under my breath, something which would have made my dear departed mother want to rap me on the knuckles.

"Sorry," Brett said, "didn't quite catch that?" He had heard very well what I had said—he was just hoping to make me blush.

I did blush, and he laughed.

"Have you seen or heard from Jack Preston in the last half hour or so?" I asked, stopping before Brett could lead me into the dining room.

"Not for a couple of hours, thank goodness. Why? Have you got something to tell him?" He eyed me speculatively.

"Oh, just something I wanted to ask him," I said. Like, *Will you let me read the manuscript before you haul it off to be examined?* But of course I couldn't say that aloud.

"I'm sure he'll be back before the evening's over," Brett said, urging me toward the dining room again. "We haven't seen the last of him, not by a long shot."

"You go on ahead," I said, disentangling my arm from his grasp as gently as I could. "I need to make a quick phone call, then I'll join you."

"You do have something up your sleeve," he said, grinning with satisfaction. "I knew it! Come on, you can tell me. What have you found out?" He gave me his best winsome-little-boy look of appeal.

"You really are incorrigible," I said. I was almost tempted to confide in him, but as convinced as I was that he was innocent of the murders, I held my counsel. I had to talk to Jack Preston first.

He stuck out his lower lip in mock pout. "Well, if you won't talk, you won't talk. Though we haff ways, you know!"

I groaned at the execrable accent he had affected. He laughed as he marched into the dining room without me.

Grasping the bag firmly to my side, I strode down the hallway toward the little television room. There was a phone I could use in there. With some relief, I gained the relative privacy of the room and shut the door firmly behind me. I set the bag down in a chair and reached for the telephone. Picking up the handset and holding it to my ear, I listened to hear whether the line was clear. It was.

I punched in the number for Jack's cell phone. I have an excellent memory for phone numbers, and I had memorized this one as soon as he had given it to me. But of course he wasn't answering it. Where the dickens was he?

Instead of talking directly to Jack, I left a message on his voice mail, namely, "Get back to Idlewild as fast as you can. I've got something I have to tell you."

As a precaution, I also called the sheriff's department in Tullahoma and asked for Jack. When I gave the dispatcher my name, she told me she'd been one of my students a few years ago, and then said, "Oh, Miss Carpenter, I'm sorry, but Jack's involved in something right now and can't be reached."

"What on earth is going on?"

She hedged for a moment. "I can't really say, but there's a situation going on in a Stop-and-Rob out on the highway, and all our available personnel are involved in it."

"So there's no telling when it might be over." I nearly moaned in frustration.

"No'm," she said, "I'm afraid not." She assured me she would see that Jack got my message as soon as possible, but she couldn't promise me he'd be able to respond anytime soon.

With that I had to be content. I just had to remain calm until Jack came back to Idlewild, and I had to do my best to resist peeking at the manuscript. I knew that if I let myself, I'd go upstairs right this minute, lock myself in my bedroom, and start reading. I didn't want to mess up any fingerprints on the paper, but of course I was dying to read it and see whether it really did contain any of the answers to the murders here.

Before I could yield to temptation, I snatched up the bag and marched back down the hall to the dining room. Inside I found Brett seated at the table with Lurleen Landry and the Bertrams. Morwell Phillips must still be upstairs with Miss McElroy.

Despite the horrors of the day, Selma Greer had provided a delicious dinner for us tonight. The woman truly was a marvel, but I figured she took some solace in being able to cook through all the madness earlier.

I stuck the bag underneath my chair, hoping the others wouldn't pay it much attention, but of course Alice saw it immediately. Her eyes lit up with a question. In response, I lifted my shoulders in what I hoped was a negative, and her eyes narrowed in suspicion. Even if she didn't believe me, she wasn't going to make a scene in front of the others.

Despite looking like she hadn't slept for two days, Lurleen made an attempt at conversation. Russell refused all gambits, although he glowered at me throughout the meal. For once, even his wife had nothing to say. It was up to Brett to respond to Lurleen, and he did his best. I offered an occasional remark, but I was too preoccupied with the potential bombshell underneath my chair to do much.

As we were finishing dessert, heavenly pecan pie topped with cinnamon-flavored ice cream, Phillips came into the room and slumped down in a chair across from me.

"How is Mary Tucker doing?" Lurleen asked him as he filled a plate for a belated dinner.

"She's been resting most of the afternoon," he said, "and I think her color is good. I'm sure she'll be fine. She just needs a bit of rest." He took a bite of Selma's excellent roast and chewed slowly. "But you know how she is. She's already talking about getting up and coming downstairs this evening. She just won't listen to sense sometimes."

"Is someone with her?" Brett asked. "Surely you didn't leave her by herself."

"Of course not! Mrs. Greer is upstairs with her," he responded testily. "I've looked after her for nearly fifty years, young man, and I know better than you do what's good for her."

"Sorry," Brett said, chagrined. "Didn't mean anything by that."

Phillips dropped his fork on his plate in disgust. "Don't mind me," he said, his voice bitter. "I'm just the errand boy. She wants to see you, by the way." He glared at me.

"Right now?" I said.

He nodded.

"Is that a good idea?" Lurleen asked. "I thought she needed rest."

"I thought so too," Phillips said, "but Mary Tucker is determined to talk to Miss Carpenter here. Why, I haven't the foggiest notion. But what Mary Tucker wants, Mary Tucker usually gets." He stabbed at a piece of roast on his plate and stuffed it in his mouth.

I dropped my linen napkin on the table and pushed my chair back. "Guess I'd better go on up to her. If y'all will excuse me." I bent to retrieve my bag.

"Just don't stay long," Phillips warned me. "No matter how much she wants to talk, she needs her rest. So don't wear her out."

"I'll do my best," I said. Holding the bag in front of me with both hands, I walked out of the room.

All the way up the stairs I felt eyes boring into my back, though I dismissed that notion for the foolishness it was. My nerves were getting on edge because of the dratted manuscript in the bag. I wished Jack Preston would get here and relieve me of the burden of it. But if he didn't get here soon, I was going to read the thing, despite the consequences.

I tapped lightly on Miss McElroy's door, and in a few moments Selma came to open it. "Come on in, Ernie," she said, her voice low. "She's been a bit fretful, wanting to talk to you. I think she's better, but she's got something weighing powerful heavy on her mind, that's for sure."

I looked past her to see Miss McElroy frowning in my direction. I came into the room, and Selma shut the door behind me. Sitting in the chair drawn up close to Miss McElroy's bed, I set my knitting bag on the floor beside me.

"We never did finish our conversation earlier," Miss McElroy said, her tone accusing me.

"No, ma'am, we didn't," I said, keeping my voice bland. "It looked like you needed to rest right then more than you needed to talk, so I left."

She harrumphed at me, but she didn't waste time arguing the point further. Without being too obvious about it, I examined her. Her color was indeed back to normal, and she seemed a bit stronger than she had been, though I wasn't too certain that she needed to be up and about just yet.

"Selma, you go on downstairs for now," Miss McElroy said. She held up a hand to forestall any protests. "I'll be just fine, and if I should need anything, Miss Carpenter will see to it."

"All right, Miss Mary Tucker," Selma said. "But you don't wear yourself out any more than you already done, you hear?"

"I promise," Miss McElroy said. "And please don't forget to pass along that message, like I asked you. Okay?"

Selma stared at her for a moment, then nodded.

Miss McElroy waited until the door had closed behind Selma, then told me, "Go lock the door. I don't want us to be disturbed."

Surprised, I did as she asked, then came back to my seat.

"I have a confession to make," Miss McElroy said. "But judging by that bag you're carrying, maybe I'm a bit late." Her mouth twisted in a grimace. "I guess you found it, didn't you?"

"How do you know it's not just my knitting?"

"You don't much look like the knitting type to me," she said tartly. "Now, are you going to get it out of the bag or not?"

"Why? Don't you think we should wait for Jack Preston?"

"Don't be ridiculous," she snapped at me. "I want to read it before they get their hands on it. Now get it out of that bag and start reading!"

Chapter Eighteen

AT THIS STAGE OF THE GAME, I had decided I wasn't going to let her intimidate me any longer. She owed me a few things—at the very least, a few explanations. I kept my tone even as I replied, "Before I read anything, you're going to answer a few questions."

That took her aback, but she had better sense than to argue. "Very well," she said grudgingly, "I suppose I owe you that much."

"Did you murder Hamilton Packer before you removed the manuscript from his room?"

Her eyes widened. "No kid gloves with you, eh, Miss Carpenter?" She surprised me by grinning. "I knew you were the right one for this job. Tough-minded, when it matters. Yes, I made a good choice."

"Thanks," I said wryly. "I appreciate the compliment, but I'd appreciate an answer to my question even more."

"Hamilton was alive and well and splashing about in the bathtub like a beached whale when I walked out of the room with the manuscript," Miss McElroy said, looking straight at me.

"And just when was that?" I asked. "We need to work out a timetable." Not to mention check it against what Alice Bertram had told me.

Miss McElroy waved a hand in the air. "I doubt it's going to matter that much, but I went upstairs just a few minutes after Hamilton. I gave him time to get in the tub, then I went into the room and extracted the manuscript."

"Did he have the door locked?" I asked.

She snorted in a most unladylike fashion. "Yes, but who do

you suppose has keys to all the doors in this house?"

I felt chastened by such an obvious answer. Nevertheless I forged on. "Where was the manuscript?"

"The great booby had left it in his briefcase, lying right there on the bed. He was just begging someone to come in and take it."

"Maybe he thought a locked door would be a sufficient deterrent," I observed.

"Perhaps," she said. "Though I'll admit it did pain me to violate the privacy of a guest in my house in such a manner. In this case, I felt I had no choice. I had to know what that manuscript contained."

"Why haven't you read it already?"

"Lack of time, and lack of privacy," she said. "There are too many people about, and with the sheriff's department searching for it, I thought I'd just sit tight on it for a while." She smiled like a schoolgirl at her unintentional pun. "How did you find it? I thought I had hidden it rather well."

"Alice Bertram saw you with it," I explained, though I neglected to tell her the circumstances under which Alice had told me about what she had seen. "Once I knew where it probably was, I went through your sitting room carefully, looking everywhere I could think of. It took me over an hour, but I finally found it."

"I'm surprised Alice didn't find it herself," Miss McElroy said.

"She tried," I said, "but she didn't have much opportunity to look for it, for the same reasons you cited for not having read it yet. Not enough time, not enough privacy."

"How much did she offer you for it?" Miss McElroy asked shrewdly.

"She never mentioned a figure," I said, well upon my dignity, "but it was a moot point, anyway."

"That goes without saying," she said. "You were going to turn it over to Jack Preston, weren't you?"

I nodded. "That seemed the right thing to do."

"So you haven't read it either," Miss McElroy observed with satisfaction.

"No, though I desperately wanted to," I admitted.

She laughed at that. "Then let's do that, right now."

"I've put in a couple of calls to Jack Preston," I said. "I didn't say precisely what I had, but I left messages to the effect that he needed to get back here immediately." At the moment, I saw no point in telling her I had no idea how long it would be before Jack could get back to Idlewild.

"Good," she said. "No doubt he'll be here as soon as he can. Time's a-wasting, then. Start reading."

"One more question," I said, stalling her a little longer. There was one more thing I had to ask her.

"What?"

"I overheard Lurleen Landry threatening you, the first day everyone arrived. What was that about?"

She looked away. "Have you asked Lurleen about this?"

"Yes," I said, "but I want to know what you have to say."

She stared at me now, but I kept my face blank. I wouldn't reveal how little Lurleen had actually told me.

Miss McElroy sighed deeply. "Lurleen has another one of her little pets that she wants me to do favors for. In this case, she wants me to see that this girl gets a scholarship. I don't think the girl deserves it. Besides, I have a candidate of my own. I told her that, and she was trying to, well, coerce me into changing my mind."

I decided to push her a little further. "What was she threatening to do?"

Miss McElroy's hands clenched on the bedspread. "She said she was going to drag out some old business to do with my husband, back when he was a law professor at Ole Miss. I managed to keep it quiet at the time, but Lurleen found out about it and she was going to use it against me, to make me change my mind."

A scandal involving Morwell Phillips? That one rocked me. I sat there and thought about it for a moment, and as I did, I recalled bits of information from all the batch of stuff that my librarian friend had compiled for me. Sukey Lytton had worked in the law library while she was at Ole Miss, and I did some rapid calculations. She probably would have been there when Morwell Phillips was teaching at the school. Sukey had had a taste for older men. Could the scandal surrounding Phillips have had anything to do with Sukey Lytton?

And if so, how had Miss McElroy hushed it up? I had a feeling I knew the answer to that one.

Miss McElroy had been watching me closely, and I doubt that I was able to hide my thoughts. I stared at her, and she sighed. "Just go ahead and read. Please," she said, her voice low.

There was no point in delaying any further. I wanted to know what the manuscript contained just as much as she did, but by now I think we both realized what we might find. And I figured that, somehow or another, she had the right to know, even before the sheriff's department. But I did make one attempt at assuaging my conscience.

"Do you have some gloves? Thin cotton ones, perhaps?" I asked her.

Though her eyes rolled with impatience, she directed me to a drawer in her ancient wardrobe. Pulling out the drawer, I beheld an assortment of gloves, in myriad colors and fashions. She probably hadn't worn most of them in decades, but there they were, just in case she ever needed them. Trying not to disturb their arrangement too much, I rummaged through until I found a pair of white summer gloves, made of a very fine cotton and embellished with small pink roses across the back. Thank goodness she had hands as big as mine. Pulling the gloves on to my hands with care, I felt almost like a girl in Sunday school again. Back in the days when I was a girl, we did wear gloves to church.

The gloves were a bit snug, but not much. Back in my chair again, I fumbled with the purple ribbon which bound the manuscript together. After a moment, I got the knot loose enough so that I could pull the ribbon off, and the manuscript lay free in my lap.

I held it up in one hand and riffled through the pages. "It's not very long," I observed. "Only about two hundred and fifty pages."

"Good," Miss McElroy said. "Then maybe we can read most

of it before Jack Preston gets here and takes it away."

Before I started reading, I finally asked her the one question that had been burning on my lips. "Why didn't you turn this over to Jack right away?"

She turned away from me. "I know I should have," she said, her voice low. "If I had, that wretched girl would still be alive, and I'd have one less death on my conscience. But I had to know, and in my own way. I've always had to do things my own way, no matter what." The bitter self-reproach in her voice surprised me. "After Katie was murdered, I was too shocked to think clearly. I should have put an end to it, right then and there, but I couldn't cope. I'm stronger now, and I'm ready for the truth."

In that moment, the full realization hit me. Miss McElroy knew perfectly well who the murderer was, but it was something she had tried not to acknowledge to herself. She had hoped—against all hope, I suspected—that she was wrong, but she could no longer deceive herself, or anyone else, for that matter.

Taking a deep breath, I picked up the first page of the manuscript and began to read aloud. "Here's the dedication. 'To Mary Tucker McElroy, for all she has wrought, so may she reap.'" My voice faltered. I glanced over at Miss McElroy, and her mouth had twisted, as if she were in pain. I turned the page. "Here's a quotation," I said, scanning it before reading it to her. "The source of her title. 'He had known the love that is fed on caresses and feeds them; but this passion that was closer than his bones was not to be superficially satisfied.' It's from Edith Wharton's *The Age of Innocence*."

That was why the title had sounded vaguely familiar to me, I realized. I had read that passage countless times, because I assigned the book frequently over the years in my senior English and honors English classes. I thought for a moment about the doomed love between Newland Archer and Ellen Olenska, and I had a dreadful premonition of the tale which Sukey Lytton's novel would reveal.

"Go on," Miss McElroy said, her voice barely above a whisper.

And so I read. The story unfolded quickly, of the passion between an older man and a young woman. The man was married to a socially prominent, wealthy woman, and the girl came from a sordid background. Though they frequently declared their undying love for each other, the man could never make the break from his wife in order to marry the girl because he felt constrained by his social position and his wife's wealth. They continued to meet and indulge their passion whenever they could, often while the girl was a guest of her lover and his wife. The girl was a talented opera singer, and the wife was well-known as a patroness of the arts who often took on gifted young persons as her protégés.

The further I read, the more depressing it got. The girl became unable to sing, she was so tormented by her lover's unwillingness to acknowledge her publicly. In despair the girl turned to other men, throwing herself at them with little discretion. She would then write long letters to her lover, taunting him with her escapades, but still he would not break with his wife.

The whole thing was wretchedly self-indulgent, but I had to admit that Sukey Lytton could write. Despite my distaste for the subject matter, I recognized the skill with which the author had constructed her story and the subtle power in her delineation of her characters.

She had spared no one. All of them were in the book: Russell and Alice Bertram, Lurleen Landry, Brett Doran. She had been merciless in exposing them, sparing them not the least shred of dignity. If I hadn't known the people she was writing about, I might have viewed the novel very differently. As it was, I felt like a voyeur.

Finally, I could take no more of it. In the middle of a sentence, I put the page down and announced, "That's enough. I can't read any more of it."

"No," Miss McElroy said, her face ashen. "That's more than enough."

I had gotten so caught up in what I was reading that I had forgotten to pay attention to Miss McElroy and gauge the effect the story was having on her. "Can I get you something?

Do you have some brandy or something like that here?" Her color, or lack of it, alarmed me.

"No," she said, her voice suddenly stronger, as if by a great act of her will. "No, that won't be necessary."

"Are you sure?" I was doubtful, but already some of her color was coming back.

"No, I don't need anything," she said.

We sat and stared at each other for quite some time. I broke the silence by asking, "Was this what you were afraid of?"

"Yes," Miss McElroy sighed. "Though it's all really my fault, I suppose."

"What do you mean? How can all this be your fault?"

"Don't be so naive," she said, her voice sharp. "Do you think that, if I had been any other kind of wife than what I've been, he would have gotten involved with that girl?"

I started to protest, but she waved me to silence. "Spare me the feminist rhetoric. I know very well he was the one who made the choice, not me, and that is well and truly his responsibility, not mine. But I never made much attempt, in nearly fifty years, to do things other than the way I wanted them. I never really gave much thought to what he wanted, because I was the one who mattered. The Good Lord forgive me for my arrogance, but it was what I wanted that mattered. Or so I thought." Tears streamed down her cheeks.

"You really love him, don't you?" I asked.

"I always have," she said, her voice breaking. "There has never been anyone else. Except myself. Perhaps I loved myself more than I loved him. And that's why I blame myself for all this. I couldn't give him enough of myself to make the difference, when he really needed it."

The tears had stopped, and she mopped at her face with the edge of the sheet. "I didn't want to believe that he had killed her, nor that he had killed anyone else. I wanted so much to believe one of the others had done it. They had enough motive, each and every one of them, because Sukey was relentless. She could never have all she wanted, so she did her best to make anyone around her as miserable as she was. I wouldn't have blamed any of them if they had killed her."

"Then why didn't you leave it all alone?" I asked. "Why didn't you let her death remain an accident?"

"Because I couldn't let well enough alone," she said. "I had to do what I thought was right, no matter what the cost to all of us. Truly a Pyrrhic victory."

"What now?" I said. I could think of nothing else to say, in the face of her bitter self-reproach.

"The choice is no longer mine," she said. "He has to decide how to end this. I just pray that he will remember how much I love him and how sorry I am." She had raised her voice, almost as if she were speaking to someone else. As I watched, she leaned forward, toward her bedside table. She fumbled, pushing aside a box of tissues and a glass of water, reaching for something behind them. I could see now what she wanted.

With a quick stab of a finger, she punched a button and turned off the intercom.

Chapter Nineteen

A MASSIVE THUNDERSTORM had rolled in, bringing the night in its wake, before Jack Preston and his men returned to Idlewild.

Morwell Phillips had disappeared from the house, but I suggested to Jack where he might find him. His body was floating in the pond, pelted by the heavy rain, bobbing up and down as the water moved in the wind.

Or so Jack told me. I couldn't face the thought of witnessing the scene for myself. Besides, I was afraid to leave Miss McElroy, even in the capable hands of Selma Greer. She wouldn't talk, even when Jack, dripping despite the rain gear he'd been wearing, came back in the house and asked her, gently, to tell him what had happened. She had retreated into the deep silence of grief and guilt from which we could not rouse her.

I had to take over and tell what I knew. I showed Jack the manuscript, and he had his men bag it and mark it as evidence. I gave him a quick summary of the contents, all the while keeping an eye on Miss McElroy across the room, while Jack and I talked near the door.

"Just wish I could have gotten here when you first called," he said, his shoulders slumped in tiredness.

"What was all the big fuss, anyway?" I asked.

He rolled his eyes. "Oh, some bubba got tanked up on beer and hauled himself off to the convenience store where his ex-wife worked. He couldn't handle the fact that she had divorced his sorry self, and he thought waving a deer rifle around would impress her." He grimaced. "And then when somebody from our department answered a call, he started threatening to kill everybody in there. So we had us a hostage situation on our hands."

"Good grief," I said, "how did it all end?"

Jack snorted. "Well, after about three hours of constant beer-drinking, bubba passed out, fortunately, and nobody was hurt." He grinned. "Nobody but bubba himself, that is. By the time we got inside, his ex-wife had taken away the rifle and was working over certain parts of his anatomy with the heavy shoes she was wearing."

"Ouch!" I said, trying not to grin. Despite the gravity of the situation here, or maybe because of it, I couldn't help responding to the comic overtones of what Jack had related.

Quelling my impulse to laugh aloud, I returned to the more pressing matter. "Jack, even if you had been here, I don't think you could have prevented Morwell Phillips from killing himself. He'd have found a way, I'm sure."

"So he was listening on the intercom the whole time?" Jack shook his head.

"Probably," I said. "Miss McElroy had already instructed Selma Greer to make sure he went into his office downstairs to turn it on. I doubt he missed much of what we talked about, or of my reading the manuscript aloud."

Jack glanced over at the bed, where Miss McElroy lay, almost asleep, her left hand clasped in the consoling warmth of Selma's. "You know, I want to be angry with her, because she could have prevented so much of this. But looking at her, I just don't have the heart."

Her doctor had come and gone, prescribing more of the sedative she was already taking. "She's one tough lady," he had said, his voice full of admiration, "but she needs some time." He then instructed Jack not to press Miss McElroy, unless she herself wanted to talk.

Jack had promised not to badger her, even though he was impatient to wrap up his investigation. For now he had to make do with me.

Selma gently disengaged her hand from Miss McElroy's and stood up. Moving quietly, she approached Jack and me. Her face heavy with sorrow, she said, "She's asleep now. Let her rest, and she'll be ready to talk to you in the morning."

"Do you want me to sit with her for a while?" I asked. Selma looked exhausted, as if she could do with a long night's rest herself.

She shook her head. "No, Ernie, I'll stay here with her. She needs me." Her eyes glistened with unshed tears. "They ain't nobody else, not now."

I felt the tears coming to my own eyes, and I blinked them away. My voice was husky when I spoke. "If you need me, don't hesitate, okay?"

She smiled, briefly. "I will, I promise. Now you and Mr. Jack go on downstairs and finish up your talking there. Looks like you could both do with something hot to drink."

Jack nodded fervently and followed me out the door without argument. Downstairs, in the kitchen, we found Brett Doran nursing a cup of coffee.

"What a mess!" he said, shaking his head at the sight of us. He got up and retrieved mugs for both of us and poured them full of coffee.

"Thanks, Brett," I said, and Jack raised his cup in salute.

"How's she doing?" Brett asked. "I mean, this must really have rocked her."

"She's taking it very hard," I said, "as you might expect. Even though I think she knew it all along."

Brett's eyes widened in shock. "You mean she knew he was going to kill himself?"

"That, too," I said. I looked at Jack, and he nodded. "I found Sukey's manuscript, and I was reading it to her in her bedroom. She had her intercom on the whole time, and I didn't know it. He"—here I had trouble making myself say his name—"was down in his office, listening. By then he realized it was all over, and he took the most expedient solution. For himself, at least."

"I still can't believe he was the one who did it all," Brett said, shaking his head. "I had Alice pegged for it, or maybe Russ. But not Morwell." He waved a hand around. "He was always a background kind of guy. You never thought of him doing anything like this. He was like part of the furniture."

"Which is how he moved around the house without anyone

paying that much attention to him," I said. "Everyone was accustomed to his going about, looking after the house, checking on guests, and so on. He wasn't doing anything unusual, so nobody paid much attention." I sighed. "Besides, most of the time, he could slip in and out of rooms, because he knew where everyone was."

I took a sip of my coffee. "Which reminds me, Jack, I need to tell you a couple of things." First, I described my little episode with the booby-trapped stairs. Brett denied having slipped the note under my door, and I assured him that I didn't believe he was responsible. Then I told them both how I had discovered the manuscript.

"I knew you had it in that knitting bag," Brett said triumphantly. He slapped the table with his hand. "I knew you weren't sitting around knitting."

"Yeah, she's not exactly the knitting type," Jack said, grinning, the strain in his face lessening a bit.

"If you're not careful," I warned them jokingly, "I might just knit you both something for Christmas."

They both twisted their faces in expressions of mock horror, and I rolled my eyes at them as I took another sip of coffee. Finally, some warmth was seeping back into my bones.

"If I hadn't been put off the track by that so-called manuscript I found in the desk in my room," I confessed ruefully, "we might have found the real thing earlier."

At Brett's puzzled expression, I quickly explained about the pile of blank paper I had found, and how it had led me down a blind alley. He tried not to laugh. I shrugged. "And that's all it was, a pile of blank paper. While we were waiting for Jack and his men to get back here, Miss McElroy did admit to putting it there, hoping it might put me off the scent for a while. Which it did."

"I shouldn't have fallen for it either," Jack said, "but your explanation seemed reasonable at the time." He took a sip of coffee. "But there are still some points to clear up, even though we know who the murderer was."

"Didn't his note explain everything?" I asked. Morwell Phillips had left a lengthy suicide note in his office for Jack, and he must have already written much of it before he had listened to me reading Sukey Lytton's manuscript to his wife over the intercom. Ever the gentleman, he absolved his wife of all blame, taking responsibility for everything that had happened.

"Not everything," Jack said. "For one thing, who rang the bell in Packer's bathroom? Phillips didn't admit to doing that."

"That would have been me." Without our being aware of it, Russell Bertram had come into the kitchen. He walked over to the table, his gait none too steady, and plopped down in a chair. "How 'bout some of that coffee?"

His diction was slightly slurred, and his breath would have done justice to a distillery. Brett jumped up and got him a mug of coffee. Russell drank it straight, like he did his whisky, practically pouring it down his throat.

"You, Mr. Bertram?" Jack asked. "You rang the bell in Packer's bathroom?"

"'S right," he said. "I did." He stared defiantly at Jack.

"Why did you do that?" Jack asked.

"Went into Hamilton's room to talk to him," he replied, making an effort to speak more clearly. "He wasn't in the bedroom, so I pushed open the bathroom door, and there he was." He shuddered. "Dead as a doornail, that knife in his back. I almost puked up my guts, right there."

"What did you do then?" Jack prompted him when he fell silent, lost in the memory.

Russell roused himself. "I didn't know what to do, at first. Just stood there and stared at him. Then I figured I'd better let somebody know what had happened. So I went around and rang the bell."

"And then?" Jack said.

"I panicked," he admitted sheepishly. "I know how it is, in a mystery novel. They always suspect the one who found the body, so I hightailed it out of there and back to my room. Alice knows. She can tell you."

"I have a question, Jack," I said.

He nodded, even as he frowned and stared at Russell.

"How did he lure poor Katie out to the summerhouse? Did he say, in his note?" I still couldn't say his name.

Jack cut a sideways glance at Brett. "Yeah, he said he gave her a note, said it was from Mr. Doran here. He made her think Doran wanted to meet her out in the summerhouse for a little fun and games. He was hoping we'd find the note and tag Mr. Doran for the murder." He shook his head. "We finally found the note. Katie had hidden it just inside a copy of Mr. Doran's novel she had on her bedside table."

Brett had gone pale, and I reached across the table to give his right hand a squeeze. He thanked me with eloquent eyes.

"One more thing, Jack," I said. "It's not really that important, but I'd like to know. Did he admit to destroying my dress, trying to scare me off?"

Jack looked puzzled. "No, the note didn't say anything about that. He did confess to trying to make you fall down the stairs, but nothing about the dress."

Russell made a snorting sound into his mug of coffee.

"Yes?" I asked. "Do you know something about it?"

He stared at me with bleary eyes. "Alice," he said. "Alice did it. She thought you were an uppity bitch, and she didn't like the fact that Mary Tucker gave you that room." He stared down into his coffee for a moment. "Alice always wanted that room, and Mary Tucker never would let us stay in it. Always put us in the room we're in now, and Alice was mad."

I ought to have known, I thought. It seemed more typical of Alice Bertram, anyway.

Neither Jack nor Brett had anything to say to that, though Brett offered me an arched eyebrow as he looked at me.

Jack stood up. "Well, if you'll excuse me, I'd better get going. Time to get back to the office and take care of some paperwork."

I glanced at my watch; it was nearly midnight. "Surely it can wait," I protested.

He shook his head. "No, gotta get it all wrapped up. Now that my men are finished outside. I'll be back sometime in the morning to talk to everybody a bit more, and to Miss McElroy, of course." He held out his hand to me. "Thanks."

I squeezed his hand before I released it. "Be careful," I said, "it's still pretty nasty out there."

Russell stood up also. "Better go on up to bed," he said. "See you in the morning."

Brett and I watched as he followed Jack out of the kitchen.

"Geez," Brett said, stretching out in his chair and rolling his shoulders, "this has been a hell of a few days."

I got up and poured myself some more coffee. My body ached with tiredness as I sat down again at the table. "I can't argue with that."

Brett regarded me with sympathy. "You're taking this pretty hard, aren't you?" he said.

I sighed. "I just feel so sorry for Miss McElroy. I wonder if she'll ever really recover from all this."

"She's tough," Brett said. "I've known her longer than you, Ernie, and she's a game old girl. I'm not denying that this is the worst thing that's ever happened to her, but she'll go on, somehow."

"Maybe," I said, "but I don't think she'll be able to forgive herself."

"She didn't do it," Brett said. "He did, not her."

I shrugged. "I know that, and you know that. But he did it *for* her, in a twisted sort of way. At least, that's what she says. He had gotten himself involved with Sukey, who was threatening to make a laughingstock of him. Not to mention what she was planning to do to Miss McElroy, with that vicious novel of hers." I shook my head. "You just can't imagine how nasty it is."

Brett laughed, bitterly. "You're forgetting. I knew Sukey, and I know what she was capable of doing. It wouldn't have surprised me in the least."

I shivered, as I suddenly recalled something Morwell Phillips had said to me. "He said to me at one point," I explained haltingly to Brett, "that he would kill Sukey all over again—or words to that effect—for what she would have done to Mary Tucker with that manuscript." I drained the rest of my coffee. "Little did I know I should have taken that for a confession."

"As my grandmother would have said," Brett cocked an eyebrow at me, "don't it beat all!"

"Amen to that!" I said.

"What do you reckon will happen to the manuscript?" he asked.

"Who knows?" I said. "Since they have a signed confession, it's probably not as important as evidence. Things have been known to get lost, and I wouldn't be all that surprised if this particular piece of evidence just happened to get damaged or lost."

Brett laughed. "I, for one, wouldn't object, that's for sure!"

I pushed back my chair and stood up. "I'm just exhausted, Brett, so I know you'll excuse me. I think it's time we all tried to get some sleep, if that's possible."

"Okay, you go on up," he said. "I'll see you in the morning."

The thunderstorm had passed on by now, and the old house was quiet as I made my way from the kitchen, up the back stairs to my room. All I heard was the creak of the stairs as I trudged upwards.

I paused for a moment outside Miss McElroy's door, debating with myself. After a moment's indecision, I knocked softly, then opened the door.

Selma looked up from her doze beside the bed, blinking as she focused her eyes on me. She wearily got up from the chair and crossed the room to stand beside me.

"How is she?" I asked, nodding my head toward the bed where Miss McElroy slept.

"Resting quietly," she said, rubbing the back of her neck with one hand.

"Why don't you go lie down for a while and let me sit with her," I said. "Go in my room and rest, and I'll call you if she needs anything."

She started to protest, but a huge yawn forestalled her. "Maybe I will," she said. "Just for a little while."

I squeezed her shoulder, then stood aside for her to leave the room. I took up her former position in the chair beside the bed and tried to get comfortable. It was going to be a long night.

I studied Miss McElroy's face in the dim glow of a bedside lamp. She had told me she had to know the truth, whatever the cost. Even when she had suspected the truth all along. Would the cost prove too much for her?

I shifted in the chair, leaning back and resting my head against one of the padded wings. I shut my eyes. It was going to be a long night.

ALSO BY DEAN JAMES

CRUEL AS THE GRAVE

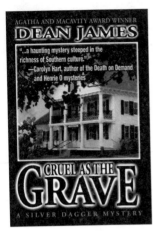

Maggie McLendon should be at home in Houston, studying for her Ph.D. qualifying exams, but a letter from her great aunt arrives, bearing bad news. Maggie's grandfather, Henry McLendon, whom she has never met, is seriously ill in Jackson, Mississippi. Maggie's father, English professor Gerard McLendon, has been estranged from his family since Maggie was an infant, but now there is perhaps one last chance for the McLendons to be reunited. The family welcomes Maggie and Gerard to Jackson, and Gerard has a chance to reconcile with his father. But a murderer strikes, savagely, and Gerard McLendon looks like the chief suspect. Maggie must sort out decades of family secrets, including the puzzle of her grandmother's death twenty-five years before and its relationship to the present crime, to arrive at the truth. But not before the killer strikes a second time. Could Maggie or her father be next on the list?

"In *Cruel as the Grave*, Dean James brings to life a family burdened by dark secrets. Determined sleuth Maggie McLendon peels away layers of hidden sadness to find the truth of her heritage in a haunting mystery steeped in the richness of Southern culture."
—Carolyn Hart

"*Cruel as the Grave* is an engaging, literate novel of family secrets and skullduggery. With a clever plot and appealing characterization, Mr. James has created the perfect English drawing room mystery set smack in the middle of steamy Mississippi. It is a witty and solid debut that will leave mystery readers clamoring for more."
—Earlene Fowler

"*Cruel As The Grave* exposes the underbelly of a Southern family, where secrets and skeletons lurk, cloaked in every imaginable guise. Well-written, deftly-plotted, and highly recommended for fans of Faulkner and others who zeroed in on the dysfunctional social structure that, to this day, continues to be concealed by superficiality and faded magnolia blossoms."
—Joan Hess

Trade Paper ISBN 1-57072-127-0 $15.00
Hardcover ISBN 1-57072-111-4 $24.50